TABLE OF CONTENTS

Chapter One

"I am searching for Avram of Bethlehem, the son of Abijah. He is said to be a big man, with broad shoulders, and very old. Do you know him?"

Before answering, the young shepherd stood silently for a moment, moving his hand up and down on his smooth staff. "I know of a herder whose name may be Avram, though most people call him 'the Lunatic.'"

"Yes. Yes, that is the one. He is my relative by marriage. Where can I find him?"

"Must be a different fellow, then. The Lunatic has no family, no one but his wife." The youth's eyes did not meet Yakov's. "Perhaps you should inquire in Bethlehem. If you offer some silver, someone may be able to tell you the whereabouts of your relative."

"If I had so much as a single coin to spare I would not be here," Yakov barked. He tamped down the air in front of him with both hands. "I understand Avram and his brother—my wife's father—had an argument years ago and never spoke to each other again. It no longer matters who was right and who was wrong." He lifted the hand of the little girl beside him. "She needs Avram's help. Please."

The shepherd took a long look at the solemn child before gesturing across the lush meadow. "The Lunatic and his crazy wife pasture yonder, over those hills. If I wanted to see him, I would keep walking that way."

"We have been wandering around all day. It seems impossible to find anyone out here in open country."

"You need not locate the Lunatic. Keep going and he will find you." The shepherd turned toward his flock and began to play a tune on his pipe.

Realizing their conversation was finished, Yakov sighed and led the little girl away. It took longer than he expected to reach the first rise. As he and the child climbed toward the crest, he glanced backward left and right across the fields stretching out behind them. He heard birds chirping and the distant bleating of sheep. The notes of a shepherd's pipe floated lightly on the air. If the weather warmed, this might be a pleasant place for a man who was not exhausted and worried.

Yakov rubbed his hands together. "It is cold out here. How much longer must I search for this madman?" It was just as well he spoke more to himself than to Channah, since she did not respond. When the climb became noticeably steeper, he lifted his head to judge the distance to the hilltop. An imposing figure stood at the summit, arms folded. Yakov stopped and shielded his eyes from the bright winter sun.

The old man's white hair stood away from his head as if trying to escape the fierceness of his weathered face. His voice had a low rumble, like far-away thunder. "Are you lost, friend?"

Even at the distance of several cart lengths, Yakov felt like the old man's eyes penetrated him. Concerned he might be in danger, Yakov took a deep breath to steady himself before replying. "I am searching for Avram of Bethlehem, the son of Abijah."

"For what purpose?"

Yakov noted the old man's impressive weaponry. He had a great iron bow slung over one shoulder, while a thick shepherd's crook leaned against a rock. A shepherd's rod was tucked into his belt, and most likely a dagger lurked beneath his tunic.

"Avram is the kinsman of my wife. I have come to put this child in his care." Yakov nodded toward Channah, who stood with downcast eyes.

The massive man grabbed his crook and strode nimbly down the hillside. Stopping an arm's length from Yakov, he took a long look at Channah. "Why?"

"When I find my wife's kinsman, I will explain the situation. I hope he will understand and help us."

"I am Avram. As you see, I am old. And my wife." He glanced back at the hilltop. "We cannot care for a child."

"Your niece Rebekah was married to my older brother. He died when this girl was still an infant. Out of respect for my brother, I married his widow in order to care for her and her child. A month ago, Rebekah was struck down in the street by a Roman chariot, a big, six-wheeled supply wagon." Yakov spat on the ground to demonstrate his disdain for the Romans. "She lived only three days more."

An old woman topped the hill and came to stand to the side of Avram. A noticeable scar ran from her left cheek and down the side of her neck. Yakov stopped speaking, expecting an introduction or some explanation for the woman's appearance. When the silence continued unbroken, he went on with his story. "It is all my wife—that is, my first wife Adah—and I can do to see after our seven children and my father." He inclined his head toward Channah. "I must find someone else to raise Rebekah's daughter."

Avram narrowed his eyes. "Find another relative. Yael and I have our hands full managing our herd."

"You are a shepherd?" Yakov asked, pretending this was new information. "A child could be useful to you. This one is sturdy and very obedient. She can fetch and carry, and I am certain she could learn to do chores to help with your sheep. She will be old enough to become a wife in a few years. Please, there is no one else willing to take her off my hands."

Something between a wail and a sob escaped from the child. Yakov slapped at the back of her head. "Stop that," he demanded.

Without warning, the woman uttered an inhuman growl and lunged toward Yakov with a short-bladed knife in her hand.

"No, Yael, no," Avram shouted. He wrapped his arms around the woman, barely preventing her from slashing Yakov's throat.

Yakov jumped backward, stumbling to a sitting position on the uneven ground. "What is wrong with her?"

Avram held the woman close to him. "Everything is all right," he said tenderly. "I will not let this man hurt the little girl." He gradually loosened his grip, at last releasing the woman. "You must forgive my wife. She is very protective of children."

"Protective?" Yakov stood and brushed debris from his tunic. "That is a considerable understatement. I could have been killed."

"Indeed," Avram agreed. "But you were not."

Yael glared at Yakov for a long moment before sheathing her knife and going to kneel in front of Channah. She hugged the child and brushed away her tears. When Avram touched his wife's shoulder, she glanced up at him and nodded.

Turning toward Yakov, Avram sighed. "Where are her belongings?"

"She has none." Yakov patted his clothing as if to confirm everything remained intact. "It is settled, then." He turned and began his departure, quickly putting as much distance as possible between himself and the threesome on the hilltop. He felt a twinge of guilt for leaving his brother's only child with a lunatic and a mad woman, but what choice was there?

Chapter Two

"How old are you, Channah?" Avram leaned against a large stone near Yael.

"Five, sir. Almost six."

"You may call me Uncle Avram. Or Uncle if you prefer something shorter." He put a hand on his wife's shoulder. "This is your Aunt Yael. I suspect she would like to be addressed as Auntie. Shall we go back to our sheep now, wife?" Avram turned toward the hilltop, but stopped at Yael's tug on his tunic. "What do you want?"

Yael pointed a bony finger at Channah's bare feet.

With a grunt, Avram hoisted the girl onto his back. "Wrap your legs around my waist," he instructed, pulling her hands across his massive shoulders.

Channah welcomed the relief of being carried. She was accustomed to going without sandals on city streets, but walking through the rocky countryside all morning had left her feet bruised and tender. When the cold wind struck their faces at the crest of the hill, Yael removed her smelly coat and tucked it around Channah before walking ahead. No longer shivering, Channah's uncertainty gave way to fatigue. She rested against Avram's thick neck and fell asleep.

At dusk, Channah stood watching Avram guide the sheep inside a low rock fence. After the last ewe scurried into the enclosure, the old shepherd rolled a large, heavy stone into the gap where the sheep had entered. "We often sleep in the pastures when the weather warms," he explained. "During the winter, the animals need the cave's shelter. Come, let us see if Yael has something for us to eat. Are you hungry?"

Channah nodded affirmatively. She had not eaten since leaving Yakov's cousin's house early that morning, but she was afraid to show too much enthusiasm. She remembered Yakov's instructions to eat as little as possible and to make herself useful in her new home. She glanced around before following Avram to the tent. Could this remote place ever feel like home?

The flat earth inside the fence formed a large semicircle around a steep outcropping of gray stone. A dark tent stood near one side of an arched opening in the rocky wall. Channah had heard stories of her ancestors dwelling in caves and tents, but she was surprised to find anyone still living in such primitive conditions.

"Sheep are easily frightened. Always move slowly and speak quietly around them," Avram advised. "Stay close to Yael or me for the time being. In a few days, the herd will become accustomed to your presence, and then they will understand you mean them no harm."

Inside the tent, Channah accepted the portion of bread and cheese Yael offered. She drank her weak wine and ate silently while taking in her surroundings. Sheepskins covered the floor of the tent, with a great pile of them stacked at the far end of the rectangular living space. The only furniture was a low shelf occupied by mismatched dishes and pots. A single oil lamp on a stand cast a dim circle of light around the brass serving tray located in the center of the tent.

As the night deepened, Channah was apprehensive about being alone with Avram and Yael. She remembered hearing her Uncle Yakov say Avram did not know the difference between real and imaginary events. Women in the family occasionally whispered Yael murdered a man. A little girl could have her throat slit and her body hidden in one of the countless caves scattered among the hills around Bethlehem. No one would ever know. Perhaps if she made herself useful, she could survive.

As soon as Avram finished his food, Channah sprang up to return his pottery bowl to the shelf. When Yael rose to put away her own dish, she gently caressed the side of Channah's face as they passed by each other. This simple act of kindness reminded Channah of her mother, and she could not prevent a single tear from rolling down her cheek. She bent her head, trying with all her might to keep the trickle from becoming a waterfall. How many times had Yakov warned her to be cheerful in whatever place he found for her to live?

A high, keening wail split the air as Yael crumpled into a ball and began to shake with sobs. Avram sighed, lifted the flap of the tent, and quietly slipped outside, leaving the two weeping females alone with each other. Channah released many days of sorrow into her tears. Obeying an impulse she neither understood nor questioned, she crept to Yael's side and snuggled against her aunt. Channah noticed for the first time that Yael's arms were scarred with the remains of what looked like many long, deep cuts.

"It will be all right, Auntie," Channah whispered. "I will work hard and eat very little."

Yael lifted her head and moaned. In one swift movement, she grabbed Channah and pulled her close. Yael rocked back and forth, cuddling Channah in her strong grip. The woman's tears continued to flow, but the racking sobs subsided. After what seemed a long time, Yael smoothed Channah's hair and kissed her on the forehead.

Eventually, Yael lifted Channah from her lap. The old woman went to the side shelf and beckoned to Channah with her hand. Yael pointed to a stack of date cakes inside a crock. Then she removed a flat rock from an iron pot buried up to its lip in the earth. She scooped out a handful of dried lentils and let them fall back. She spread her hands toward the shelf, where other jars, pots, and crocks sat in haphazard rows.

"Are you showing me you have plenty of food?" Channah was relieved when her aunt nodded affirmatively and smiled. Not knowing what else to do, she kissed Yael's hand.

Together they made Channah a bed of fleece, with Channah following her aunt's nods and hand gestures. When they were done, Yael topped the pallet with a coverlet of finely woven wool. Then she began to stitch pieces of leather, occasionally holding up her work to measure it against the sole of Channah's foot. A pair of boots, similar to those Avram and Yael wore, soon took shape.

Channah sat hugging her knees to her chest, watching her aunt sew and wondering what lay ahead of her with these peculiar people.

Chapter Three

The first light of dawn streamed into the tent when Avram threw back the doorway flap and boomed, "Good morning. The sun is rising, and so must we."

Channah rubbed her eyes and slipped from the snuggly warmth of her bed. She pulled on the new boots, wiggling her toes in their soft fleece. Remembering her promise to be helpful, Channah hurried to her aunt's side and did her best to assist in serving dates, almonds, and cheese for the morning meal.

"No more bread?" Avram spat a date pit into his bowl. He shrugged with his eyebrows when Yael's shake of her head answered his question.

Yael's hand motions mystified Channah. Her aunt held her hands parallel to the ground and waved them back and forth. Then she held up seven fingers.

Avram nodded and murmured, "Ah, you may be right, Yael. I think today is the Sabbath." He inclined his head toward Channah and asked between bites, "Did you keep holy days in your father's house?"

"We did not go to the well or to the market on the seventh day," she answered.

"Was that the only difference between the Sabbath and the rest of the week?"

Not certain of the correct answer, Channah gave the question a moment's thought. "Sometimes men would come and visit with Uncle Yakov. Mother and I would leave them alone and keep very quiet behind the house."

"Yael and I are lax in our religious observations. Sheep do not know one day from another. Wolves, either, for that matter." He used a rock to break open an almond. "Still, I am relieved to know we are not imposing our heathen ways on a devout child."

Since she could not bring herself to refuse food, Channah was certain she needed to find some other way to avoid being a burden. She watched as Avram rolled back the stone gate that morning. He called to the animals as if they were human and walked away with the sheep following behind. Yael waited until the enclosure was almost empty, and then she took Channah's hand. They walked behind the flock, with Yael now and then using her staff to give stragglers a nudge in the right direction.

Later that morning, Yael led Channah near Avram, who sat on the ground with a sheep on her rump between his legs and a small knife in his fist. Yael used her hands to indicate Channah was to remain behind and then slowly walked away.

"What are you doing, Uncle?"

Avram kept his eyes on his work. "I am trimming back her hooves."

Her uncle's tone of voice revealed no impatience. Therefore, she risked another question. "Why?"

"An overgrown hoof collects dirt and dung, which can cause fever and swelling. Neglected sheep can die from infected feet."

"Does the trimming hurt them?"

"No." Avram glanced toward Channah and gestured with his knife. "Her hooves are like your fingernails, thicker of course. As long as I am careful not to trim too deeply, it is painless."

Channah edged closer. "Could I do it?"

"I'll teach you someday if you like." Avram released one hoof and grasped another. "You will need to grow stronger hands first." He turned the ewe upright and rubbed her wool. "There you go, Little Twin, all trimmed up."

After sheathing his knife, Avram asked, "Are you interested in learning how to care for a herd?"

"Yes, Uncle."

"Why?"

"You and Auntie have plenty of food."

Avram covered his mouth and shook with laughter. "Bless me," he said after recovering his composure. "I'd forgotten how honest children are. Very well. This afternoon, I will begin by teaching you something simple. For now, go and see what Yael is doing. If she has made a campfire, then she plans to bake bread and you should help her. If she is sitting and gazing into the distance, return and let her be."

Later that day, Avram allowed Channah to sit by him while he anointed the head of a ewe he called Wanderer. "Rub the oil all over her head. Gently massage a good coating all around inside her ears," he said. "Apply pressure with your thumbs, but not too so much that you hurt her. The oil will keep insects from taking up residence in there."

Channah was thrilled when her uncle let her spread the olive oil he poured on a sheep's head. "I think this one's name is Little Twin," she said.

"How do you know?" Avram re-did the ewe's left ear but did not scold Channah.

"Because you said her name this morning. She has a black spot on her nose."

The old man smiled. "You are correct, although Big Twin has the same spot."

Since her uncle did not seem to mind questions, she asked, "Do all of the sheep have names?"

"Yes," he replied. "When you have been with them longer, you will see how individual they are. My sheep are like my children."

Avram released Little Twin, and his body stiffened. He held up a hand, as if to signal for silence. He snapped his face to his left, appearing to listen intently.

Channah sat motionless, catching the faint melody of a shepherd's pipe in the distance.

After a moment, Avram arose. He put away the oil and stashed his bag of supplies in the hollow of a rock. "We are about to have company." He slung his iron bow over a shoulder. "Go and bring Yael. I want the two of you near me when we greet our visitor."

When Channah leapt to her feet, Avram put a hand on her shoulder. "Remember to walk, and do not be afraid. One man is no threat against your Auntie and me."

As she made her way across the meadow, Channah saw Yael coming to meet her. "Uncle Avram says to come."

Yael nodded and tapped her ear. Though Channah had no idea what the gesture meant, she followed her aunt's sedate pace toward the vantage point where Avram now stood.

"Are you lost, friend?" Avram asked the well-dressed man riding a donkey up the hill.

The man smiled as he slid off his mount. "Greetings. I do not exactly where I am, but I would not describe myself as lost, either. I simply decided to ride out and enjoy the countryside, perhaps see if the wildflowers have started to bloom."

"Taking a ride?" Avram's face revealed no emotion. "On the Sabbath?"

The man lifted his chin and led his donkey nearer. "Only the Pharisees abide by those old-fashioned rules these days, and I suppose devoted Sadducees as well." He smiled. "I have nothing against those who practice the old ways, so long as they do not try to make me conform." He jiggled the leather reins in his hand for a moment. "I left my home early and have not eaten since. Do you have some spare food you would be willing to sell me?"

"Leave your animal and come." Avram gave a slight nod to Yael. She frowned before turning to pick her way down the gentle slope.

Chapter Four

In view of the sheep, but still some distance away, Yael offered a tray of bread and cheese to the stranger. He and Avram sat on the ground cross-legged, facing each other. "Wine?" Avram held up a flask.

"Yes, thank you." The stranger ate slowly, with his eyes darting left and right. "You have a fine herd. Have you been a shepherd long?"

Avram poured a portion of wine for his guest and another for himself. "All of my life."

Yael sank to the earth, a short distance behind the stranger. Following her aunt's example, Channah sat nearby. She watched Yael unobtrusively unsheathe her knife and hide it in her lap, beneath a fold of her tunic.

"I should introduce myself." The stranger took a gulp of wine. "I am Samuel, son of Mattathias, from Hebron."

"You are a long way from home."

"My father is a wool merchant. He is thinking of expanding our business." He made a sweeping gesture toward Avram's flock. "Very soon it will be time for shearing." He munched a chunk of bread before adding, "The taxes on your bounty will be very high."

Avram nodded.

"Everyone says these hills are riddled with caves," Samuel said. "Since you are constantly out in the fields, you probably know where many of them are located."

Folding his arms, Avram replied, "My time is occupied managing my sheep. I do not go exploring."

"I understand." Samuel ate a few bites before speaking again. "I heard about a shepherd near Hebron who became quite wealthy. He hid his wool in caves at shearing time. Later he sold it in secret, out of the tax collector's sight."

Channah watched Yael ease her hand into the fold of fabric where her knife rested.

Samuel drank more wine. "I do not suppose you know of anyone doing such a thing here?"

Avram stared at his visitor for a long while. "A man who would attempt such a scheme is a fool." He stretched his arms. "I did know a baker who tried to cheat on his taxes. He was scourged with whips and thrown into prison. As far as I know, he is still there. Care for more wine?"

"Yes, thank you. I must say it is excellent." Samuel held out the metal cup to Avram.

"I make wine the way my grandfather did. We ferment the grapes in ram's blood. It adds a rich smoothness to the flavor."

Samuel quickly jerked the cup back to his chest. "On second thought, perhaps I should be going. Thank you for sharing your food with me." He took a coin from a small leather pouch.

Avram waved his hand. "Keep your money. My hospitality is free."

As he rose and shook out his tunic, the stranger said, "I am in your debt—uh—what was your name?"

"My name does not matter." Avram stood and took up his shepherd's staff. "Good day, my friend." After walking with Samuel to the top of the hill, Avram took out his pipe and began to play a tune.

Channah helped to pick up the remains of the stranger's meal and followed Yael to the little spring near the meadow. Whenever her anxiety about the aunt and uncle began to subside, some unsettling remark reminded Channah how terribly odd they were. "Auntie, does Uncle Avram have to kill a sheep to make wine? Or does he just take some blood from a wound?"

Yael grinned and made a sound something like a chuckle. She shook her head and waved her arms, but Channah could not gather any understanding from her aunt's movements.

Later that afternoon, Avram stretched out on the ground in the shade of a boulder and went to sleep. Channah lingered with her aunt. Several times each day, Yael channeled water from the nearby spring to a large rock basin carved into the ground. Earlier, Channah had asked Avram if she could teach the sheep to drink from the spring or the small brook it fed. With a smile, her uncle explained the silly animals feared running water. Therefore, she assisted Yael to rupture the little earthen obstruction to allow the water to flow. When the hollowed-out depression was full, they repaired the dam to keep the sheep's drinking water still.

Channah watched with fascination as Yael slung a small rock, chasing away a big black bird who pecked at a sheep. "You missed him," Channah observed.

With a cocked eyebrow, Yael pointed toward a scrubby tree in the distance. She selected a small stone and slung it, hitting the middle of the tree's trunk. Then Yael handed her slingshot to Channah and again pointed toward the tree.

From Yael's gestures, Channah understood she was to try her hand. She picked up and discarded several small rocks before Yael chose one for her. After placing the smooth stone in the sling, Channah whirled it above her head, imitating Yael's earlier motions. When Channah launched the rock, it thudded to the ground near her own feet instead of speeding toward the tree.

Instead of laughing or scolding, Yael stood behind Channah, put her hands on the girl's arms, and demonstrated the correct way to make the rock fly toward the target. Although Channah never hit the tree, she enjoyed the feeling of accomplishment when a stone landed anywhere near it. After she tired of the game, Channah handed the slingshot to her aunt. Yael pushed Channah's hand back, motioning for Channah to tuck the sling into her belt. Though she wished for better words, "Thank you, Auntie," was the best she could do. The simple gratitude appeared to be sufficient when Yael beamed at her.

As the three of them sat at their evening meal, Channah stared into her cup of wine mixed with creek water. Remembering how Yakov made sure everyone in his household expressed their appreciation for the food he worked hard to provide for them, she lifted the cup and looked at the reddish liquid. She would taste blood if she drank. Suddenly aware of Yael's eyes on her, Channah slowly brought the wine to her lips.

Yael frowned. She tapped noisily on the side of her cup.

23

"What?" Avram asked, lifting his gaze from his food.

Yael pointed at Channah, who still sat trying to force herself to take a sip of wine. Avram had a puzzled look. Then his sudden explosion of laughter seemed to shake the tent.

"Oh, child," he said, as he caught his breath. "Surely you know there really is no blood in the wine." He giggled, sounding more like a girl than a man. "Bless me. Channah, if you believed what I said this afternoon, perhaps our visitor did as well." He laughed again. "My reputation as a lunatic is intact."

Growing more solemn, Avram said, "You see, there is more to raising sheep than watching over the herd. People can be more dangerous than any wild animal. That man who rode up on the donkey today? He is quite capable of bringing us trouble." The old man set his plate aside with a sigh. "His name may be Samuel, and perhaps he comes from Hebron. It is equally likely that everything he told us was a lie. My guess is that he was sent to spy on the shepherds in this area to make sure we are paying all the taxes we are supposed to."

Channah struggled to understand. "He is a Roman?"

"No," Avram said. "I know he is a Judean from the way he spoke." He exhaled loudly. "I expect the Romans to mistreat us. We are a conquered people, after all. But when brothers betray each other ..." He shook his head. "Ah, well, we shall hope this 'Samuel' is nothing more than a dishonest and very foolish tradesman."

Soon after eating, Avram bade them a peaceful night and went outside. With no prompting, Channah

24

prepared her bed as Yael had shown her when she first arrived. There were so many questions she wanted to ask, but she knew her aunt did not give explanations. If she wanted any information beyond a simple yes or no, she would have to ask Avram.

Chapter Five

Each evening, Channah assured herself the next day would bring a messenger with news that Yakov had changed his mind and wanted her to return home. However, more than a week passed before Channah saw any human being other than her aunt and uncle. One morning, Avram charged into the tent with his usual announcement of the sunrise, but Yael remained on her bed.

Avram knelt beside his wife and spoke words Channah could not hear. He rose and glanced around. "Auntie is not feeling well," he said. "Eat something and pack up our food portion for today. You and I will do the work today, child." He glanced toward his wife. "I am certain we can manage."

Channah filled a leather bag with cheese and the remains of yesterday's bread. When her aunt opened her eyes, Channah went to her bedside. "Do you want something to eat?"

Yael extended an arm from her covers and waved away the notion of food. She took Channah's hand and gave it a weak squeeze before pulling the blanket to her chin.

When Avram led the flock from the enclosure, Channah tried to keep the stragglers moving as Yael normally did, hoping she did not make a mistake. She kept busy during the morning with chores such as diverting running water into a still pool for the animals to drink. When the ewe named Little Twin cried out, Channah found the foolish animal lying on her back. She gently rolled Little Twin to one side, remembering her uncle's earlier comment that a sheep on its back was unable to arise without assistance. Little Twin jumped to her feet and bleated what Channah took to be an expression of gratitude.

Soon the sheep were resting in the shade of the few scrubby trees. Channah wandered toward the spot where Avram sat dozing. He jumped when her footstep in a bed of pebbles made a crunching sound.

Avram scanned the horizon, his eyes darting here and there. "I used to be able to stay awake after standing watch at night, one of the many lost benefits of youth." He stretched his arms and yawned. "You have watered the animals?"

"Yes, Uncle." Channah was proud of her morning's work. "They are resting now."

"So I see. I think someday you may be as skilled a shepherdess as my sweet Yael. She was so eager to learn, always asking questions, most of them beginning with why."

Surprise allowed words to fly from Channah's unguarded mouth. "There was a time when Auntie could speak?"

"Oh, my, yes." He stared into the distance. "And she sang like a turtle dove cooing. All day long, humming and singing, telling me stories to pass the time. That was years ago, but I can still hear her voice in my mind." Avram stood and took up his staff.

Channah pondered this new information. "What happened to make Auntie stop speaking?"

Avram turned his fierce eyes on Channah, his nostrils flaring from deep breaths. After a long moment, his face softened. "You do not know. Of course not." He tapped the end of his staff on the ground. "It was long before you were born. Yael's mother was ill, and she went to the village to take care of her. Naturally, she took the baby along because he was still nursing." His pause was so lengthy Channah began to think her uncle would not complete his explanation. Then, as abruptly as he had stopped, Avram took up his narrative again. "Yael fought them, but she was no match for armed soldiers. They murdered our little son, and they almost killed her, too."

"The Romans are evil."

"No disagreement there. These were King Herod's men." Avram shook his head.

"But why, Uncle?"

"Who knows? Fear. Insecurity. Insanity. The mighty king had Bethlehem's baby boys slaughtered so no one of them could grow up and take his crown."

Channah cringed when her uncle muttered a curse she occasionally heard in the marketplace, using a word no one ever dared to speak in Yakov's home. She sat staring at her lap, where her hands twisted at her tunic. Her shadow reminded her the sun was almost directly overhead—time to serve the midday meal. She stood to announce her intention. "Now I—"

Avram quieted Channah with a hand motion. He stood motionless, turning his head to face the light breeze. After a long moment, he broke into a smile. "There will be three of us eating."

Channah unloaded food to the two trays she had with her. In the distance, she heard a shepherd's pipe. Turning toward the sound, she was stunned to see a man approaching on a donkey, piping a merry tune. Perhaps Avram was not only insane but was also possessed of a demon. How else was he able to predict the arrival of strangers? Nevertheless, she prepared the trays, while wrapping her own portion of food in the corner of her shawl.

"Caleb, my friend." Avram barely waited for the man to dismount before embracing him. "Surely spring must be here if you are out and about."

The thin man's hair and beard were gray. Unlike Avram's unruly locks, Caleb's were scraggly and spare. "Greetings, Avram. I trust I find you and Yael in good health."

"My wife is resting today, but for the most part she is doing well. The arrival of this child has brightened her life." Avram pointed. "Channah, daughter of my niece Rebekah. Yael and I will teach her shepherding skills."

"It is good you finally consented to pass on what you know." Caleb inclined his head in Channah's direction. "Listen to this old man, child. He knows everything there is to know about caring for sheep."

"Yes, sir."

"You will take refreshment, I am sure." Avram settled cross-legged on a level piece of ground, and Caleb sat down facing him.

Channah set the trays of food before the men, serving the guest first, then her uncle. She squatted nearby, ready to perform any required serving tasks and to clean up afterwards.

After Avram poured the wine, he asked, "How is your son?"

"He still lives in the wilderness. I see him rarely." Caleb cleared his throat and picked pieces of crust from his bread. "I assume we shall be doing business at shearing season."

"I see no reason why not," Avram answered.

"Since we have been friends for so many years, I will warn you that the tax collectors are growing more suspicious than ever. If we are caught, you know as well as I the consequences are severe. On the other hand, the rumor is they will take an even higher percentage than last year."

Avram nodded.

"There are days when I wonder how much longer I can continue my business." Caleb sipped his wine with closed eyes. "I am getting too old to keep outwitting these tax men."

"I know what you mean, my friend. I would sell my sheep and move to the village if there was anyone to take care of Yael when my life is done."

"I understand. The Lord was wise to take Zara before me. Now I am responsible for no one but my worthless hirelings and my runaway son. I once expected he would carry on as a wool merchant when I sleep with my fathers, but I doubt that will ever be."

"So we are just two tired old men who have lost all hope. More wine?" Avram filled his and Caleb's cups. He held the container out to Channah, but she nodded her declination. He set the wine to the side and folded a chunk of bread around the last of his cheese. "The tax collectors are not fools, and too many men do not guard their tongues. Consider this. Not more than two weeks ago, a man who claimed to be a wool merchant came through here. Although he did not directly ask me to do anything illegal, the offer was clearly implied."

"I trust you made no mention of me." Caleb held his cup suspended between his mouth and the serving tray.

"Of course not." Avram snorted. "I fed him and sent him on his way convinced—I hope—that I am a lunatic, as anyone from around here could tell him."

"You could rid yourself of that reputation, my friend. All you have to do is admit the possibility you had a dream."

"I know what I saw as well as you do." Avram brushed bread crumbs from his flyaway beard. "It was real."

"No doubt our memories have grown dim," Caleb insisted. "By now you must be uncertain what, if anything, happened so many years ago."

Avram tipped his cup upward and drained the last of his wine. After wiping his mouth on a sleeve, he raised his chin. "It is as clear as if it took place last night. Besides, why should I care if some say I am mad? Perhaps people will think twice before they come near me. Even tax collectors."

While the men shared a laugh, Channah retrieved the empty trays and cups. She wanted to linger and listen but feared being reprimanded if she appeared too interested in a grownup conversation. Reluctantly, she took the dishes to the spring, all the while wondering what mysterious thing Avram had witnessed.

Chapter Six

The next morning, Yael arose as usual and went to the pasture with Avram and Channah. Her face had a pinched quality to it, but Channah was unable to guess whether her aunt was still sick or not. Yael wept when the first spring lamb was born that day. She brushed away tears while showing Channah the use of a gentle touch to clean the newborn's face. Then she demonstrated how to encourage the new mother to bond with her baby.

"Ah, an early lamb." Avram knelt beside his wife. "Can it be springtime already?"

Yael nodded her agreement, still dabbing at her eyes.

"There will be strangers in the hills soon," Avram said. "Next time we get supplies, I will buy Channah a shepherd's pipe and show her how to play it. I should have taught her sooner, but the new season has crept up on me." He put an arm around Yael. "It is good for you to have this child's company until the tax collectors go back to their houses in town." He turned his head back to Channah. "I am depending on the two of you to take care of each other."

"Yes, Uncle," Channah replied, although she did not understand what he meant.

"In a year or two you may be strong enough to help me shear the winter wool away." Avram stroked his beard. "Have you ever pulled the string of a bow?"

"No, Uncle. Never."

"Of course not, living in the city you would have no need." He held out a fist. "Here, push my hand to the ground."

Although Channah applied all the muscle power she could muster, Avram's arm hardly moved.

The old man chuckled. "You will have to defend yourself with a rod and a slingshot for the time being, but they will suffice. I have seen Yael use her rod to bring down a swooping hawk." Avram inclined his head until it rested against Yael's shoulder. "She is quite a woman."

Without taking her eyes from the sheep, Yael lifted a hand to caress the side of Avram's face.

After the sheep were settled and the evening meal was finished, Avram pushed aside a sheepskin to expose the bare ground that formed the tent's floor. He began to dig with his knife, eventually uncovering a small wooden chest. Channah watched with fascination as her uncle withdrew a handful of coins. He put the money into the soft leather pouch he kept tucked into his belt and re-buried the chest. "No one is to know about my box of coins, Channah. It is our secret, mine and Yael's, and now yours." He stood and smoothed over the earth with his foot before replacing the sheepskin rug.

Yael packed bread, which Avram took when he went outside. Then she moved a good quantity of food into the center of the tent, along with a few pots and dishes.

"Is Uncle hungry so soon after eating?" Channah asked. Yael responded with a number of hand gestures Channah did not understand. Before long, Yael dragged her bedding outside.

Channah followed her aunt to the tent's opening. "Are we going to sleep in the sheepfold?"

Yael tapped her chest and pointed to the spot where her pallet lay. Then she extended a hand to Channah and shrugged, which Channah took to mean she had the choice of sleeping inside the tent or outside. She fetched her sheepskins and placed them immediately next to Yael's.

Channah snuggled into her bed of soft wool, drawing her coverlet under her chin in the crisp night air. The full moon infused the landscape with a soft, silvery light. As Channah gazed up at the bright moon and numberless stars, she thought she had never seen anything so mysteriously beautiful. She fought to stay awake to continue enjoying the peaceful delight of this night, but she could not keep her eyes open long.

The next morning, Yael led the herd to a pasture just as Avram customarily did, except she tapped lightly on a small drum instead of calling out to the sheep. The day passed uneventfully. Everything went according to the established routine except for Avram's unexplained absence. That evening, Yael and Channah bedded down in the sheep enclosure as they had the night before.

Before the sun rose the next morning, a noise interrupted Channah's sleep. She rubbed her eyes and propped herself up on one elbow. A short distance outside the stone fence, Avram dismounted from a donkey cart. He wrapped the leather reins loosely around a sturdy branch and climbed into the compound.

Yael sprang from her bed and greeted her husband. When Channah grabbed the corner of her bedding to drag it inside the tent, Yael placed a staying hand on her shoulder.

"We are moving to higher ground today," Avram explained. "Or more precisely, you and Yael are moving. I will get you settled and come back for shearing."

Normally, a good number of the sheep slept under the shelter of the cave's wide mouth while the others bedded down out-of-doors, but still inside the rock fence. As instructed, Channah helped Yael keep the cave sleepers in place while Avram removed the boulder and led half of the herd a short distance away. Once the sheep were separated, Yael took charge of the outside flock.

Avram dumped a roll of dried grass from the donkey cart into a wooden feeding trough. "That should be enough to sustain them until Caleb comes later on," he muttered. Channah helped him load the cart with the provisions Yael had gathered in the middle of the tent the previous evening. Avram tossed the bedding on top of the loaded cart.

"Are you ready, Yael?" Avram helped his wife climb over the high side of the chariot. She stood braced against the front, which reached almost to her armpits, and took the reins Avram lifted to her. The donkey was slow to discontinue grazing, but Yael finally coaxed him into a half-hearted walk.

"Come, Channah." Avram retrieved his shepherd's staff from the stone wall. "Help me get the sheep to their new pasture."

"But what about the rest of the herd?"

Even in the dim light, Channah could see Avram's broad grin. "Their fleece and lambs will be taxed. Meanwhile, you and Yael will keep these wooly ones out of the publican's sight." He chuckled as he made his way up the rocky slope, calling to his sheep to follow.

Avram set a brisk pace, always winding upward. Channah encouraged the stragglers from behind, and Yael drove the cart at a great enough distance to keep the donkey from frightening the sheep. The caravan had to hold up more than once for Avram to rescue a sheep who got into one sort of trouble or another, such as becoming entangled in a thorn bush. The stops never seemed long enough to Channah, but she knew there was no point in complaining.

Chapter Seven

Avram was able to travel more swiftly on his return trip, driving the donkey downhill and not having a flock of sheep to be concerned with. Even with the girl to help and provide companionship, he worried about being separated from Yael. If all went well, he would finish his business with the tax collector soon.

Caleb was outside his house when Avram arrived before dawn. After the two men nodded their greetings, Avram handed the reins to his friend and leapt from the cart. He unhitched the donkey while Caleb fed the animal a bag of grain. When Avram started to push the cart away, Caleb whispered, "Leave it."

Avram ceased his movement and raised a questioning eyebrow.

Caleb leaned close. "Go before the sun rises. There were soldiers and strangers in the village yesterday, and I have no idea why."

Grabbing his staff, Avram walked briskly away from Bethlehem. Renting Caleb's cart to haul hay was legitimate. Still, it was best to avoid contact with Romans. A wily soldier might ask enough questions to figure out Avram's use of his friend's donkey and cart took longer than a simple delivery. Besides, he needed to get back to the sheep still enclosed in his winter fold. He knew from years of experience how anxious his animals became with even the slightest change in their routine.

Since he had not stopped to draw water at the village's public well, Avram planned his route to take him by the nearest natural spring. He drank his fill of the gurgling water and munched on dried fruit as he continued making his way through the familiar terrain toward home.

During a journey through the hills, Avram typically played his pipe to announce his presence. On this occasion, however, he used his knowledge of fellow shepherds' habits to avoid being seen. Even those Jews who cheated on their own taxes were not above betraying a fellow countryman. There were always a few scoundrels hoping to sell information to the Romans. The safest approach was for no one other than Caleb to know about his recent trip to conceal half his flock from the publicans.

Although he longed to take a long rest, Avram knew he had many things to do that morning before the shearers arrived. He collapsed his tent and stowed it deep inside his home cave. Then he took his sheep—those not in hiding with Yael—and a few supplies to a pasture he used only when strangers were around. At one end of the wide valley, an overhanging cliff provided adequate shelter for the sheep. Some years ago, Avram had erected a stone enclosure against the shadow of the cliff, not far from a little brook that supplied fresh water.

As expected, Caleb arrived with two helpers and with a tax official. "Greetings, Avram bar Abijah." He made no move to embrace his old friend.

Avram matched Caleb's formality to underscore the illusion their association was nothing more than business. "Peace be upon you and your house, Caleb of Bethlehem. I expected you earlier."

"Yes, we were unavoidably detained," Caleb said. He glanced upward. "We must work quickly before the light fades."

"Quite right. I have prepared a patch of soft ground near the pen. Do your young men know how to position and restrain the animals?"

"This is their first shearing, but I have instructed them in what to do." Caleb motioned to his workers, and they hurried toward the paddock.

Avram lifted an eyebrow but did not comment. Turning to the tax man, he asked, "Do you require any assistance?"

"No," the slender fellow replied. "I shall keep account from that little rise yonder. Less dirt and stench from that distance."

"As you wish." Avram did not bother to restrain scorn from dripping into his words. "Let us get to work, then."

While Caleb and Avram laid out their tools, the tax assessor unrolled his carpet and meticulously arranged his writing materials on it. Meanwhile, the hired helpers hauled water from the stream to fill a wooden trough. Avram separated a ewe and led her to Caleb's assistant. "Let's get her as comfortable as we can. That will minimize her struggling."

The young man nodded but did not move. With a sigh, Avram sat the sheep upright. "Kneel behind and hold her this way." He demonstrated his words and then stepped aside as the youth took hold of the sheep. Shaving the wool from the sheep's belly proceeded slowly because Caleb's helper could not keep the wiggling animal still.

Avram brought a second sheep to the shearing place. "Are you as inept as your friend?" he asked the short, stocky youth.

"We are not friends," the lad replied.

"Your gain." Avram squatted and put one arm on the sheep. "You have seen how this is done. Go ahead and put her into a sitting position."

With considerable grunting, the young man wrestled the uncooperative ewe into a sitting position on her hind end. Just as Avram scraped his knife down her belly, the sheep sprang from her captor's grasp, somehow managing to kick the helper in the face before making good her escape. The young man screamed a curse and hurled a rock, narrowly missing the sheep's backside.

Avram grabbed the young man's tunic and jerked him close. "It is good your stone-throwing ability is as pathetic as your shearing skills." He held the blade of his knife almost touching the helper's bleeding nose. "Harm one of my sheep, and I promise you will regret it."

"Peace." Caleb stopped his work and glared at his friend. "The ewe is not hurt."

"I will bring another sheep," Avram said, relaxing his grip on the young man's tunic. "Wipe your nose before I return. Bloody fleece will not bring as good a price."

After Avram walked away, Caleb's helper said, "My father warned me this old man is crazy. Now I see for myself that he spoke the truth."

The other young man dabbed at the oozing blood. "Forgive me, Caleb. I am going home. No wage is worth putting up with this lunatic."

"He is harmless," Caleb replied. "If you do your work well, you will have no trouble. Merely show respect for him and treat his animals gently."

"Gently? That cursed ewe kicked me in the face. I would like to use a thick rod to teach her some manners. And that old fool who owns her as well." The youth stood and shook out his tunic. "I hope my mother can get the bloodstain out of my clothes. I will see you back in Bethlehem."

"Wait until this sheep is shorn," the other helper said. "I will go with you."

"Put her on her backside so I may continue," Caleb advised. After the sheep was positioned, he resumed cutting away her thick winter wool. "Surely you will not leave two helpless old men to do all this shearing?"

"Helpless?" The idle helper puffed his cheeks and exhaled with a snort. "The lunatic may be old, but he is as strong as an ox. Did you see how he lifted me by my tunic? Filthy old viper."

Caleb worked in silence until the ewe's fleece finally fell away in one piece. The newly-shorn sheep frisked away, leaping as if she was relieved to be rid of her burden of wool. Caleb stood and stretched his back. "One done at least." He turned to his helpers. "I cannot pay you if you desert me."

"You should give us something for the work we have done and for traveling all the way up here into the hills," the blood-spattered youth protested. "Not to mention my injury."

His companion tugged at his sleeve. "Come, let us go before the madman comes back with another of his precious sheep. My father will give us some coins when I explain we were in fear for our lives."

"There is no danger here, only hard work. Is that not your real objection?" Caleb muttered as the young men walked away.

Bringing one of his sheep with him, Avram sauntered toward Caleb. "Departing so soon?" he asked, nodding toward the helpers' retreating backs.

"Alas, we must do all of the shearing work ourselves." Caleb rinsed his knife in the trough. "Regardless how much I offered to pay, those two were the only ones willing to help me do your shearing. Your reputation is well known, and now you will again be the subject of village gossip."

Avram shrugged. "I will hold Skinny Fleece while you shear." He put the ewe on her rump. "If the publican is still here when she is done, I will bring a yearling, the one we shall roast for dinner."

"So the next sheep is for eating." Caleb began working on Skinny Fleece. "I see the tax collector has stopped the boys, and he is speaking with them."

Chapter Eight

"Curse those worthless helpers you brought with you," Avram said loudly, as he positioned the ewe.

"They are no worse than the rest of today's young men. None of them want to work hard." Caleb grunted. "How do you expect me to get the wool from this animal if you cannot hold her still?"

"Am I a magician?" Avram uttered a curse as the sheep squirmed and struggled against his grip.

The publican wandered closer. "How long is this shearing going to take?"

Avram looked up at the official. "Far longer than it would if this merchant had brought some competent help."

"You blame me?" Caleb shouted. "You are the one who drove the strong young men away. You and your evil temper."

"I do not wish to spend the night out here," the tax collector said. "You must work faster."

Caleb moved the fleece aside and washed his knife. "We are old men. You cannot expect us to move with the speed of our youth."

"We are not quick enough?" Avram released the shorn ewe and stood. "Since you are so knowledgeable, you should demonstrate for us how this is done."

"I know nothing of this kind of work and have no wish to learn," the publican replied.

After Avram went to fetch another sheep, the tax collector turned to Caleb. "The shepherd is a disagreeable old man, but at least he is honest."

"Oh?" Caleb asked, wiping sweat from his face to cover a grin. "How can you be certain?"

"I have counted his sheep and compared the number to last year's records. His herd has grown at the expected rate." He sighed. "You cannot imagine how many of these ignorant shepherds try to hide their new stock, thinking no one will discover their deceit." He inspected his own left hand, turning it over and back. "What they fail to realize is that we tax collectors have a great deal of discernment. I am able to tell immediately if a man is lying or telling me the truth."

Caleb sat back on his heels. "Amazing."

"Yes. These foolish backcountry shepherds have no idea how easily we see through their clumsy attempts to cheat on their taxes."

"Apparently not." Caleb nodded.

Returning with a young sheep in tow, Avram knelt and settled the animal before Caleb. "Try to work fast enough to satisfy the demands of your government," he growled.

Caleb ran his thumb along the sharp edge of his knife. "I have no need for you to tell me how to do my work, old man." He began to scrape the yearling's underside. "Now I will show you how swiftly I can move."

"I do not know how the two of you tolerate the smell of these animals." With that remark, the publican turned and began to walk away.

Before the tax man reached his perch, Avram pulled the sheep's head upward. He nodded to Caleb, who severed the animal's jugular with one deft swipe. "You idiot!" Avram roared. "Look what you have done in your careless haste." He set the bleeding sheep aside and drew his dagger. "Now you will pay."

"You crazy old fool." Caleb jumped to his feet, brandishing his shearing knife.

Avram stabbed at Caleb, who stepped aside just in time.

"Stop it," the publican yelled, running back toward the two men. He pushed them apart, panting to catch his breath. "What are you doing, trying to kill each other?"

Avram glared at Caleb. "This jackal cut my yearling's throat."

Caleb attempted to lunge at Avram, but the publican held him back. "You are a snake," Caleb growled. "How can I have a steady hand at shearing when you cannot hold your sheep still? If you had the strength of a young man, I would not have cut the ewe."

"If I had the strength of my youth, you would be as dead as that sheep yonder." Avram pointed his knife at the lifeless carcass.

"Calm down, both of you," the publican demanded. "If you have a grievance to settle over the dead animal, take it to court. In the meantime, even out here in this remote pasture, you are to live peaceably, as Rome has decreed."

"Even the Romans recognize a man must defend himself," Caleb said.

"Rome," Avram muttered. He spat on the ground and put away his knife. "I expect compensation for my loss when we settle up for the purchase of my fleece."

"You should be the one to pay, Avram." Caleb threw his shearing knife to the ground. "You ran off all my help, and now I must spend the rest of this week doing a job that should have taken only two or three days."

While the men continued to argue, the tax collector returned to his carpeted refuge. He bent over, writing without looking up.

Avram and Caleb removed the fleece from another animal, stopping frequently to complain about one another's technique. After one more sheep was sheared, Avram declared the rinsing trough needed to be refreshed. He and Caleb quarreled stridently about which one of them was responsible for hauling water.

The publican packed his writing materials and rolled his carpet before approaching the two feuding old men. "Based on the number of sheep and the yield from the sheep the two of you have managed to shear, I have calculated the taxes you owe." He handed both Avram and Caleb a scrap of parchment with a number written on it. "You know how this works. Deliver payment to me within a week. Good day."

Avram shook the parchment at arm's length. "This tax is too high. I will have nothing left to buy grain when the grass withers. My sheep will die. You cannot collect taxes from dry bones."

Caleb did not wait for Avram to finish speaking before he began to protest. "How can you imagine we will harvest so much wool? See what sparse coats most of them have. Besides, I have expenses, workmen to pay, and tools to maintain. A man has to eat, you know."

While both Avram and Caleb pled their respective cases, the publican smiled and walked away. He loaded his donkey and quickly disappeared over the nearest hill.

The men stopped their complaining and sat on the ground. "The publican lasted longer than his predecessor. Wine, my friend?" Avram asked.

"With pleasure," Caleb answered.

"If you dress and roast the yearling, I shall see if I remember how to shear sheep."

Caleb nodded. "No one can cut a fleece better or faster than you, Avram." He smiled. "That is, unless you allow a stranger to restrain the animal."

"I must have some sleep soon. Even so, we should be able to finish shearing the herd by the time the moon rises tonight."

Caleb lifted his cup of wine. "To friendship."

Chapter Nine

Caleb came to the summer pastureland to collect the great mound of fleece Avram harvested from the hidden sheep. After he departed, Channah saw no one but her aunt and uncle. Most of the time she was content, although there were evenings when she wished for a friend to sling stones with or even one of her cousins to talk to.

Shunning the dark cave, Channah made her bed in the fold among the sheep, enjoying a sense of wellbeing she had never known before. As the summer progressed, Yael showed her how to make bread and cheese and how to use a rod as a weapon. Avram taught her to trim wool tags and help ewes with difficult births.

Although the days continued to be warm, the nights eventually became chilly. One morning, Yael took the tunic Channah normally wore and gave her a ragged castoff instead. Channah wondered why, especially when she noticed her aunt was also wearing a threadbare garment.

The day was further set apart when Avram asked Channah to help him separate the male lambs into the paddock while the remainder of the flock went to graze. "I will be going to Bethlehem today, delivering these young rams to Caleb," he said. "As always, he will help me to keep half of them out of the tax man's view." He rubbed a hand over his upper arm. "Cooler days are coming. While I return, we will move back to our winter home."

Yael nodded in agreement and then drew Avram aside. Channah watched as the couple engaged in their peculiar variety of communication. After many hand motions, Yael grabbed a small stick and drew in the dirt.

Channah could hear Avram's voice but could not make out his words. She wanted to linger, to know what the discussion was about. However, since leading the herd to each day's pasture had become her job, she called to the sheep and began to walk away. She saw Yael pat several lambs before turning away to follow the ewes.

After the sheep ate and drank, they rested in the grass. Yael sat with her knees drawn up and her forehead resting on them. Channah wandered near her aunt, already missing Avram's conversation. When Yael lifted her head, Channah saw tears glistening on her aunt's cheeks.

Channah wished for some way to comfort Yael. Knowing none, she sat beside her and slipped an arm around her aunt's slender waist. Yael hugged Channah's shoulders. They sat motionless for some time, with Channah wondering what secret sorrow made Yael weep. "I once cried for my mother every night, but the tears did not bring her back to me. Now I make up songs and stories. Would you like for me to sing to you?"

After Yael nodded and brushed at her wet face, Channah borrowed a tune she often heard in her Uncle Yakov's home. She sang about a beautiful woman who married a handsome man and had a little girl both of them adored. After the song ended, Yael patted Channah's hand and returned to the sheep.

Channah sat for a moment, surveying the calm beauty of the scenery. She breathed in the cool mountain air, certain someday she would have a good husband, someone who cared for her with the tenderness Avram showed Yael. She plucked a wildflower and studied its petals, vowing her own daughter—when she had one—would never be forsaken or feel unwanted.

After the evening meal, Yael planted seeds in pots while Channah watched with intense interest. She wondered what her aunt planned to grow, but she knew such a direct question would be hopeless. Channah looked forward to Avram's homecoming, which would allow for occasional conversation.

***

It was almost sunset a few days later, when Avram returned. He had an enormous basket strapped to his back and led a donkey laden with supplies. Yael grinned and clapped her hands when her husband opened the basket and held up new tunics. "Channah, you will have to use your belt to take up some length until you grow a bit taller," he said. "The young weaver does not pay as much for used tunics as his father did." Avram shook his head. "Typical."

Peering into the basket, Avram muttered, "Now, let's see. Is there anything else I should unpack?" Yael bent beside him to look inside. "Ah, yes." He pulled out a small leather pouch and handed it to his wife.

After a peek inside the pouch, Yael smiled and handed it back to Avram. She pointed from him to Channah and back.

"Auntie wants you to have this." Avram grinned as he handed the pouch to Channah.

Not certain what to do, she ran her fingers over the smooth leather.

"Open it," Avram said.

Loosening the drawstring, Channah explored the inside of the pouch with her fingers. She pulled out a small jewel on a silver chain. Afraid to breathe, Channah held it up and admired the golden color. Was it truly for her?

Yael took the necklace and slipped it over Channah's head. The jewel hung almost to her waist. It sparkled in the waning light.

"It is a topaz." Avram cleared his throat. "Something you women and girls value, I suppose."

Channah hugged Yael tightly. "Thank you, Auntie. I've never seen anything so beautiful."

Next, she kissed Avram's hand. "Thank you, Uncle."

"You have brought joy back into our lives, child." Avram shuffled his feet. "Well, I suppose you two have everything ready to return to the winter pastures tomorrow." He glanced around and wiped his eyes on a sleeve. "I will go now and see to the donkey."

Chapter Ten

Channah was thrilled when Avram assigned her to lead the herd to their winter quarters. On the first morning of their journey, she stood waiting with most of the sheep on a small plateau, accessible only by a narrow ledge. Meanwhile, her uncle guarded the top of the steep path that wound down into the valley, permitting only one or two sheep at a time to travel on the narrowest part of the passage.

Before they set out, Avram stressed the importance of keeping a keen watch as they crossed this treacherous territory. Although the sun had shone brightly at first light, a fine mist now made the terrain slippery. The shadow of a tall mountain peak and the gathering clouds made the morning feel more like twilight to Channah. She skirted the perimeter of the herd, nudging the sheep into a tighter grouping.

At last the slow descent was almost complete. Channah could see Avram lying flat, leaning his upper body over a ravine to rescue a sheep that had lost her footing. Some distance behind, Yael was picking her way down the ledge, leading the reluctant donkey.

At the same moment she heard a low growl, Channah caught a flash of movement in her peripheral vision. She whirled around to see a mountain lion leap on the back of a ewe. "Uncle!" she screamed, not concerned about frightening the sheep by shouting. Tingling with fear, Channah pulled the slingshot from her waistband. She hurled a sharp stone, scoring a direct hit on the predator's head—though not striking the eye she aimed for.

The stunned lion released her grip on the sheep. Instead of running away, the ewe crumpled to the earth. Channah took a step backward as the mountain lion stood and swiped a paw across her face. The apparent confusion lasted only an instant.

The lion turned toward Channah. It felt as if the two of them were locked together in wordless communication. Channah saw an angry hostility in the depths of the mountain lion's eyes, and she felt a paralyzing terror.

With as little movement as possible, Channah closed her fingers around another stone, never breaking contact with the beast's fearsome greenish-yellow eyes. A jumbled mass of thoughts flew through her mind. *The slingshot is not sufficient. A direct hit on the nose might chase her away. I am not strong enough to kill the lion with my rod. I am going to die.*

As soon as Channah eased another stone from her pouch, the rock slipped from her hand and ricocheted off her toe. The lion glanced at the sheep's bleeding carcass, then turned back and took a tentative step toward Channah. While desperately feeling inside her pouch for another stone, she heard the sound of rushing air. The lioness screamed, leapt straight up, and then sprawled on the ground, shot through with an arrow.

Avram came running and crushed the mountain lion's head with one blow of his rod. "I believe the arrow killed her, but I want to be certain." Then he rushed to kneel beside Channah and held her close. "Are you all right, child?"

"Yes, Uncle," she managed to choke out before bursting into tears. Before long, a weeping Yael joined them in a three-way hug.

Avram disengaged and went to the ewe the lion had attacked.

"I tried to save her," Channah said with a trembling voice.

After examining the sheep's body, Avram shook his head. "She could have recovered from these wounds. The poor little thing died of fright." He moved to the lion's carcass and began to drag it away. "I will guard the sheep while the two of you bring the donkey."

Earlier, Channah relished leading the herd. Now relieved to be under her aunt's protection, she stayed close to Yael as they climbed to the ledge where the loaded donkey stood grazing. "I was afraid," she confessed. "I should have known you and Uncle would not let the lion get me."

Yael wiped her eyes, nodded, and squeezed Channah's hand.

Although the rest of the day was uneventful, Channah was still shaken that evening. After sunset, Avram slept while Channah and Yael kept watch over the sheep. They sat on a flat rock, back to back, high enough to spot any unusual activity. After munching on dried fruit and cheese, Channah grew restless. Normally, she would have wandered around among the sheep. However, because of the earlier encounter with the mountain lion, she was reluctant to leave her aunt's side. Instead, Channah told Yael a story about a shepherd girl whose sheep spoke and sang songs with her—but only when other people were not around to hear them talk.

When the twilight faded, Yael shook her husband awake. With a yawn and a stretch, he left the fleece pallet and drank a cup of wine. As soon as he disappeared into the darkness, Channah and Yael snuggled into the still-warm fleece.

Late the following afternoon, Channah spied a shepherd bringing his sheep down the mountain. If she continued in the direction her uncle set for their descent, the two herds would converge. She waved her arms to get Avram's attention before pointing toward the other flock. She could see her uncle had already lengthened his stride to move through the sheep toward her.

"We will rest and let the herd graze on that smooth place yonder." Avram pointed with his staff.

"But Uncle," Channah protested, "the other shepherd is going to that same spot. Our sheep will become mingled."

"The animals know who to follow when we separate." Avram smiled down at her. "You still have much to learn, child." He waved to the approaching shepherd. "The company of a fellow herder and his family will be most welcome after our summer of solitude. See? Bringing up the rear? A woman and some children are with him."

Channah was disappointed to find only little boys with the shepherd's family. She slung a few stones with them before joining the women. "My aunt does not speak," Channah explained. "But she hears and understands what you say. We have been pasturing our sheep in the high country this summer, my Aunt Yael, Uncle Avram, and I. Now we are going home to the hills near Bethlehem."

"As you can see," the young woman said, "my husband and I also are shepherds. Our winter home is in a valley on the other side of Bethlehem." She adjusted her

56

long scarf over her nursing baby. "Your uncle's name is Avram? I have heard there is a man by that name who works in this area." Her eyes darted to where the men stood. "Perhaps there is more than one."

Yael held up one finger, pointed to her husband, and then displayed a single finger again.

"I believe my aunt is indicating Uncle is the only shepherd by the name of Avram in our area." Channah remembered her uncle was known as a lunatic. She watched the woman shift as if uneasy. "He has been teaching me about sheep. My other relatives refused to raise me, but Uncle Avram and Auntie took me in." She hoped the woman understood that her aunt and uncle were good people, even if they were somewhat peculiar.

The shepherd's wife focused her attention on her infant, giving every appearance of forgetting Channah and Yael were there.

"May I hold your baby after he finishes nursing?" Channah asked.

"She," the woman said with a smile. "My little daughter Lilia." She rubbed the baby's stomach. "She should be full by now."

Chapter Eleven

The men and boys watched over the sheep while Channah helped the women prepare the evening meal. The shepherd's wife asked Channah many questions about Yael's method of making fresh bread in a lidded pot over an open fire.

After eating, the two families sat cross-legged in the deepening twilight, while the men talked. They complained about high taxes and bashed all levels of the Roman government. At one point, the young shepherd's wife whispered to Channah that she should discontinue refreshing the wine in the men's cups. Attempting to strike a balance between the woman's wishes while still responding to Avram's upheld cup, Channah served refills more slowly than normal. She did not see that her lack of speed diminished the laughter the men shared after each comment on the stupidity of Roman administrators.

Channah helped her aunt put away the pots and eating utensils. As soon as possible, she squatted near the young mother, drawn by an unexplained fascination with the woman's baby.

"It was a night not much different from this one," Avram said, seeming to continue a conversation with the other man. "Later in the year, cold but not bitterly so. My wife was in the village."

When Avram held his cup away from his body, Channah scurried to fill it immediately. Regardless of the young mother's wishes, she did not want the flow of her uncle's words to be interrupted. She had never heard him talk about his past, and she wanted to learn the rest of his story.

Cradling his wine cup in both hands, Avram gazed into its depths. "I joined two other young fellows to share the work of caring for our sheep. All of us had small flocks, nothing like the large herd I have now." At last, he took a sip of wine but continued to stare into his cup. "The three of us sat and talked while the moon rose that night. But then, a most peculiar thing happened, what the Romans call an 'eclipse.' The moon remained in the sky but slowly disappeared."

The younger man nodded. "I have been witness to such an event once. It was a marvelous sight."

"The darkening of the moon was only the beginning of the amazing events of that night." Avram took a gulp of wine. "We sat in the thick darkness, the other shepherds and I, in awe of what we had seen. Then, suddenly, there was a great burst of light." He put his cup aside. "It was as if a star soared from above and rested just above where we were." He turned his face upward. "Looking at the light was not painful the way looking into the sun is, yet it had equal brilliance." Avram grasped his companion's arm. "And then, I saw an angel floating in the light, suspended above the earth, standing on the air as it were."

The previously jovial young shepherd spoke in a somber tone. "What did he look like, this angel?"

"Like a man, somewhat, but taller I think. It appeared he had wings, but it may have been the aura of the light encircling him." Avram pointed upward. "As you might imagine, I was scared to death. We all were. And, do you know what he said?"

The young man shook his head. "No idea."

"'Fear not.' The first thing he told us, 'Fear not.' He said he had news for us, and all of a sudden the sky was filled with angels or some sort of Heavenly beings. A thousand times more of them than all of the sheep in my herd and yours. These creatures made music, but they were not exactly singing, not like humans anyway. It was—I cannot say—indescribable."

"You said your name is Avram?" The young man scooted back a slight distance.

"Yes. I am the Avram often referred to as a lunatic. But, listen to me, these things really happened. It was not a dream. I know because the angel told us the anointed one was born that night. In Bethlehem, as foretold in prophecy."

"Perhaps I should move my flock forward."

"Hear this first," Avram insisted. "The other men and I ran all the way to the village. We found a newborn child, just as the angel told us, in a stable. The baby's mother had laid him in the manger, on the straw meant for the cattle to eat. Every detail was exactly, precisely as the angel specified, right down to his description of the way the child was wrapped up. I knew that night our Messiah had come." Avram bowed his head and spoke softly. "That was more than twenty years ago, but I remember it as if it was yesterday"

"Twenty years?" The young man narrowed his eyes. "If the child you speak of was indeed our liberator, then why are we still ruled by the Romans? Where is our Messiah now?"

"They killed him. King Herod—not the imbecile who rules now, the one who called himself 'the Great'— had him murdered. Him and all of the other baby boys in Bethlehem." Avram's voice dropped until it was barely audible. "Every one of them. Including mine."

"I cannot thank you enough for sharing your wine with me, Avram. It has refreshed me more than I expected." The young shepherd stood and glanced around. "I remember now my wife suggested we not waste good moonlight in sleep." He stepped back. "If you will forgive me, meaning no disrespect, I feel we must move on."

"Bah," Avram snorted. "I pose no threat to you, nor does my wife. You may believe what I say or not. It makes no difference to me."

"Please do not think I doubt anything you have told me, good sir. No, not at all. But my wife has not seen her family for months, and I know she is anxious to get home as soon as possible."

"Yes, I see her eagerness to resume your journey." Avram gestured to the shepherd's wife, quietly dozing with the baby fast asleep in her lap. "Go in peace if you will. Or let your family have a night's rest. The decision is in your hands. Meanwhile, I will guard our sheep." With those words, Avram stalked away.

Channah lay on her fleece, trying to make sense of all she had heard. Finally, she understood why everyone said Avram was insane. When Yael shook her awake the next morning, the other family and their sheep were nowhere to be seen.

Chapter Twelve

Channah was surprised by a feeling of happiness when she caught sight of the entrance to the cave that served as Avram and Yael's winter haven. "Home," she exclaimed, bringing smiles to the faces of her aunt and uncle.

"Yes, home," Avram agreed. He stopped and took a long look. "Someone has been here in our absence."

No matter how hard she squinted in the dim afternoon light, Channah could not see what prompted her uncle to think there had been an intruder.

"Yael, Channah, wait here. I will see if they are still inside." Avram strode through the rock-walled sheepfold to the cave's entrance, his rod in one hand. Soon he emerged and beckoned them forward with a wave of his hand.

Channah immediately noticed the wooden shelf had been turned over. The remains of a broken pot lay nearby.

Avram bent to move a heavy stone, revealing food containers still buried in the cave's soft earth. "It appears our visitor was a small animal, not a human." He straightened. "Nevertheless, I will move our valuables to another location. I have thought for some time my little box might be safer somewhere else, and this convinces me."

As soon the evening meal was consumed, Avram dug up the wooden chest. "Yes, it is all here," he muttered. He stood and shook dust from his tunic. He turned to Channah. "Come with me, child, and help me with this chore."

While Yael remained behind, Channah followed her uncle out of their compound.

"Pay close attention to the path I take to this little cave." Avram pointed to his right. "You know that is the way to our pastures, but we will go in the opposite direction." He led her around rocks and up a steep incline. "If anything happens to me, you and Yael must sell off enough sheep to get the herd down to a size the two of you can manage. These coins will provide you additional security. Do you understand what I am telling you?"

"Yes, Uncle," Channah responded. The thought of being without Avram's protection unsettled her.

"Now, see that rock formation there, the one that looks like a great fist?"

"The one with the scrubby tree growing from its thumb?"

Avram nodded. "Yes, that is the one. But do not depend on the tree. Remember the size and shape of the boulder. When you hold out your hand and it can no longer block the rock from your view, turn to this side." He followed his own directions. "Behind that triangular, dark stone formation, there is a small opening that leads to a cave. I can enter it only by crawling. You might be able to squat or bend enough to walk inside." Avram walked around the stone he described and pointed to the cave's entrance. "Now walk to your left twenty steps. That is where we will bury the chest."

Peeking inside the cave before following her uncle, Channah saw nothing remarkable. "How do you know of this cave, Uncle?"

Avram drew a deep breath. "When I was your age, I wandered throughout these hills and valleys, always curious." He began to dig. "Yael and I took refuge in this little cave once, but that was many, many years ago. Now how many paces am I from the stone that hides the cave's mouth?"

"Twenty, Uncle."

"Good." He continued to deepen the hole as he spoke. "Never tell anyone about this place, Channah. Nor about this box of coins. No one, not even your Uncle Yakov. Especially him, I should say. If—God forbid—Yael and I fail to survive until you are grown and married, you may bring your husband here and take the box." At last he settled the wooden box into a thigh-deep hole.

It was dark by the time Channah and Avram made their way home. Although she knew her aunt and uncle were elderly, she had never thought about the possibility they might die before she was old enough to take care of herself. Avram's solemn words concerned her for a while before she went to sleep that night. However, when their little family resumed a normal routine the following morning, she did her best to put thoughts of death out of her mind.

After the weather turned crisp, Avram made a two-day journey and returned leading a fine ram behind him. He patiently acquainted his ewes with the male he called Big Man.

After the evening meal, Channah sat with Yael's arm around her while her uncle took out a stone and began to sharpen his knife. Avram glanced at Yael, who nodded and smiled. He cleared his throat and began to speak of producing lambs as being somewhat like Yael growing vegetables.

"God has put sheep seeds inside rams. Big Man will plant his seeds inside the ewes," Avram said. "Together they will make the lambs, what you might call their little flowers." He went on to explain the necessity of planning the ram's time with the ewes to assure lambs would be born in the springtime, giving them the longest season possible to grow strong before facing winter.

Keeping his eyes on the work of honing his knife, Avram asked, "Do you understand what I have told you, Channah?"

After a moment of reflection, she replied, "Yes, I see what you have said, Uncle. But why does God not let us plant lambs in the soil, instead of growing them inside of the ewes? Then we could harvest them the way Auntie does her cucumbers. It seems that would be much easier for everyone, especially the sheep."

Yael put a hand over her mouth, but not before Channah saw the grin she attempted to cover.

Avram stood and sheathed his knife. "God's wisdom is different from ours. He does as he pleases, and I do not pretend to understand his ways." Cutting his eyes toward his wife, he muttered, "As I warned you, Yael, the child is too young to understand. I am hardly able to be a father at my age. I cannot be a mother also." He exited the tent without looking back.

Channah wondered what she had done to displease her uncle. She grasped her aunt's hand. "Was I wrong to question the ways of God?"

Yael shook her head to indicate a negative answer. She smiled and pulled Channah into a hug.

Chapter Thirteen

After eight years of working with the sheep, Channah was well acquainted with the daily routine. Activities varied only with the seasons, which repeated themselves in an endless winter-summer-winter-summer pattern. This particular day began as ordinarily as any other. Channah awoke early and lay snuggled in her fleece, enjoying a drowsy rest before Avram's announcement of sunrise. Her reverie was interrupted by what might have been a moan from Yael's side of the tent. Channah lay still, listening, wondering if she actually heard something or dreamed it. After a moment, she heard the sound again.

Channah threw the covers aside and went to kneel beside Yael. "Are you not feeling well, Auntie?" she asked.

Yael pointed to herself and then to her bed, a sign Channah knew meant she and Avram would care for the sheep without her aunt's assistance that day. By the time her uncle came in from the sheep pen, Channah had the morning meal prepared.

Avram patted Yael and tucked her blanket around her shoulders. He ate quickly and without speaking, as he typically did. Channah knew her uncle would become talkative later. First thing in the morning, however, his typical communication was his wish not to communicate.

Humming a tune as she watered the sheep, Channah was unaware she was not alone until a shadow fell across her shoulder. She whirled away, preparing to flee. Despite the gray streak in the man's beard, Channah recognized a familiar face. "Uncle Yakov?" She exhaled, and jammed a hand against her thumping heart. "Good afternoon."

Yakov nodded an acknowledgment of her greeting. "Where are the old shepherd and his wife?"

"Auntie is not feeling well today. Uncle Avram is just over the rise and across the pasture. I will take you to him."

Channah rinsed her muddy hands and struck out toward the rock where Avram normally stationed himself during the afternoon. Although Yakov's appearance was a surprise, Channah was glad to see him. Visitors always brought interesting news of the world beyond the grazing fields, breaking up the predictability of everyday life.

Near the familiar rock, Avram squatted on his haunches. He looked up briefly from the ewe whose hooves he was trimming. After a glance toward Channah and Yakov, the old man turned his eyes back to the animal positioned between his knees and continued his work.

"Good day, Yakov." Avram neither rose nor made eye contact. "I had begun to think you were no longer among the living, since we have not seen or heard from you all these years. Will you take refreshment?"

Yakov frowned and licked his lips. "Yes, I would like something to eat and drink. It is a long walk to this place from where I live."

As she arranged what remained of the day's provisions on a tray, Channah regretted not bringing extra food for the day. She worked as quietly as possible, hoping not to miss any of the conversation between the men.

"I have come to take the girl home."

Yakov's words almost made Channah drop the wine jug. After eight years with Avram and Yael, the pastureland *was* her home.

The calmness of Avram's voice somewhat reassured her. "When?

"Now," Yakov replied.

Channah placed food before Yakov and handed him a jar of wine. Avram released the ewe and turned to accept his portion of wine. Her serving duties done, Channah squatted a short distance away.

With his eyes riveted on Yakov's face, Avram took several sips of wine in silence. When he finally spoke, his voice was almost a growl. "This is a rather sudden turn of events." He sat his drink aside, still staring at the younger man. "We hear nothing from you for years, and then you show up and announce you are taking Channah away. Why?"

"This was always our agreement, sir," Yakov replied. "When I—"

"Agreement?" Avram cocked an eyebrow. "We had an agreement? I thought you simply abandoned a helpless orphan to an old man and his ailing wife. I must be too senile to remember there were terms." He folded his arms. "Yael and I have taught Channah to be a highly skilled shepherdess. Now that she has learned her trade, it seems only fair for her to remain with us and help care for our sheep. Otherwise, why have we fed, clothed, and trained her for the past eight years?"

Yakov leaned forward, hands on his knees. "I am a poor man from a poor family. I am grateful you have raised

Channah, but repaying you with anything more than gratitude is completely beyond my means. I spend everything I make to support my big family."

Avram reached for his wine and took a long drink. After wiping his mouth on a sleeve, he spoke softly. "If you already have too many mouths to feed, why do you wish to add our girl to your household? She should remain here where there is plenty of food."

"After a great deal of effort, I have found a husband for her, and he is anxious to be married as soon as possible."

Channah was so stunned she could hardly breathe. How many lonely evenings had she longed for a home, a husband, and—even more—children of her own?

Instead of speaking, Avram closed his eyes and bowed his head.

After a long moment of silence, Yakov continued, "You have no idea how hard I had to work to arrange this pending marriage for Channah. No one wants to join with a poverty-stricken family."

"She is so young," Avram said without opening his eyes.

"She is almost fourteen, the perfect age for marriage." Yakov scraped his last remaining bread crumbs together and tossed them into his mouth. "If this opportunity slips away, there may never be another."

Avram rested his forehead in his hands. "Gather the sheep, Channah. We will return home early today. You must prepare to go with your uncle, and I must tell Yael you are leaving us."

Chapter Fourteen

Channah hated missing the conversation going on between the men, but she obeyed Avram's instruction to get ready to go home. Despite taking as long as she dared to put away wine jars and trays, all she managed to hear was her prospective husband's name.

Enos. She whispered the name as she herded Avram's flock toward their home paddock. Is Enos tall, she wondered, or short and stocky like me? Maybe he has black hair, or perhaps tawny, sun-streaked locks. Regardless of appearance, Channah was certain her husband would adore her in the same way Avram cared for Yael. Enos had seeds to plant in her. Then, like a healthy ram and ewe, the two of them would bring forth their child. A girl, Channah hoped, but a son was all right as well. A baby boy would be frisky, like a new lamb. No doubt her husband had relatives to talk to, and perhaps Avram and Yael would manage to come and visit on occasion. Channah was certain she was about to begin a season of great happiness.

Avram put a hand on Yakov's shoulder as they and Channah followed the last of the sheep into their enclosure. "Wait here with the girl. I must prepare my wife."

Channah spread fresh straw for the sheep to sleep on and checked the water level in the drinking trough. When there was nothing else to do, she stood in awkward silence.

At last Yakov spoke. "Why are you so inappropriately dressed?"

Channah searched for an answer. "This is what I always wear, Uncle."

Yakov shook his head. "These shepherds may have allowed you to run wild out here in the wilderness, but you cannot go into the city with your hair uncovered."

On cold winter days, she sometimes took her sleeping blanket into the pasture and draped it over her head and shoulders. Was it possible Yakov expected to encounter bitter weather on the walk back to Jerusalem?

As she tried to decide what to do or say next, Avram emerged from the tent. "Come and speak with your Auntie, Channah." He held the flap aside, indicating Channah was to go inside. "I will show Yakov the inside of the cave where the sheep pass the night."

As soon as Channah stepped over the threshold, Yael embraced her in a hug that seemed it would never end. When it finally did, Channah noticed her aunt's eyes were red and puffy.

"You've been crying, Auntie."

Yael nodded, then picked up a leather bag and pointed to the shelf where Channah kept her things. Together they packed the spare tunic, an old pair of boots, and a slingshot. Each time Yael wiped away her tears, she patted Channah's hand or arm.

"May I take the blanket from my bed tomorrow morning?" Channah asked, remembering Yakov might wish for her to wear something on her head.

Yael agreed with her quick little nod. She drew an imaginary circle around her neck, puzzling Channah for a moment.

"Ah, the jewel." She always wore her topaz, but tucked it inside her garment to prevent catching it on a hoof or thorn bush. Channah pulled the necklace outside her tunic. "This is the best gift you and Uncle ever gave me."

Yael held out her hand, palm up. Channah slid the chain over her head and slowly surrendered her only jewelry. *Will she take the necklace, now that I am leaving?*

Wiping her eyes, Yael pushed two small silver coins and the topaz necklace into the bottom of her knife's scabbard. Yael replaced her knife, which hid the money and jewel. She held the scabbard out to Channah.

After a series of hand motions, Channah finally understood that she was to take Yael's knife and keep her necklace hidden. She surrendered her own knife to Yael, thinking the scabbard with its hidden compartment was an extravagant gift, since Yael's knife was much finer than hers. Once Channah's belongings were packed, the two of them began to put together the evening meal. As usual, Channah baked bread while Yael assembled the remainder of the food. They had done this task together for so long there was no longer any need for communication.

"Everything will be fine," Channah said, when Yael continued to weep. "I am going to be married. My husband will take care of me, and Uncle will be here with you."

The evening meal passed with sporadic conversation, but nothing of interest to Channah. While Avram and Yakov spoke of how they hated the Romans and the heavy taxes they imposed on Israel, she thought only of Enos. After the men retired to the sheepfold, she crept into bed, certain she was too excited to fall asleep.

As she lay awake, Channah felt twinges of regret as she realized this was the last time she would lie in her soft fleecy bed. The morning meal would mark the final familiar intimacy of cooking with her Aunt Yael. No more races to see if she could make Avram swell with pride when she sheared a sheep faster than he. Nevertheless, in the city she would go to festivals and markets with the women of her new family. Her husband would cherish her, and their children would warm both their hearts.

Channah spent a restless night. Each time she fell asleep, she awoke excited and eager for morning to come. At last, the sound of voices outside the tent assured her daybreak was about to arrive. Although she could hear Avram and Yakov speaking, she could not strain her ears enough to understand their words. Suddenly they began to shout, filling the air with curses.

When Yael arose and began preparing the morning meal, Channah folded her blanket and rolled up her fleece bedding.

Avram threw aside the tent's flap and stomped inside. "Channah, come and help me with the sheep."

After a furtive glance toward her aunt, Channah followed Avram out of the tent and into the sheepfold. With a jerk of his head, he motioned toward the cave.

Meanwhile, Yakov stood at the far corner of the sheep enclosure with his back turned.

Avram made his way through the milling sheep before turning to face Channah. "Child," he said quietly, "Do you remember where the coins are buried?"

"Yes, Uncle," Channah replied.

"Repeat the directions to me."

"Beyond the triangular rock formation, go to the mouth of the small cave and then go twenty paces to the left. Do you want me to fetch the box for you?"

"No. No." Avram shook his head. "But I want you to remember always where it is. If you are in trouble and you cannot find Yael and me, take what you need from the coins." He lowered his voice. "And never forget, Yakov must not know I have anything of value." He glanced toward the cave opening. "He is an evil man."

"Yes, Uncle. I will remember everything you have told me. What is it you want me to help you do with the sheep?"

Avram put his hand on her shoulder. "Nothing, child. Nothing at all. I hope you know what joy you have brought your Aunt Yael and me. God be with you, little Channah." He turned and walked swiftly from the cave.

Mystified by Avram's peculiar behavior, Channah shrugged and followed him.

Chapter Fifteen

Yakov and Avram ate the morning meal in silence, never once looking at each other. As soon as Avram went outside, Yakov said, "Come along, Channah. We must begin our journey."

Channah stuffed her blanket into her bag, on top of food Yael must have added when no one was looking. She hoisted the strap over her shoulder and embraced her aunt. Last night her only thoughts were about becoming a wife and mother. This morning, the reality of leaving her aunt and uncle overshadowed her excitement about the future.

When Channah left the tent, she saw the stone gate was rolled aside, with Avram standing in its place to restrain the milling sheep. Channah and Yael approached Avram, and he gently took his wife's arm from the girl's shoulder. As Channah passed through the gate, she saw that both her aunt and uncle had wet cheeks. Not knowing what to say to comfort them, she kissed each one's hands and touched them to her forehead. Then she turned and hurried after Yakov, who was already walking away.

"That old man is crazy," Yakov sputtered after he and Channah had covered a short distance. "What did he say when he took you into the cave?"

"He told me I have brought joy to him and Aunt Yael," Channah replied. She reasoned this was a truthful answer, since her uncle had indeed spoken those words. However, she did not make any mention of the coin box.

"Who does that old fool think he is, anyway?" Yakov continued. "Threatening me. I should have taken his rod away from him and beaten him senseless with it."

Channah followed a few steps behind Yakov, enjoying the red wildflowers blossoming on every hillside. A gentle breeze intermittently tossed tendrils of loose hair around her face. It was strangely unsettling not to have a flock of sheep to tend, but she was confident Avram would make sure the animals were fed, watered, and protected. She turned her thoughts to her upcoming marriage, wondering how long she would have to wait to become Enos's wife. Were her cousins and Yakov's wife even now cooking up a feast for a grand celebration?

The sun burned away the morning dew as the pair strode silently toward the city of Jerusalem. Yakov mopped his brow. "Do you have anything to eat?"

"Auntie sent food for at least two good meals."

"Any wine?"

Channah stopped walking and rested her bag on the ground. "No, sir. There are springs of water all around, though."

"We could die of thirst before we find water." Yakov sank to the ground. "I am exhausted from so much walking."

Channah noticed Yakov's breathing was labored, though not raspy as Yael's often was. After surveying the landscape, she pointed to her right. "Yonder may be a spring or brook."

Yakov drew up his knees and rested his head on them. "How would you know that?"

"I cannot be certain," Channah replied. "But there is a line of greener, lusher plants over there. The bushes always gather themselves around water."

"Go and find out. I will wait here."

Glad to be relieved of both Yakov and her bag of possessions, Channah went to investigate. She marveled that her uncle was tired from nothing more than walking. With a glance over her shoulder, she tried to calculate his age. She knew Yakov was not as old as Avram, though both of them seemed ancient to her. What about Enos? She thought seventeen or eighteen would be about right, although she had no information on which to base her guess.

When Channah returned to report she had found water, Yakov was stretched out on the ground, resting on her blanket.

"I suppose we have to go over there to drink," Yakov grumbled.

"Yes," Channah agreed. When she retrieved her blanket and put it away, she realized all of her packages of food had been opened. The tunic she and Yael folded so carefully was now in disarray.

Yakov stuffed a date into his mouth and dusted his tunic. "You must learn how to walk."

Channah looked at her feet and then back at her uncle. "I walk every day."

"I mean in a ladylike fashion. You should glide along gracefully instead of bouncing up and down. Also, stop swinging your arms around. It is undignified."

Memories flooded back to Channah as they trudged toward the water. During the years with the shepherds, she had forgotten how strictly Yakov controlled his home. Now she recalled his precise rules for everything from the place where each household item was stored to an elaborate procedure for washing hands. Unsettled by such thoughts, she shifted her mind to a daydream about the dwelling she and Enos would share as soon as he came to claim her.

As the sun tracked across the sky, Yakov and Channah passed by a flock of sheep. Although there was no physical resemblance, the sight of the shepherd reminded her of Avram. Uncle would need help when the ewes began to give birth. Was Yael strong enough to go to the grazing field with him? Channah smiled at the thought of lambs soon frolicking in the pasture.

In the distance, two men on donkeys made their way over a hill. "We are nearing the city," Yakov said. "Cover your head."

Channah stopped, put down her bag, and shook out her blanket. She draped it over her head, remembering a veiled woman she once saw once traveling with a wool merchant. "I cannot see," she remarked.

"Not like that," he shouted. "You look like a harlot. Did those crazy sheepherders teaching you nothing? Cover your hair, but not your face."

Thinking Yakov was more peculiar than Avram by far, Channah pulled the blanket from her head, folded it into a triangle, and did her best to achieve the desirable appearance.

"Better," he said, glancing around. "I hope no one saw you before. Now tie the ends under your chin. Tightly. Make sure your hair is covered up until we are inside my house."

"Yes, sir." Although she occasionally wrapped herself in a blanket when the weather was bitter, wearing a covering on her head on a mild day soon became uncomfortable. The knotted wool scratched the skin of her neck, and her peripheral vision was restricted. She vaguely remembered her mother grabbing a light, airy scarf to cover her head when leaving home. Soon she would no longer be under Yakov's authority. Enos, like Avram, would pay no attention to her clothing. Or, if he did notice, he would go and buy her pretty things to wear.

Inside the city gates, Channah recognized the narrow streets leading to the house that once belonged to her grandfather, then to her father. Having no sons at the time of his death, her father's possessions passed to his younger brother Yakov. She and her mother were part of Yakov's inheritance.

Yakov's wife turned and stared when her husband and Channah entered the house. "You have returned."

Not certain whether the words were addressed to her or to Yakov, Channah smiled and stepped forward, anticipating an embrace. "Greetings, Aunt Adah."

Adah stretched out a stiff arm to maintain the distance between them. "You stink of sheep. We must hurry and get you cleaned up."

Chapter Sixteen

Avram remained sitting in the pasture, holding a lamb, as he watched Caleb ride toward him. When his old friend came near, Avram raised a hand in greeting. "Good to see you, Caleb."

"And you as well." The old man grunted as he dismounted his donkey. After dropping the reins, he groaned and sank next to Avram. "I remember when I could walk to this pasture from the village and not even be out of breath. Now it is all I can do to ride out here."

Avram poured a cup of wine and passed it to Caleb. "Refresh yourself." The old shepherd sipped his own drink before reaching for his knapsack. "I have fruit and dried fish. Will you eat?" Without waiting for an answer, Avram spread a blanket before him and dumped the bag's contents. "I have no bread to offer you. It is not worth the effort to bake for only one. Have you heard my sweet Yael is gone?"

"The spice seller told me. He could not remember the name of the young man who told him. I suppose it was another shepherd." Caleb nodded. "I was greatly saddened."

Holding up a dried fig, Avram stared at the fruit and replied, "At least she had an easy passage. She went to sleep one evening and did not awake the next morning." He turned the fig over and over before putting it back on the cloth. "It broke her heart when that cursed Yakov took Channah away from us." He took a handful of almonds and began to munch. "I gave her a proper burial in a little cave she used to like, and then I sealed it to keep the animals out."

"How are you?"

With a bowed head, Avram said, "I cannot tend so many sheep by myself. Selling off half my flock would attract the tax collector's attention, and certainly raise questions I cannot answer." He took a gulp of wine. "But it does not matter. Nothing matters any more. I have no reason to go on living, Caleb."

"I felt the same when my wife passed on. God chose to leave you and me here and gather our women to Himself. You have been ordained to go on. Therefore, you must."

"I am under judgment. That must be the reason everyone I care for has been taken away. My son, my wife, and the child I thought of as my daughter." Avram poured himself more wine.

"My friend, you are grieving now, but eventually you will be able to see the great blessing you enjoyed by having a good wife who loved you. As for judgment, I cannot believe you are cursed. We were within the law. Vengeance is not murder. An eye for an eye and a tooth for a tooth." Caleb looked into his cup as he swirled it round and round for a while. "I have sold my business to a man from Jerusalem. He knows nothing of the schemes we have carried out to dupe the tax collectors over the years. I am sorry we cannot be together at shearing time, but as you can see I am too crippled to work any longer."

Avram sighed and tossed a pebble. "I am sorry for your pain. As for me, I care nothing for profit any more. Before, I worked hard because I wanted Yael and the girl to be provided for. I expected Channah to inherit my flock and see after my widow when I died. I planned to find the girl a husband eventually, when she was older. A shepherd, someone who would care for her and help her with the sheep. Then that jackal Yakov took me by surprise." Avram's shoulders slumped. "He sold her. I am certain of it. He grew angry and refused to answer when I asked him if he received a bride price. I should have slit his throat. His body ought to be sealed in the hidden cave, not Yael's."

Caleb lifted his eyebrows. "You had the opportunity?"

"I did. I sat and watched the wretch sleep for hours. More than once I took my knife in my hand. He should be on his knees, thanking God he was spared." Avram shook his head. "Too many people in the city knew he was coming to fetch Channah. The authorities would have investigated. Yael and the girl would have been drawn in."

"Murder always ends badly," Caleb said with downcast eyes.

Avram stared into the distance. "Yes."

After draining the last of his wine, Caleb held his cup in both hands during a long silence. Finally, he cleared his throat and spoke. "My son Nathan has come back to Bethlehem."

"He has given up the life of a nomad?"

"No." Caleb shrugged and put his cup aside. "The crazy preacher he followed is dead, beheaded by Herod as I understand it. So he has taken up with an even more eccentric rabbi. Nathan says this one is the Messiah." He exhaled and set his cup aside. "He wants me to go to Galilee to ask his master to heal my aching joints."

"Surely you will not make this futile journey. You and I know what happened."

"Nathan and I can live for some time on my savings and the proceeds from selling my business. After that, I can only hope to die in peace, in the company of my son. He is all I have." Caleb stood and shook out his robe. "It pains me to leave the only home I have ever known, and I mourn to think you and I will never see each other again." He fidgeted with the ends of his sash. "We are the last two."

Avram rose and the men embraced silently.

Brushing aside a tear, Caleb took the reins of his donkey. With Avram's assistance and a loud grunt, he struggled into the saddle. "May the Lord bless you and keep you."

"Farewell, my friend." Avram stood watching Caleb ride away over a distant hill. Then the old shepherd drew a deep breath. "And may God have mercy on our souls."

Chapter Seventeen

At sunset Adah and her married daughters Zillah and Lillian took Channah to the mikvah to prepare for her wedding. Following the attendant's instructions, she stripped naked and waded into the cool, bubbling spring water. The cousins spoke a blessing before Channah immersed and scrubbed herself vigorously.

"All right," Adah announced at last. "You may get out of the bath now."

Channah swaddled her shivering body in the generous length of cloth the attendant held out. Zillah inspected Channah's hands. "Her nails do not need to be clipped. They are short enough already."

Doing her best to keep still while the attendant combed her wet hair, Channah cut her eyes toward Adah. "Tell me what you know of Enos."

Adah nudged the attendant aside. "Let me finish her hair. See what you can do to soften her feet." She tugged at a tangle. "What is there to tell? Enos is a man. He will be a husband and provide for you. I do wish your face showed less evidence of being in the sun."

"Do you know what it means to be married?" Lillian asked. She and her sister giggled.

Channah smiled with anticipation. "Enos will plant his seed inside of me, and we will have a baby."

"You talk like a midwife. What do you know of such things?" Adah made a clicking noise with her tongue.

"Uncle Avram taught me about breeding sheep," Channah insisted. "I have delivered countless numbers of lambs."

"You are well removed from that man's insanity now. However, I will pray you conceive immediately." She tapped the comb against Channah's head. "That would please your husband greatly."

"Yes, a child will make everyone happy." Zillah bent over a leather bag, pulling out scarves. "I brought some of my old mantles. Father said our family would be shamed if she had no proper head covering when she goes to her husband's home. I must agree that wearing a blanket on her head looks ridiculous, and besides, it stinks."

Lillian rubbed olive oil on Channah's face. "This will make your skin shine." She turned toward her sister. "You said everyone? Do you think Keren will be glad when Channah gives Enos a son?"

"Keren is never happy. I have never seen the woman smile." Zillah chuckled as she pulled out a faded blue scarf. "Channah, you may have this one. I have no need of it anymore."

"Who is Keren? Does she belong to Enos's family?" Channah was curious about her new relatives.

Lillian and Zillah stopped what they were doing and exchanged a glance.

Adah tossed the comb onto a table. "No more of this idle talk. It is time to get our bride dressed. Zillah, where is Channah's tunic?"

"We have her outfit all assembled." Lillian held a tan tunic out to Channah. "Here, put this on first."

Happily complying with her cousin's instructions, Channah slipped into her wedding garment, flipping her damp hair aside to avoid getting her dress wet. "This is nice," she said, patting the smooth fabric. She swirled the skirt around her ankles. "And look how long it is."

Lillian bit her lip, but not before Channah observed her amusement.

"City dwellers do not wear knee-length tunics such as the one you had on when you arrived at my home," Zillah observed.

Channah cast her eyes downward. Although her new attire seemed elegant to her, she suddenly realized her wedding clothes were drab in comparison to the way her cousins and aunt were dressed.

"Your coat goes over your robe." Lillian helped Channah don the sleeveless outer garment. "And now your mantle."

Adah stood in front of Channah, adjusting the drape of the mantle, tugging at the neckline of the robe. "Well, now, you look lovely." She rested a hand on Channah's shoulder. "Gather our things, Zillah. We will add her wedding veil just before Enos comes to claim his bride."

"When will he come, Aunt Adah?" Channah's excitement pushed aside all thoughts of clothing.

"His arrival is supposed to be a secret." Adah smiled. "I can only say you would be wise to prepare to go to your husband's home this evening."

Channah thought of Avram and Yael, realizing they would not be in attendance at her wedding. "I shall be a bride tonight?"

"You have been betrothed for a year now. There is no reason for any further delay," Adah replied. "Come along, girls."

Upon arrival at Yakov's house, Channah discovered her travel bag sitting near the doorway. When she started to lift it to her shoulder, Adah tapped her arm. "Leave it. One of my daughters will bring your belongings when we follow your wedding procession."

For what seemed to be a long while, Channah sat cross-legged on the smooth earthen floor, in a circle with her cousins and Adah. Zillah worked on her embroidery, while Adah and Lillian repaired clothing.

"This feels like the Sabbath," Zillah commented.

Adah nodded. "Except we are permitted to do work today."

"Perhaps Enos has forgotten this is the day of our wedding," Channah said. Her relatives exploded with laughter.

Outside, there was a sudden noise—musical instruments, singing, men's voices. Yakov appeared at the doorway. "It is time."

Although Channah found it difficult to see through the heavy veil that covered her head, she tried to glimpse her groom. She saw only dark outlines of numerous people.

"Enos the son of Jedidiah has come to claim his bride," someone announced. The man speaking sounded pleasant to Channah. Was he her soon-to-be husband?

Channah recognized Yakov's voice next to her. "Give me your hand."

After she complied, Yakov led her through the jostling crowd. Like a flock of sheep, she thought. How she wanted to throw off her veil and join the merriment. However, she knew doing so would immediately subject her to Yakov's wrath. The noisy party wound its way from Yakov's house, through narrow streets, and outside the city walls.

Soon Channah stood next to Enos underneath a cloth canopy held aloft on wooden poles. The words of blessing were barely concluded before someone started serving food and wine. In the midst of the chaotic celebration, Enos led his bride away from the crowd.

In the seclusion of the house, Channah pulled off her veil and stared at her husband. He was considerably shorter than most men, only half a head taller than her. His face was dominated by his curly black beard and huge brown eyes. Although his limbs were thin, the trunk of his body was round and thick. Channah thought he resembled a giant frog, an idea that made her smile. She found the silence awkward and finally said, "I thought you were younger."

Enos took a backward step. "I expected you to be beautiful, but then I suppose I should know by now not to believe anything Yakov says." He cocked an eyebrow. "I am only thirty-five."

She was not at all surprised when he behaved like an eager ram with a ewe in mating season.

Chapter Eighteen

The wedding celebration went on for days. The men danced while the women clapped and cheered. On one occasion, someone handed Channah a large cup of wine, even though she had not asked for it. Spotting an elderly dowager leaning on a cane, Channah asked her, "Do you care for some refreshment?"

"Oh, thank you. I cannot take the cup until I sit down. Bring the wine and follow me."

The old woman wobbled through the crowd, finally wandering into the house and taking a seat on a storage chest. "Ah, this is much better." She reached both hands for the cup of wine. Instead of the genteel sip Channah expected, the woman took a great gulp. "Good wine," she commented, after wiping her mouth. "I am Peninnah, your husband Enos's great aunt."

Channah smiled. "I am so happy to meet my new kin. I am Channah, the bride. May I fetch you something to eat?"

"What a sweet girl you are. I do not have enough hands to manage my cane and gather food and drink, and I am ready to nibble."

"What do you want?" Channah was happy to have someone to talk with and something to do. So far, she had been unsuccessful in her attempts to engage the women celebrating her marriage. They either ignored her entirely or excused themselves from her presence quickly. Peninnah's wrinkled face brought Yael to mind, further putting Channah at ease.

Peninnah's reply interrupted Channah's thoughts. "Bring me a little bit of everything they have."

Channah drifted past trays piled high with food. Following Peninnah's instructions, she took samples of everything, including several items she could not identify. Topping off the loaded bowl with a stem of grapes, she made her way back to Peninnah. When she saw no suitable surface on which to set the food down, Channah sank to the floor and balanced the bowl on her drawn-up knees.

"You took me at my word to sample everything, I must say." Peninnah took a handful of stuffed olives. "Here, share this bounty with me. It is not easy to be the second wife. I know. I was one. You must give your husband a son immediately. Then you will gain everyone's respect."

Stunned, Channah was unable to accept what she heard. She glanced over her shoulder to see if anyone appeared to be listening. Then her words came out slowly, with a breath between each one. "Enos has another wife?"

"Ah, no one told you. Forgive me for being the bearer of these tidings." Peninnah patted Channah's head. "Yes, Enos and Keren have been married these nine, or maybe it is ten years now. I forget exactly how long it has been." She dipped into the food bowl and popped a morsel of something unknown to Channah into her mouth. "Enos was not so prosperous then." She lifted her cup as if in a toast to the walls surrounding them. "Now, he has a thriving business, a fine home, and a lovely wife. Everything a man could ask, except he has no son. No one to keep his lineage alive." Peninnah leaned toward Channah. "That is why he has finally decided to take another wife. So you can bear his heir."

"Nothing would please me more," Channah affirmed truthfully. "I long to be a mother."

"I seem to be out of wine." Peninnah held out her cup.

Channah set the food bowl on the floor by Peninnah's feet and sprang up. "I will get more for you. Is there anything else you want?"

"Perhaps another portion of roasted lamb."

Returning with a full cup and a generous container of meat, Channah pretended not to notice Peninnah tucking a handful of almonds into her bosom.

"Now let me tell you the secret to conception." Peninnah took a tentative sip, followed by a generous swig of wine. "It is dove breast."

Channah's eyebrows shot upward. "Excuse me?"

"Dove breast," Peninnah repeated. "At the evening meal, eat a female dove's breast cooked in olive oil." She shook her head. "You will find yourself pregnant in no time. This is how I gave my Simeon twin sons."

"I have never heard of that," Channah admitted. "I fear I am ignorant of city ways." She took a few grapes from Peninnah's food bowl. "With sheep, we let a ram in with the ewes at the right time. Then the spring lambs naturally come along."

"There she is," Peninnah whispered with her cup in front of her lips.

Since her companion spoke softly, Channah did the same. "Who?"

"Keren. Enos's wife."

Channah looked in the direction of Peninnah's nod. She caught sight of a woman with regal bearing at the doorway. Her creamy skin contrasted with her glossy black hair and dark eyes. "Has anyone seen Enos?"

Someone behind Channah answered, "He is in the courtyard, I believe."

Keren's glance swept around the large room, resting briefly on Channah. And then she was gone.

Channah gazed at the place where Keren stood a moment earlier. "She is very beautiful."

"What are good looks to a barren woman?" Peninnah sniffed.

An old woman wandered near. "Greetings, Peninnah." She nodded toward Channah. "And you must be the bride. I am your husband's cousin, Shiloh."

"I am honored to join your family." Channah stood. "May I fetch wine for you?"

"No, my husband and I are leaving soon, since we live a day's journey from here." Shiloh put a hand on Channah's shoulder. "Before we go, I must warn you not to eat meat until you become pregnant. Your body cannot digest meat and grow a new infant at the same time." She tapped her belly. "I should know. I gave birth to five sons."

Channah glanced at Peninnah, then mumbled, "Thank you for advising me."

"Certainly, my dear." Sporting a wide grin, Shiloh embraced both Peninnah and Channah. "I must be on my way now."

Peninnah picked at the grapes in her bowl. "Shiloh knows nothing." she muttered after her kinswoman disappeared through the doorway. "Her great-great grandmother was a Canaanite."

Chapter Nineteen

Keren snatched the cup from Channah's hands. "That is mine. Is it not enough you have stolen my husband's affection? Must you also have my dishes?"

"Forgive me," Channah answered. "I did not know the cup was yours."

"Now you do." Keren's face was breathtakingly lovely, despite the scowl she perpetually wore. She placed the cup back in the chest where the kitchenware was stored and took out another. "This one is more suitable for you."

Channah took the cracked cup and dipped it into the water jug. She drained the cup and then swallowed the handful of water that leaked into the palm of her hand.

"Here, make yourself useful." Keren held out a stick with a stiff bouquet of grasses tied to one end.

Turning the implement over several times, Channah looked up at her husband's other wife. "What is this for?"

Keren took the broom from Channah's hands. "You cannot truly be as ignorant as you pretend to be." She began sweeping the floor with vigorous strokes. "This is how to use a broom. Were you raised in a cave?"

"I have slept in caves and under the stars in the pasture. Most of the year, though, our home was a tent." Channah thought hard. "How does that affect one's ability to stir up the dust?"

Rolling her eyes, Keren replied, "You are supposed to be sweeping floor tiles so they will be clean. Use broad strokes to loosen the dirt, and then sweep it outside." She thrust the broom toward Channah. "Now, hurry and finish this simple task. There is much to be done, and I do not intend to spend the whole morning telling you things even a child knows."

Channah took the broom and tried to imitate Keren's sweeping technique. "Oh, I see. The dust is like a flock that must be herded through the doorway."

"Is that all you know anything about? Sheep?"

"I suppose so."

"Pity."

"But sheep are interesting. My Uncle Avram spent years teaching me how to care for them." Channah tried to imitate Keren's sweeping technique. "Oh, no, little stone. You cannot hide under the chest." She poked the broom at a tiny pebble to send it flying toward the threshold.

"After you finish sweeping the floor—if you ever do—take the bedding up to the rooftop. Unroll the mats and place them side by side to soak up the sun. But before the bedding, go and milk the goat. I assume you know how to milk?" Keren tossed her head to flip a glossy lock of raven hair over a shoulder. "I have laundry to attend to."

Channah thought it made more sense to have an earthen floor than to install baked clay tiles that needed sweeping. Nevertheless, she held her tongue and did her best to push every particle of dust out the door. In a short while, the large one-room home she shared with Enos and Keren had a clean floor.

She hummed a tune while doing housework, only slightly affected by Keren's disagreeable attitude. From the rooftop, Channah looked across the dirt road to Enos's tanning yard, hoping to catch sight of her husband. She saw steam rising from huge pots, loaded carts arriving and departing, and workers going to and fro. Enos was nowhere to be seen. No matter, he would return to the house at the close of the business day, and everything would be fine.

Sure enough, as the sunlight began to fade, the activity in the tannery slowed to nothing. Enos burst through the doorway and announced, "I am home."

Keren rushed to greet Enos. "Oh, husband, how pleasant to have your presence with us."

Seeing Keren's example, and remembering Yael's reaction when Avram came near, Channah hurried to embrace Enos. "Greetings, husband," she murmured shyly.

"Can I not walk into my home without being fawned on by women?" Enos fussed.

Channah was uncertain whether to believe Enos's words or trust his broad grin. He draped an arm around her shoulder and drew her nearer. "And how is my little wildflower this evening?"

"I am well," Channah replied with downcast eyes. A strong odor clung to Enos, the same smell that occasionally wafted from the tanning yard during the day.

Keren swung a hand toward the low table in the middle of the room. "Your favorite evening meal awaits you."

Setting aside the scroll he carried under his arm, Enos washed his hands in a small stone basin and stretched out next to the table. Channah set freshly baked bread before him while Keren served him a plate of lentils and vegetables. Since Keren waited until the Enos was eating before helping herself, Channah did likewise. In Avram's tent, everyone sat cross-legged at meals. However, following Enos and Keren's example, Channah reclined by the low table's edge. She propped herself up on her left elbow, and used her right hand to eat.

Enos wiped his face with a square of linen cloth. "You will go to the market tomorrow."

"Yes, husband." Keren dabbed at her mouth with the same piece of fabric Enos used, and handed it to Channah. "What is it you wish me to buy?"

"Get Channah some nice clothing. I will not have people think I cannot afford to dress my wife decently."

Keren pressed her lips together while her eyes flicked to Channah and back to Enos. When she spoke, her voice has a slight tremor in it. "As you wish." Keren stood and began to clear the table.

Channah leapt up to help with the dishes, but Enos reached for her hand. "Let Keren take care of the housework. I want you to stroll through the tanning yard with me. I will show you the source of my wealth.

"Now the first thing we do when the hides are delivered is smear the flesh side with a slaked lime compound," Enos explained as he guided Channah through the large processing enclosure. "Then we fold up the skins and set them aside until the hair loosens."

Channah was overwhelmed with foul odors, but she did not interrupt Enos's lecture.

"When the skins are ready, my men scrape away all the hair and flesh. Next, we plump the skins in a lime bath. Now we can go to the courtyard, and I'll show you my vats."

Only too happy to go outside, Channah breathed deeply to clear the fetid air from her lungs.

"The secret to my fine leather is my unique dung wash. The smell of dung and urine are offensive to people who live inside the city walls, but they crave the softness and beauty of my finished products." He laughed and threw an arm around Channah's shoulder. "Some of the Pharisees say tanning is unclean. I enjoy thinking of them poring over the scrolls I have softened with my special solutions."

The couple walked through the tanning yard, where skins were arranged in neat rows. Each skin laid on its "back," with the legs tied together to form a neat bundle. Channah tried to concentrate on her husband's continuing description of his superior tanning business. However, the stricken look on Keren's pretty face kept intruding on her thoughts.

Chapter Twenty

"Where are you going?" Keren whispered.

Holding up a leather pouch, Channah said, "To do the milking." Although she had been a member of Enos's household only six months, she had assumed care of the family animals from the first day.

Keren slipped from her bed and tiptoed across the room, casting a backward glance to the mat where Enos lay snoring. "No," she mouthed. She dragged Channah by her elbow from the house into the courtyard. "Did you forget this is the Sabbath? Again?"

Channah did not know how to answer. Now she remembered Enos closing the tannery early the day before so his workers could get home before sundown. Nevertheless, the old habit of tending sheep every day of the week was hard to break. Explaining Avram and Yael did not observe the day of rest might cause Keren to think ill of her uncle and aunt, perhaps even get them into trouble with the authorities. "I can be forgetful sometimes," she said at last.

Keren sighed. "Are you so slow you are not aware Philip the Greek comes and milks the goat each Sabbath?" Keren glanced toward the door. It remained shut, and there was no noise to indicate the man of the house was awake. "How long must I remind you every week not to light the cooking fire in the courtyard or do any labor whatsoever? Surely you have learned by now that my husband is concerned about keeping up appearances."

With a shrug, Channah set the milk pouch by the door. Enos worked on the tannery's accounts every Sabbath, but he did so inside the house. He made it clear on more than one occasion that she was not to discuss anything about their household with women she encountered at the stream where she drew water nor on those rare occasions when she accompanied Keren to the market.

Keren sat on the ground and leaned against the back wall of the house. "We shall wait here in the courtyard until Enos awakens. Then we will eat the bread you baked yesterday."

With nothing better to do, Channah sat next to Keren, leaving an arm's length of distance between them. She marked the passage of time by the sun's slow ascent into the morning sky. All the while she imagined what Avram and Yael were doing at home. When the silence weighed on her, she dared to ask Keren, "Do you ever see your family?"

"No." Keren continued to look straight ahead.

Although Keren's brief answer did not encourage further conversation, Channah could not resist an additional comment. "I miss my aunt and uncle." Sudden, unexpected tears filled her eyes. One escaped and rolled down her cheek before she could brush it away.

Keren's flawless face revealed no trace of emotion. She rose and took a deep breath. She began to walk away, but turned to look down at Channah, who was still sitting on the cool earth. "You are a wife now, and soon you will be a mother. Your childhood is over. Forget the life you had before and grow up."

Channah continued to sit alone, hands clasped around her drawn-up knees. She pondered Keren's last remark while watching Philip the Greek stride across the open field behind the house, headed toward the animal shelter. He was tall and muscular, and his chiseled face was framed by a cluster of golden curls. Although Channah knew Philip was a Roman soldier's slave, he looked free as a mountain goat this morning, swinging his arms and whistling a tune.

Doodling in the dirt as Avram liked to do, Channah wondered how long she must wait to conceive a child. Keren and Enos seemed to assume she was pregnant or soon would be. However, her monthly bleeding continued without interruption. She wondered if she was cursed, as Enos's relatives whispered Keren was. Feeling sorry for herself, she once again felt tears welling up in her eyes. Rather than give in to her frustration, Channah decided to go in search of something to eat.

Inside the house, Enos sat on the floor beside the central table, arranging parchments beside a large leather scroll. He grunted to acknowledge Channah's "Good morning." Meanwhile, Keren lounged on her bed, applying a creamy substance to her face.

Channah helped herself to a portion of cold bread. Rather than irritate Enos by asking him to share the table space, she perched on the kitchenware storage chest to eat. She tried to push down the discomfort caused by Keren's eyes following her every move. The silence was broken only by the scratching of Enos's quill and the occasional braying of Enos's donkey from outside.

When someone rapped at the entrance, Enos slid the parchments under his unrolled scroll before responding.

Keren quickly rose and hurried to sit next to Channah on the chest.

"Good Sabbath, Joab," Enos said, throwing the door open wide. "I did not see you coming. I was too engrossed, instructing my wives on the Holy Scriptures."

The man grasped Enos's forearm. "Help me. My wife is in labor."

"What can I do about that?" Enos cast a frown toward the chest where Channah and Keren sat. "Perhaps another neighbor has a wife who has given birth and will know what to do. Ask one of them."

"No," the man insisted. "There is no time to go from house to house, searching. Send your women to my wife before it is too late."

Channah stood and murmured. "We must go."

"You need a midwife." Enos waved a hand toward Channah and Keren. "These two know nothing."

"The midwife lives too far away, and she will not come on the Sabbath anyway. I must get back to my wife and little ones. There is no time to find someone else." The man tugged at Enos's sleeve. "Please, I beg you."

Enos sighed heavily, then put on a wide smile. "Never let it be said that Enos the tanner refused to help his neighbor in time of need." He jerked his head toward the door. "Go and make yourselves useful."

Keren reached for her mantle, which dangled from a peg on the wall next to the door. Channah followed suit.

Since her scabbard was hanging underneath her scarf, she took it along as well.

Joab was already walking swiftly toward his house, which was visible not far down the road that separated Enos's home and his tanning yard. With her short legs, Channah had to trot to keep up. Before long, the sound of a scream flowed from the neighbor's house. Although excessive haste was considered beneath a man's dignity, Joab broken into a run. "Hurry!" he shouted over his shoulder.

Shuwshan lay on a low couch, moaning and clutching at her pregnant belly. Nearby, a placid toddler sucked her thumb. A girl of about three years sobbed loudly. Joab picked up the smaller child, and took the little girl's hand. "Do what you can," he said. "She has been in hard labor since the middle of the night." He took his little girls outside, while his wife let out a terrible shriek.

"Something is wrong," Shuwshan said weakly. "I had my other two babies with much less laboring time."

Channah glanced around the house to locate items she needed. "Find a basin and fill it with strong vinegar," she said to Keren. "If you find no vinegar, use wine."

"I have no idea where they keep things," Keren answered, wringing her hands.

Shuwshan pointed to a chest. "Vinegar is there."

Keren glanced toward the chest but did not move. "Why?"

"Because that is the way Uncle Avram taught me. Stop wasting time," Channah commanded the woman who

106

had ordered her around for the past six months. "Pour a basin full of vinegar and then dampen a cloth with it."

Kneeling beside Shuwshan, Channah spoke calmly, as if assisting a ewe giving birth to a lamb. "Do you know what is keeping the baby from coming?"

Keren set the vinegar next to Channah and backed away. Channah wiped perspiration from Shuwshan's face. Then she soaked her hands and knife in the vinegar.

Between moans and cries, the suffering woman said, "I think he may be turned wrong."

Doing her best to remember Avram's explanation of how birthing sheep differed from humans, she asked, "The baby's head is supposed to come out first, correct?"

"Of course," Keren answered from across the room.

Channah pressed down her anxiety and smoothed Shuwshan's hair back. "Spread your legs for me." She could see the child was at the point of immediate birth. All she could think was what she would do if a lamb did not come out feet first as it was supposed to. She knew she had to reach inside this woman and position the baby for birth. Otherwise, both mother and child might die.

"Please!" Shuwshan whispered.

"I must turn your baby," Channah explained, surprised at the calmness in her voice. "This will not be easy for you. Come and assist me, Keren."

With Shuwshan screaming the whole time, Channah felt one of the baby's feet, pushed it away, found what she hoped was its shoulder, and somehow turned the tiny body so it could emerge head first. That task done, she pulled the woman's hips to the edge of the couch and caught the perfect baby boy when he came forth rather quickly.

"You have a son," Channah announced, but Shuwshan had already curled up and gone to sleep. "I need your help," she said over a shoulder to Keren. Receiving no response, she managed to tie and cut the umbilical cord. She wiped the baby clean, assuming a human did not lick the afterbirth from their young as a mother sheep was expected to do.

Joab rushed into the house. "I heard a baby's cry."

"Your son." Channah wrapped a length of cloth around the baby and handed him to his father.

"Praise God." Joab went to his wife's side. "We have a son, Shuwshan." He sat on the side of the couch and nodded toward the far corner of the room. "What happened to her?"

Surprised to see Keren sprawled on the floor, Channah investigated. She rolled Keren onto her back and rubbed her arms until she began to revive.

"I think she must have fainted."

Keren's voice was barely audible. "I cannot stand the sight of blood."

Chapter Twenty-One

Although Keren often complained about Enos's snoring, Channah hardly noticed it. With their husband gone to Caesarea, however, she awoke with an awareness of the unusual nighttime silence. Unable to return to sleep immediately, she thought about the long day ahead of her. It was the Sabbath. Therefore, she and Keren would be unable to draw water from the river, cook, or shop at the vegetable market. She turned over and snuggled into her bedding, but a curious noise from outside kept her from returning to sleep.

Channah propped herself up on an elbow trying to detect the source of the sound. It sounded as if someone was digging in the courtyard, but that made no sense. A loud "maaa" solved the mystery. That contrary goat must have escaped from her pen. Fumbling as quietly as she could manage, Channah located her sandals. She opened the back door softly to avoid awakening Keren and slipped into the moonlit courtyard. Sure enough the goat was chomping on the mandrakes Enos insisted on planting. "No!" she whispered.

The goat looked her way briefly and then continued to chew.

"You naughty nanny!" Channah grabbed an ear and pulled the goat toward the shed. "Your master will be furious with both of us when he sees you have eaten his mandrakes," she fussed, as if the animal understood or cared.

Channah shoved the uncooperative goat inside her pen and pushed the gate shut. She was about to go back to the house when she noticed the door to the barn was closed. The door was supposed to be open in all but the most severe weather, to allow the animals to go back and forth between the pen and their shed at will. With a sigh, she trudged to the stable and pulled on the door.

It took considerable strength to drag the heavy door open, but the creaky hinges finally gave way. Channah gasped and clapped a hand over her mouth, stunned to see two human forms writhing on a bed of straw.

The man rolled aside and sat up. "Oh," Philip the Greek said. "We were not expecting a visitor."

Keren leapt up, pulled her hemline down, and used her fingers to comb straw from her hair. Without a word, she swept past Channah and out of the stable.

Philip the Greek slowly put his clothing in order. "I suggest you milk your own goat today, even if it is your Sabbath. I just remembered I have urgent business in the city." Philip touched her cheek on his way out. "Let me know if you ever get as lonely as Keren. I will be more than happy to help you feel better." He smiled and disappeared into the pale pre-dawn.

Channah sank into the straw, her mind overwhelmed. When the goat wandered inside and began to munch, she decided to harvest the animal's milk under the cover of darkness. She had the rest of the day to worry about what would happen when Enos returned home.

Keren was on her bed sobbing when Channah went inside the house. After some time, her shock and anger subsided, and she wanted to comfort Keren. What would Yael do? Auntie never spoke, but her gentle touch was comforting. Finally, unable to stand the tears, she went and silently put her arms around the distraught woman.

"It was my idea for Enos to take another wife." Keren sniffled later, while nibbling her cold bread. "I had no idea how hard it would be. My only thought was to fulfill my husband's wish for a son."

Channah concentrated on her breakfast and said nothing.

"Philip thinks I am beautiful the way Enos once did. I was so desperate for a man to make me feel worthwhile." Keren pushed her food aside. "What do you suppose Enos will do to me?"

It was the question Channah had struggled with all morning. "He will be livid."

"What he cannot stand is that he will be humiliated," Keren said. "I am certain he will divorce me, because he is so concerned about the opinions of other people. He will be compelled to show he is not a man to be trifled with." She chewed her lip before asking, "Do you hate me, Channah?"

"No. There is no one I can say I hate." What a peculiar question, coming almost a year after they became members of the same household.

"I would not blame you if you did." A single tear rolled down Keren's cheek. "I know I have been mean to you. I am jealous because Enos favors you over me."

"He did at first," Channah observed. "Not so much anymore. He is frustrated that I am not yet pregnant." She sighed. "He has mentioned many times that bearing his son is my sole purpose. I want a child as much as Enos, maybe more, and I do not understand why it has not happened."

Keren nodded. "Enos has been most fortunate in his business. Yet he has bought himself two barren wives. Ironic, is it not?"

"Bought? What do you mean by that?"

"Do you not know?" Keren cocked her head to one side and stared at Channah. "No, of course, you know nothing of the bride price Yakov collected for you. Tanners are not desirable husbands, and Enos wanted a pretty wife." She wiped away a tear. "My mother was poor, and so she and Enos struck a bargain."

Channah was curious. "Did you agree?"

"I knew nothing of the arrangement until my wedding, much like you." Keren laughed mirthlessly. "But Enos was kind to me, and I foolishly allowed myself to have some affection for him. He is easily offended, and I have learned to step lightly where his pride is concerned." She studied her splayed fingers. "I suppose you might say I learned to love him, as my mother told me I should. I even believed he cared for me as well." She took a deep breath and exhaled. "But all he wants now is to make money and have a son. He has the money, despite the amount he spent for you—a fertile young woman of sturdy stock to produce his male heir."

Channah swallowed the last of her bread without tasting it. "I know I have disappointed Enos by not becoming pregnant. He has made that clear more than once." Now it was her turn to sigh. "I wish I knew some way to hurry up my conception. The mandrake plants did not work their promised magic, and now the goat has eaten them."

Chapter Twenty-Two

As usual, Channah cooked the next day's evening meal in the courtyard. As she slid the fresh bread from the little brick oven, she heard the braying of Enos's donkey. She dusted her hands together and hurried toward the stable to take care of the animal.

She took the donkey's reins while Enos dismounted. "Greetings, husband. It is good to have you home once again."

Enos puffed his cheeks and exhaled. "I am exhausted. Travel is hard, but I saw amazing sights in Caesarea. There must have been a hundred ships in the harbor." He looked toward the courtyard. "You have fresh bread just out of the oven? Good. I am hungry."

Channah led the donkey into the stable, removed her saddle, and checked the water level in the drinking trough. "I am happy to welcome you home," she said to the donkey. "You can see you have plenty of fresh straw." As she began to brush the donkey's coat, she tried to put away the memory of seeing Keren and Philip in this place. "Stay still for me, and I will sing to you."

"You speak more around animals than you do with other people."

When Channah jumped, Keren said, "I did not mean to frighten you."

"No one but me ever comes to the stable, except when the gentile comes on the Sabbath." Channah was embarrassed by her unintended reference to Philip the

Greek. She continued to curry the donkey until curiosity overcame her. "What did Enos say?"

Keren pursed her lips. "He told me no one makes better bread than you. I think he went on to mention how fine his new bronze vats are and how tired he was. The next sound I heard was his horrible snore."

"He does not know?" Channah forced her eyes and hands to focus on the donkey.

"About Philip? How could he possibly know? Surely you do not think me a big enough fool to confess." Keren came and stood nearer Channah. "It appears you did not inform Enos, either."

"Me? How can I—no, I did not speak of what I saw."

"Well, then. Let us both try to forget the whole incident. Telling Enos of my indiscretion would only put him in a foul humor. I would deny everything, and it is not worth the Greek's life for him to own up to what we did. Who knows? Perhaps Enos would believe me if I said you merely had a bad dream. Or that it was you in the shed with Philip, not me." She edged closer. "Please, Channah. I am desperate. Keep my secret, and I swear by all of the gold in the temple I will never again treat you like a soiled rag."

Keren retreated to the house without waiting for a response.

Stunned by Keren's outrageous innuendos, Channah finished grooming the donkey. She sang the promised song to the animal, but her mind was troubled. If Enos had to choose between her and Keren, which one would he believe? She did not want Keren to be divorced and turned out of the house, nor did she relish that fate herself. Now that she was known to be barren, Channah was not sure where she stood with her husband.

The following day, Channah was surprised to find the morning routine went on as before. Enos arose just after dawn, wolfed down some breakfast, and rushed across the road to the tanning yard.

Keren surprised Channah by inviting her to accompany her to the market to buy vegetables. They walked home with their neighbor Shuwshan, who allowed Channah to carry her beautiful six-month-old baby.

"I have not seen you at the market before," Shuwshan commented, as she handed the boy to Channah. "You can see what a fine, healthy boy Joshua is. I cannot thank you enough for delivering him. I fear both of us would have died if you had not come to our aid when you did."

Not knowing how to accept praise, Channah mumbled, "Keren and I were glad we could help."

Keren laughed shortly. "I was willing, but falling into a dead faint did nothing to bring this little one into the world. It was all Channah."

That evening, Enos boasted about the improvements he was making to his tannery. "Someday I will be the most prominent purveyor of leather goods in all the land," he predicted. "Not every woman is fortunate enough to marry so capable a provider." He sighed loudly. "Even so, a man must have a son to carry on his name." Enos scowled. "And neither of my wives seems to be able to do her duty as a woman."

The most astonishing event of all occurred the following Sabbath. Philip the Greek came and milked the goat as he did every week. When he passed near the courtyard where Channah stood admiring her cucumber plants, he nodded a businesslike greeting in her direction. Then he went on about his work, just another hired hand doing his master's bidding.

Chapter Twenty-Three

Avram sat in the shade of a boulder, watching someone walk across the pasture. When he determined the lone traveler intended to approach him, he stood and shaded his eyes with one hand. There was something familiar in the stranger's gait, something that reminded Avram of a man he never expected to see again.

Avram squinted against the mid-morning brightness. "Perhaps I really am a lunatic," he muttered to himself. "That man yonder looks for all the world like my old friend." When the traveler was close enough to address he said, "You must be Caleb's son, Nathan."

"Is the sun in your eyes, or have you grown blind in your old age? How can you not recognize me, as many years as we have known each other?"

"Caleb?" Avram stepped forward to embrace his friend. "Is it really you? Last time I saw you, you could barely walk. Now you stride along like a youth. What has happened?"

"It is a miracle." Caleb smiled and clapped Avram on the shoulder. "I have so much to tell you. I hardly know where to begin."

Reaching for his wineskin, Avram declared, "Why not start with a cup of wine?"

Caleb squatted on the bare earth while Avram poured wine and set bread and cheese on a food tray.

"I see you have learned to bake." Caleb tore a chunk of bread and chewed it slowly. "Not as good as the girl used to make, but tasty nevertheless."

"No, I have not taken up cooking. A baker comes through now and then to peddle bread." Avram sighed. "The hills are becoming crowded." With a grin, he added, "It is just as well you went out of business when you did. Too many pairs of eyes nowadays." The old man sat beside his friend, their backs against the shading rock. "Enough trivia. I must know how you regained your health."

With a smile, Caleb began his story. "I left Bethlehem, thinking I would never see the village of my birth again. I sold everything I owned except a few items of clothing and my donkey. I rode him to Galilee, and Nathan walked beside us." He shook his head. "It was an extremely hard trip. At times, I thought I would not survive it. When we arrived in Capernaum, Nathan wanted us to go immediately to his teacher, the man they call Jesus. I told my son I had to rest first, but he was insistent." Caleb stopped talking to eat a hunk of bread.

"You never were any good at getting to the point," Avram observed.

Caleb cut his eyes toward Avram. "Jesus is the Messiah. He is the savior promised to us in prophesy. He healed me." He thrust his arms upward. "He not only took the pain from my body. He healed my soul. Can you imagine it, Avram? He took away my guilt and gave me peace."

Avram drew a deep breath. "The anointed one was sent to us that night when the angels came to the fields and told us he was born. And then we went and saw him, in that stable." He lifted his eyes upward. "I was filled with such hope. All of us were." He exhaled and sipped wine. "But you also know quite well what happened. You saw the corpses of the baby boys Herod's soldiers threw into the ditch." He rubbed his forehead with a gnarled hand. "Our Messiah is dead."

"Yes, I know what happened as well as you do. For years I saw the bodies in nightmares. Not just the children, but mothers and fathers who tried to stop the killing as well." Caleb put a hand on Avram's forearm. "They left Yael for dead in that trench, Avram. But she lived. Maybe that is what happened to him. Or maybe God raised him up again. I cannot explain him, any more than I understand how the night sky can instantly be filled with angels. I only know this Jesus of Nazareth speaks the truth."

"Nazareth? That hotbed of ignorant rebels? Have you forgotten the prophesy we learned as boys? The chosen one was to be born in Bethlehem." Avram refilled both his own cup and Caleb's. "Dishonest fellows spring up now and then, claiming to be the one. They gather followers for a while, and then they fade like the morning mist. You have seen this more than once in your lifetime."

Caleb sipped at his wine. "After the many years I have lived, you still take me for a fool. I know about the false ones. But tell me, what proof did they offer? The ailing come to Jesus from all over." Caleb waved an arm. "Blind men, lepers, demon possessed. He heals every one of them." He stabbed a finger in the air to emphasize his next three words. "Every. Last. One. Nathan claims his teacher even has the power to breathe life back into the dead."

"And people call *me* a lunatic." Avram's bushy eyebrows shot upward.

Turning his body to face Avram, Caleb spoke quietly. "You once made a vow. You said I could have anything I asked of you, if only I would help you do what needed to be done."

"How can I ever forget? Their young faces haunt my sleep. One strangled in his bed, another stabbed in the street at midnight, two fed to the wolves in the wilderness. One by one I took vengeance on the soldiers who carried out the slaughter." He bowed his head. "My rage was so great I bloodied not only my own hands, but yours as well."

"I now claim the promise you made to secure my assistance." Caleb put a hand on Avram's shoulder. "Go and listen to Jesus. Hear what he says, and see what he does. Do this one thing, and I will make no further attempt to persuade you about him."

"Be reasonable, my friend. Even though my herd is smaller now than it was before, I cannot leave my sheep to travel to Galilee."

Caleb smiled and nodded. "I knew that would be your answer. However, Nathan and I are prepared to care for your animals while you are gone. Surely the two of us together will be able to keep up the work of one broken-down old man."

Avram scratched on the ground with a finger for a while. At last he spoke. "I will do as you ask, but only to honor my vow to you, my friend."

Chapter Twenty-Four

Channah was relieved to remember it was the Sabbath. She did not feel well, due to her monthly time of bleeding coming upon her during the night. For once, she would not mind being idle all day. Enos sat at the table muttering over his accounts, while Keren combed her hair.

When Channah went to the basin to wash herself, Keren looked up at her with an unexpected smile. *How lovely she is when she does not wear a frown,* Channah thought. *Her face has the glow of an angel.* She started to comment but stopped herself when she remembered Enos demanded silence when he was working inside the house. After completing her morning cleansing, she went into the courtyard, as was her custom on the Sabbath.

Soon Keren came outside and sat beside her near the wall opposite the house. "What a beautiful morning this is."

Surprised to hear an optimistic comment from the normally dour Keren, Channah replied, "Yes, spring is the best season of all. Soon the wild flowers will bloom and the lambs will be born."

"And not long afterward we will celebrate the coming of a son to this house."

"No." Channah ducked her head. "I always hope, but my monthly bleeding has started."

"I know." Keren patted her arm. "I saw you swaddling yourself just now."

Blinking back tears, Channah said, "Enos is probably right. I am barren."

Keren threw her head back and smiled brilliantly. "It is Enos, Channah. Not us. He is the one who cannot produce a child."

"Why do say that?"

"Because I am pregnant."

Channah's eyes widened. She covered her mouth to keep from shouting. "Are you sure?" she whispered through her fingers.

Nodding and giggling, Keren spoke softly. "You and I bleed at almost the same time. Only I skipped last month. Now it is your second period when I have not bled." She grinned. "The last few mornings I have awakened feeling queasy. Then the nausea goes away in the afternoon. Channah, I am going to have a baby."

"I am certain Enos is pleased."

"I have not yet told that dirty jackal. All these years, he has made me feel worthless, cursed, less than a woman. But it was him, all along. Now he will puff out his chest and bellow like a bull, claiming he has begotten a son. Yet an unclean gentile has shown me the fault lies with our husband."

Although they were across the courtyard from the back door, Channah was careful to keep her voice quiet. "Do you mean to say your baby may belong to Philip the Greek?"

"I am certain of it."

Channah sat for a moment, trying to take in the surprising developments of the morning. "When will you tell Enos? About the baby, I mean."

"I have not yet decided." Keren tossed up an eyebrow. "Maybe I will wait until he makes a cutting remark about my womanhood." She laughed. "A great burden has been lifted from my shoulders."

"How excited you must be, to have a child growing inside of you."

Keren shrugged. "I have never longed for motherhood as you do. But I am relieved to have the curse of barrenness removed from me." She smiled and shook out her hair. "And now I know I never deserved the shame Enos heaped on me."

Speaking barely above a whisper, Channah leaned closer to Keren. "Does the Greek know?"

Keren's smile vanished. She glanced toward the stable, then back toward the house. "No, and he must never find out."

"But, Keren, the man comes every week to milk our goat. In time, your pregnancy will show. Surely he will notice and possibly suspect the truth."

Keren drew a breath and exhaled it slowly. "He comes very early in the morning and does not stay long. I will take care to stay inside until after he has come and gone. He will not dare approach our house." Her eyes moved to the stable again. "We must make sure Enos never finds out he is not the father of our son."

When Channah did not speak, Keren grasped her hand and urged her. "Promise you will keep my secret."

"I will not tell Enos," Channah answered at last.

"Thank you." Keren gazed into the distance. "He will be better off not knowing. He will be glad to have a child, and everything will work out fine."

After Keren went into the house, Channah sat alone. Keren's deception made her uneasy, but there seemed to be no way to avoid being the senior wife's conspirator. If only she could go into the pasture, sit with her uncle, and talk through the messy situation. Avram would know what to do.

A few days went by. Then, one evening at mealtime, Keren said, "I saw our neighbor Shuwshan at the market this morning. She said her baby does not sleep well, and I suggested she give him a few sips of wine at bedtime."

"Who are you to advise a mother on the care of her son?" Enos growled. "What do you know about raising children?"

"Why, nothing," Keren answered, with lowered eyes. "I suppose I have a lot to learn before our baby is born."

Enos held his wine suspended before his lips for a long moment. Then he carefully set the metal goblet on the table. "What are you saying?" He inclined his head toward Channah. "Are you pregnant at last?"

"No, husband."

His eyes flicked to Keren. "What is the matter with you? Are you deliberately trying to spoil my digestion?"

"Not at all." Keren smiled at him. "I am with child, Enos."

"You, Keren? After all this time?" Excitement rippled through his words. "Are you sure?"

"As certain as I can be until my belly begins to swell." Keren patted her stomach. "Which should happen soon."

"Oh, my wife!" Enos exclaimed. "My dove. How I have longed to hear this news from your lovely lips." He raked a hand through his hair. "I will engage the best midwife in the whole country to attend to my son's birth. Channah, you must take care of all the household chores from now on. Keren must not exert herself. I must go and arrange for the carpenter to make a fine cradle. Oh, my." He rubbed his hands together. "I have many plans for this boy."

Chapter Twenty-Five

Avram stood by the side of the road as a small group of people walked toward him. A ragged man stopped and grasped Avram's sleeve. "The teacher healed my leprosy." The man stretched out his hands. "See? My skin is as clear as a baby's. I can go home to my wife and children. I can live a normal life again." He dropped his arms to his side. Moving away, the man shouted, "Praise God!"

"Wait," Avram called. "What teacher?"

"Jesus," someone replied.

"The one from Nazareth? Where is he?"

A prosperous-looking fellow with an armload of ivory and gold bracelets pointed across the road. "Down by the lake."

After waiting for the group to pass by, Avram crossed the road and climbed through a shallow ravine. Beyond a small embankment, on a plain that sloped gently toward the lake, he spied a group of people near the water's edge. He took his time circling toward the gathering, taking note of the situation as he advanced.

As many as two dozen women tended a campfire, stirring pots as if preparing or cleaning up after a meal. Not far away from the women, forty or fifty men sat on the ground. Like schoolboys, the men were arranged in a semi-circle around a speaker. Soon the man on whom all eyes were focused stood and walked away alone, skirting the shoreline.

Since no one challenged him, Avram joined the men. "Are you hungry, friend?" one of them asked.

"I have no money." Avram pressed his arm against the pouch slung under his clothing. He was wary of letting strangers know he had coins.

"We are happy to share what we have with you. The master calls me Peter."

"Avram the son of Abijah, from Bethlehem. I am searching for a teacher called Jesus, from Nazareth."

Peter smiled and gestured toward his companions. "We are his followers, but he has gone somewhere to be alone and pray. We may not see him again until sunrise. You are welcome to spend the night with us, although we will camp here out in the open instead of going to an inn."

"I am a shepherd." In spite of his determination to remain aloof, Avram warmed to this man. "Most of my nights are spent under the stars."

"Our master has a great affection for shepherds," Peter assured him. "Come and refresh yourself with some food. We have eaten, but my wife and the other women will find something to sustain you."

One of the women ladled soup and brought it over as soon as the two men squatted near the fire. She bent to offer the bowl to Avram.

"Thank you." Avram's eyes met a striking face. "Woman, do I know you?" he asked. "Forgive me, but I have the feeling we have met somewhere."

"I am from Nazareth. Have you been there?"

"No." Avram continued to stare into her luminous amber eyes. "This is the first time I have been this far from my village of Bethlehem." Realizing he was being impolite by staring, he dropped his gaze.

"My husband's ancestors came from Bethlehem," the woman said. "My son was born there."

Avram concentrated on the woman's face again. "Now I know where I have seen you. I am one of the shepherds the angels sent to worship your child in the stable in Bethlehem. You probably do not remember me, since it has been over thirty years." At last, Avram accepted the bowl of soup she offered.

"A woman does not forget a night such as that one." She straightened, placing a hand on her hip. "You and your friend ran ahead of the other shepherds. You were so out of breath you could barely speak of the angels at first. Later, you cradled little Jesus in your arms and told me of your own infant son."

"You said Jesus?" Avram looked left and right. "Your son is this teacher who heals people?"

"The same." Mary resettled the end of her scarf across her shoulder. "The baby in the stable is a grown man now."

"But soldiers came to the village. They killed all of little boys under two years old, my own son among them."

Mary shut her eyes and nodded. "My husband took our little family to Egypt before the terrible massacre happened. I learned about the slaughter, but not until much later." She wiped away a tear. "What a heartbreaking tragedy."

129

"He is alive?" Avram pushed his hair back with both hands. "The one the angels announced was not murdered with the other babies?"

She smiled the same beautiful, serene smile Avram remembered from many years ago. "Jesus is still with us," she assured him.

As Mary returned to the group of women, Avram stood and began to pace.

"Are you all right?" Peter rose and clapped Avram on the shoulder.

"I was so sure the soldiers killed him." Avram could not stand still. "I took vengeance on one on behalf of my son, but then tenfold more because they robbed our people of our deliverer." He looked upward. "How horrific to learn I was wrong."

"Jesus teaches us we are forgiven when we confess and sincerely repent."

Avram shook his head. "You do not understand. I do not attend the sacred festivals or present sacrifices. For years I have routinely violated the Sabbath, and I cheat on my taxes. Worst of all, I have committed murder. Several murders." He pulled his cloak closed. "I must go. I should not be in the holy one's camp."

"Stay." Peter put his hand on Avram's sleeve. "You are welcome here, and he will show you the pathway back to God."

Hesitating, Avram whispered, "I am too old to change, and I have done far too much evil to be forgiven."

"You will find neither of those things holds true if you follow my master. What do you have to lose if you eat, spend the night with us, and tomorrow meet Jesus?" Peter sat again, and beckoned to Avram to join him. "Meanwhile, my friend, sit and let me tell you how he changed my life."

Later that evening, Avram wrapped himself in his cloak and settled near the other men for the night. His body was tired, but his mind refused to close down. Finally, he gave up trying to sleep and sat gazing out at the dark water. Having never seen the constant movement of a lake before, he rose and walked along the shoreline for a closer look. Soon the reflection of the full moon began to shimmer on the gently lapping waves.

As he strolled barefoot at the shallow edge of the water, Avram became aware he was not alone. A sidelong glance revealed a muscular physique. After a few steps, the stranger said, "You cannot sleep."

Though normally distrustful of people he did not know well, Avram felt comfortable talking to this young-sounding man. Surveying the moonlit landscape, he said, "I have never seen water like this. Creeks and rivers rush toward lower ground, but the restlessness of this level lake is something new to me."

"Yes," the stranger agreed. "It is something like the soul of a man longing for God, but resisting Him at the same time." After a few more steps, he asked, "Did you come this far to see the lake?"

"No."

"What, then?"

Avram pondered the question. "I started with the intention of discovering how someone deceived my friend. Yet, all during my travels I have asked myself how Caleb—my friend—was healed if the one he met was an imposter." He stopped walking and turned toward the water. "I met a woman tonight who cast a new light on everything I have believed for thirty years." He searched the stranger's face in the dim moonlight. "I suppose now I am searching for forgiveness for all I have done."

The stranger put a hand on Avram's shoulder. "You have found what you seek, my son."

Chapter Twenty-Six

"I have never been so miserable," Keren complained as she sat on her bed.

Channah stopped hulling almonds and went to Keren's side. "It will not be long now. Do you want me to rub your feet?"

"Yes." Keren edged her heavy body into a reclining position. "I cannot sleep. My legs are so swollen I can hardly walk, and I still have the pain of childbirth to endure."

"I would gladly bear the child for you if I could," Channah said as she poured a soothing lotion into a hand and massaged it into Keren's puffy ankles. "Soon you will be delivered. Then we will have the laughter of a little one to brighten our home."

Keren shifted from her back onto one side. "Has Enos told you the name he has chosen for the baby?"

"No." Channah chewed at her lip for a moment. "He hardly speaks to me anymore."

"Now you know how it feels to be cast aside, as I was when Enos took you as his second wife."

"None of that was my doing." Channah was weary of feeling like an unwelcome intruder in her home.

"Still." Keren seemed to ignore Channah's words. "If you have not come, I would never have realized I was blameless. Anyway, I merely make the point that I am a good wife." She sighed. "I only hope Enos appreciates what I am going through to fulfill his wish for a son."

Channah wiped her hands. She could not honestly say Enos had any sympathy with Keren's endless complaints. "He is as anxious as you for the baby to come." When Keren began to doze, she returned to preparing the evening meal. Marriage turned out to be nothing like her expectations. In the beginning Enos was attentive if not tender. Now Channah felt both he and Keren treated her more like a servant than a member of the family.

Going to the courtyard to bake fresh bread, Channah looked toward the distant hills and wondered if she would ever see Yael and Avram again. She allowed herself a few moments of longing for her old life as she patted out small rounded loaves on the baking paddle. Enos had a spacious home, but its single room was less to Channah's liking than a small tent filled with love. Sliding the paddle into the oven, she recalled thinking she would attend festivals in the city. However, Enos went alone to the occasional celebrations, even leaving his wives behind when he went to a recent family wedding. Except for brief encounters with neighbor women at the river or a rare trip to the vegetable market, Channah spoke with no one except her husband or Keren. She never expected that living near the city would turn out to be lonelier than herding sheep in the country.

No matter, she assured herself. Any day now, their household would be blessed with new life. As the mother, Keren would naturally take care of the baby, but Channah looked forward to times of holding, cuddling, and caring for him.

Channah heard the sound of Enos's voice inside the house as she pulled her perfectly formed loaves from the oven. She breathed in the aroma of the fresh bread, in no hurry to go inside. Suddenly, Enos burst into the courtyard. "See to Keren!" he shouted, hurrying toward the stable. "I will get the midwife."

Momentarily taken by surprise, Channah watched her husband throw open the shelter's doors. Ordinarily, she would go and saddle the donkey for Enos, but this was clearly not an ordinary situation. She ran inside the house, leaving the bread sitting beside the oven.

Not sure what to do, Channah poured a basin of vinegar and tossed her knife in to soak. She responded to Karen's sharp yelp by dampening a rag and laying it across her forehead. "Try to stay calm," she said. "There is nothing to fear." How she hoped what she said was true.

Keren moaned occasionally but cried out as the periodic birth pangs struck. Drawing on her experience with sheep, Channah stroked Keren's hand, wiped her brow, and hummed a soft lullaby during the quiet periods between the pains.

"Where is that cursed midwife?" Keren asked, panting for breath.

"She is on the way. Enos rode his donkey to fetch her."

"What if the baby comes before she gets here?" Keren shrieked.

Remembering to remain calm, Channah assured her, "I delivered our neighbor Shuwshan's son, and I can help you if the midwife does not arrive in time."

"Shuwshan had other children. This is my first baby." Keren's face contorted. "And I promise you, my last."

When darkness fell, Channah left Keren's side long enough to light the lamp that stood on a high stand near the center of the house. At last, Enos arrived and hustled the midwife through the entryway ahead of him. Keren's high-pitched scream eliminated the possibility of polite greetings. Channah took the midwife's cloak and set her bags by Keren's bed. "I am Channah. I will do whatever you wish to assist you."

"Call me Eder," the midwife said, settling herself on a stool near Keren. "You may begin by giving me something to eat."

"Get this baby out of me now," Keren pled.

"All in good time," Eder mumbled.

Channah scurried to fill a bowl of broth for the midwife.

Enos spoke from the far corner of the room. "I am hungry, too."

When she served Enos his soup, Channah could see he was perspiring. "This is not my bowl. Why did you put my food in Keren's dish?

"Forgive me, husband." Channah took the offending bowl from Enos and exchanged it for the one he ate from daily.

Between gulps, he asked, "Why is there no bread?"

Realizing the loaves were still sitting in the courtyard, Channah went outside to fetch them. Doing her best to keep from showing her irritation with Enos, she served him two of the cold fist-sized portions. "In all the excitement, I forgot about the bread."

"Careless." Enos stuffed half of a loaf into his mouth. As soon as he finished eating, he announced, "I am going across to the tannery. Let me know as soon as my son is born."

Channah went to sit by the midwife, who by this time was embroidering a length of cloth.

"Help me!" Keren cried out.

Eder seemed to ignore Keren's plea. The midwife's needle kept going in and out of the fabric. She stopped only long enough to point at Channah. "Be a dear, and unpack my birthing stool. It is in the largest bag."

Channah complied immediately.

Leaning toward Keren, Eder said, "You have to get off your bed and onto the birthing stool, dear."

"I cannot." Keren's voice was barely audible.

Channah leaned over Keren. "Please try. I will help you."

"Anything to end this—Ohhh!"

With Channah's assistance, Keren managed to position herself to the midwife's satisfaction. At last the baby's head began to emerge. Eder guided the baby into her waiting hands, and the long-awaited child was born.

Keren lurched back onto her bed while the midwife tied and cut the umbilical cord. When Eder coaxed a cry from the newborn, Keren asked, "Is he all right? Ten fingers and ten toes?"

"She is perfect," Eder replied. "Here," she laid the baby beside Keren. "You may inspect her."

"A girl? I have not given Enos the son he wants?" Keren began to cry. "Take her away."

Following Eder's instructions, Channah cleaned the baby. Meanwhile, Eder attended to Keren.

The door flew open, and Enos burst inside. "He is born? I heard a cry."

"You have a fine, healthy daughter," Eder said from Keren's bedside.

Enos stood in the doorway with the lamplight flickering across his stunned face. "A daughter? Are you certain?"

"I have been a midwife for fifteen years," Eder replied without looking at Enos. "I know the difference between a boy and a girl."

Enos moved slowly from the entrance to the bed where Keren lay weeping. He stood there for a moment, and then muttered, "How could you shame me this way?" He took coins from the leather pouch tied to his waist and thrust the money toward Eder. "Here are your wages. I really should not have to pay you, since you did not deliver a son." Enos turned on his heel and strode out of the house.

After Channah closed the door Enos left ajar, Eder said, "Am I God, that I should determine the sex of a child?" She tucked away her coins before leaning to smooth back Keren's hair. "Perhaps your next one will be a boy." With that, she began to gather her things. "Keep the baby warm, and make sure she nurses often."

Chapter Twenty-Seven

Keren allowed the baby to suck at her breast, although she turned her head away from the infant the whole time. Afterwards, Channah took the yawning babe in her arms and cuddled her. "Did Enos tell you her name?"

"Do you actually think he ever considered the possibility of a daughter?" Keren pulled the blanket to her chin. "I am going to sleep now." She turned toward the wall and closed her eyes.

Channah kissed and cooed at the baby, amazed at how tiny her ears and fingers were. "You are the most beautiful thing I have ever seen," she whispered. With Keren sleeping and Enos not home, she decided to let the baby sleep with her instead of using the fancy wooden cradle. That arrangement would keep the babe warm, as the midwife instructed. Besides, what newborn lamb would want to pass the night in isolation? As Keren so often reminded her, sheep are not people. Nevertheless, Channah had no other experience to draw on.

Three days passed before Enos returned home. He came in just after sunset, as if being gone several nights in a row was normal behavior.

"Good evening, husband." Channah needed no effort to infuse her words with joy. Taking care of the baby gave her abundant happiness.

Enos grunted and nodded a greeting. "I hope you baked bread for the evening meal."

"We have fresh loaves, still warm from the oven." She hurried to set out the bread, along with goat-milk cheese, dried figs, olives, and honey—foods she knew Enos favored. While her husband ate, Channah took bread and cheese and offered them to Keren, who remained on her bed.

"Is she sick?" Enos motioned toward the bed.

"She is still weak from giving birth."

Enos dribbled honey on his bread. "The slave woman I pay to gather dung for me had a child last month. She was back at work the next day."

Not wishing to displease either Keren or Enos by seeming to support the other, Channah ate without speaking. Then she decided to ask the question that was uppermost in her mind. "What name have you decided on for the baby?"

"Ask Keren. She can name her daughter whatever she likes. It is no concern of mine."

The next morning after Enos left for the tannery, Channah restrained herself as long as she could. Finally, she asked Keren, "What name will you give the baby?"

"Who cares what she is called?" Keren threw her blanket aside and sat up.

"I care."

Keren scowled at Channah. "Where are my good sandals?"

"Your shoes are there, beside you." She watched Keren comb her hair for the first time since the baby was born. "Shall we call her Rachel?"

"Rachel? Meaning ewe? You will never get past being raised in a tent with sheep."

"Uncle Avram told me one of the founding mothers of our nation was named Rachel."

Keren flipped her hair over one shoulder. "Give her the name Jezebel for all I care."

Channah shrugged, trying to mask the excitement she felt at being the one to choose the baby's name. She heard Rachel fussing and brought her to Keren to nurse. "She is hungry."

Keren sighed. "She is always hungry."

"That is good. A lamb who refuses to eat will not thrive." She enjoyed watching the baby suck, though she wished she could be the one to provide nourishment. "We should ask Shuwshan for advice on caring for our child." Channah observed Keren's face intently as the spoke, wondering if referring to Rachel as "ours" brought forth any resentment. Detecting no reaction, either positive or negative, she breathed a sigh of relief.

"You may speak with Shuwshan if you like." Keren shifted the baby to her other breast. "I have no interest in anything she has to say."

Channah calculated her earliest opportunity to encounter Shuwshan. "If I do not see her at the river in the morning, I will go to her home."

"As you like," Keren said without emotion.

Although Keren regained her strength in a few days, she continued to show no interest in anything or anyone outside herself. Occasionally she went shopping at the vegetable market but claimed to be too tired to do anything else. Channah did not mind doing the work required to maintain the household, but Keren's withdrawal left her even lonelier than before. Lacking anyone else to converse with, she talked and sang to Rachel all day.

As soon as Enos came home each evening, the focus of the household shifted to him. Channah knew to have her husband's evening meal prepared at sundown so food could be set before him as soon as he arrived home. After eating, Channah and Keren rubbed Enos's shoulders, cut his nails, combed his hair, or listened to his tales of how he outsmarted someone in a trade. All the while, Channah attempted to keep Rachel quiet to avoid her husband's complaints about living in a house full of noisy females.

Cuddling the sleeping baby in her arms after dinner, Channah cooed, "Rachel is so beautiful. When she is old enough, I would love to go and show her to my aunt and uncle."

"Who is that?" Enos asked. "Yakov?"

"No, the one who raised me, Uncle Avram."

"The sheepherder?" Enos narrowed his eyes. "No. I will not be shamed by permitting my family to associate with people of a lower class. It would look bad."

Channah did not answer. She kept her eyes on Rachel and rubbed the back of her hand against the infant's soft cheek. She knew she could not see Yael and Avram often, but she had previously nourished a hope Enos would allow her to go and visit them someday.

As the weeks passed, the household settled into a familiar routine. Channah took care of Rachel, only turning her over to Keren for breast feeding. Once too often she came inside after feeding the animals to find Keren sitting idly by while Rachel cried. Thereafter, Channah took the infant with her any time she went outside the house. The baby smiled and gurgled while Channah sang and milked the goat. She rode on Channah's hip or nestled into a long scarf tied around her caregiver's chest.

"Look at this," Channah said when she met her only friend at the river one morning. "Rachel has sprouted a tooth."

Shuwshan set aside her water pouch and chucked Rachel under the chin. "I am not surprised. She is about four months old?"

"Exactly." Channah loosened the cloth sling she used to carry the baby. "Four months yesterday." She jiggled Rachel to coax a smile. "She hardly ever fusses. So I should have known something was bothering her the last few days. Now I see it must have been the little tooth breaking through."

"Channah." Shuwshan took up her pouch and dipped water from the river.

"Yes? Why the grim face all of the sudden? Is there something wrong with Rachel's tooth?"

"No. The baby is fine. But there is something else I think you should know." She bit at her lip. "I owe you my life, and my son's as well. If you had not come the day he was born, I believe both of us would have died."

"I was happy to help."

Shuwshan nodded. "You are a very kind person." She poured water into the jugs sitting on her small wheeled cart. "Promise me you will never reveal how you learned what I am about to tell you."

"I promise." Channah removed her sandals. There was no one other than Shuwshan with whom she could share information anyway. "What is it?"

After glancing left and right, Shuwshan lowered her voice. "Your husband is actively searching for another wife."

Channah stepped barefoot into the shallow water and filled her pouch. "He wants a son more than anything. I suppose he has given up hope of getting one from Keren. Or me." She sighed.

"Just remember, you never heard this from me." Shuwshan dipped more water, while Channah hugged Rachel close and wondered why the news had to be a secret.

Channah watched Enos carefully that evening. She noticed nothing remarkably different about his behavior. Although she had been busy all day, at bedtime she pondered whether her husband's decision would have any effect on her or—more importantly—on Rachel. Fatigue overcame her before she reached any conclusions, and she fell asleep.

After Keren trudged off to the vegetable market the next morning, Channah swept the floor and sang to Rachel. She was still humming when Keren burst into the house, tossing her bag of cabbages and squash on the floor.

"That jackal Enos is seeking another wife," Keren shouted. "Everyone knows. Everyone but us. What is to become of me now?"

Picking up the bag, Channah peered inside. "These look good." She stepped around the baby to place the vegetables on the table. "Why are you upset at the thought of Enos taking another wife?" She waited for an answer from Keren, but when none came she added, "She will be company to us, and she can help with the housework."

"What if she is beautiful?" Keren laced her fingers into the hair on the sides of her head and swayed back and forth. "I must be cherished, be the apple of someone's eye, even if that someone is only an ignorant tanner." She dropped her arms to her sides. "Oh, you do not understand."

Suddenly bold, Channah replied, "I understand more than you think. I understand that Enos is disappointed in me and probably regrets our marriage. I understand that nothing I do seems to change how he feels." She picked up the baby. "But now we have Rachel to love and care for."

"Love." Karen spat the word as if it burned her mouth. "I once thought I knew what that word meant. Now the only thing I know is that another wife cannot give Enos the heir he craves. That could only happen if—" Her eyes widened. She stood very straight and slowly turned her face in the direction of the tannery. "All he wants is a son. So be it." She sat on her bed and began to comb her hair.

146

When Rachel began to whimper, Channah took her to Keren. "Time to feed the baby."

"No." Keren held up a restraining hand. "No more nursing. She will get no more milk from me."

"What?" Channah stared at Keren in disbelief. "Rachel is only four months old. You cannot mean that you want to wean her so soon."

"There is no other way. I cannot conceive while nursing a baby."

Puzzled, Channah dared to speak on a forbidden subject. "But you said Enos is unable to give us children."

Keren fluttered her eyelids, took a deep breath, and exhaled noisily. "Yes, Enos is barren, if that term applies to a man. There is no doubt in my mind."

"Then how can you become pregnant?"

"How do you think?" Keren resumed combing out her locks.

"But the Greek no longer comes to milk on the Sabbath. Now it is that bent-over fellow with a white beard. Surely, you would not ..." Channah was at a loss for the words to complete her thought.

Keren snorted. "No, that old man is probably no better than Enos at begetting a son. But men are fools. Sooner or later one of them will offer me an opportunity, and I shall take advantage of it." She took up her polished brass mirror and smiled at her image before turning toward Channah. "Are you shocked?"

Although the answer was a definite affirmative, Channah simply replied, "My only concern is Rachel. I wish you would nurse her for a few more months."

"On my wedding day, my mother warned me not to expect to get everything I wish for." Keren cocked her head and puckered her lips at the mirror.

Chapter Twenty-Eight

Channah found evenings somewhat stressful, due to the challenge of keeping the house quiet enough for Enos. However, her days were filled with the joy of watching Rachel grow and learn. The baby showed no ill effects of relying on goat milk for nourishment. She clapped her hands and swayed while Channah sang to her of frisky lambs and fields of wild flowers.

No one other than Channah seemed to notice when Rachel sat up on her own. Despite showing little interest in motherhood, Keren began to talk more and spent less time lying in bed.

"Channah, pack me food for three or four days and have my donkey ready to travel first thing in the morning." Enos's instructions during an evening meal caused Keren to stop eating and raise her eyebrows.

There was a slight tremble in Keren's voice when she asked, "Are you going to the seaport for new equipment?"

"No." Enos stroked his beard. "I have other business to attend to."

Well before sunup the next morning, Channah arose to feed the animals. She saddled the donkey and slung two bags of provisions over the its neck—one for her husband and another for the animal. Although she was curious, she resisted asking Enos where he was going. By now she had learned her husband shared whatever information he wanted his wives to know on his own schedule.

Enos was hardly out of sight when Keren sprang out of bed and dressed in her best robe and coat.

"Tomorrow is the day the farmers sell their produce," Channah remarked.

"Then I will go to the vegetable market tomorrow." Keren used a finger to smear a dark substance on her eyelids. "Today I am going inside the city walls to shop."

"For what?"

Keren touched her lips with a creamy, reddish substance. "I will know what I want when I see it."

As soon as her essential morning chores were done, Channah took Rachel into the courtyard behind the house. "There is no need to bake bread today, and no one will notice if we make a mess," she said, speaking to the baby as if she were another adult. "So you and I are going to make pickles from the abundant cucumbers from our garden."

Channah sat Rachel down with a wooden stirring stick and her favorite plaything, a small copper pot. With a cry of delight, the child began to beat on the pot, pausing between each ping to laugh at the noise.

"Perhaps you will have a drum when you grow up. Aunt Yael had a little one, and she used it to signal her sheep to follow. Auntie could not speak, you know." Channah glanced toward the hills. "You would love her, and she would adore you also. Someday I will teach you how to sling a stone, the way she taught me."

As Channah assembled her vinegar, spices, and crocks, she was surprised by Enos's entry into the courtyard. "Why, husband. I thought you would be gone several days."

"Cursed Romans." Enos dropped his donkey's reins. "The Zealots attacked some soldiers and killed most of them. So they have closed the road I was traveling—no traffic is allowed in or out until they catch the rebels." He removed the food bags and tossed them on the ground. Then he pointed toward Rachel. "Why is she making that irritating noise?"

Channah grabbed the stirring stick from Rachel's hand. "I think she likes the sound."

Rachel reached for her stick. When Channah put it behind her back, the baby resumed her drumbeat on the pot with the palm of her chubby hand.

"I hate wasting all of my preparations for my journey," Enos removed his cap, shook it out, and returned it to his head. "But I will have the satisfaction of seeing how my employees behave when they think I will be away. What are you doing?"

"Making pickles" Channah picked up Rachel and led the donkey toward the animal pen, while Enos disappeared into the house. Although she yearned to know her husband's planned destination, she knew he would resent being questioned.

After placing Rachel on a bed of straw, Channah unsaddled and began to rub down the donkey. Keeping the active, curious baby away from the goat and out from under the donkey's feet proved impossible. Finally, Channah put the child on her hip and continued working one-handed.

Enos stuck his head through the doorway. "Where is Keren?"

"She went inside the city walls to shop for something or other," Channah answered.

"Alone?" Without waiting for an answer, Enos left.

Satisfied the donkey was well situated, Channah tapped Rachel on the nose. "Slight change of plans, sweet girl. We will be baking bread today after all."

By the time Channah returned to the house, Enos was gone. She set a batch of dough to rise, washed and fed Rachel, and put away the pickling spices. As the afternoon wore on, she became concerned that Keren had not yet returned from the city. She remembered Shuwshan's caution not to go into town without companions—a warning Channah never thought to take seriously, with her days centered in Enos's house. Today, Shuwshan's words haunted her. She should have gone with Keren and put up pickled cucumbers tomorrow.

Unsure why she felt so troubled, Channah took the precaution of making Enos's favorite lentil soup for the evening meal. Although Keren had never before been gone all day, Channah sensed things would not go well if Enos found her missing when he came home. A feeling of dread crept into her mind and refused to release its grip.

Rachel, normally the happiest of children, seemed to catch Channah's apprehension. The baby became clingy and whiney, constantly reaching her arms up to be held. Lifting the baby into her arms, Channah asked, "Are you about to cut another tooth, sweet girl, or just worried about your mother? Soon you will be able to talk and tell me what bothers you." She cuddled Rachel close while putting bowls on the table with her free hand.

Channah brought freshly baked bread in from the courtyard. She bent to place the loaves on the table when Keren burst through the front door. Her dress was torn, her face bruised, her hair a tangled mess.

Automatically clutching Rachel, as if to protect her from the evils of the world, Channah whispered, "What happened to you?"

Keren flew to Channah's side and grabbed her forearm. "You must help me. Hide me. Something. Enos must not find out."

"Must not know what?" She reluctantly set the baby on floor. "Here, let's wash your face. Were you robbed? Did someone assault you?" Channah poured water into the basin and dabbed at Keren's discolored face with a strip of rag. When Keren took the cloth from her hand, she fetched a comb. "Let me fix your hair."

"He will kill me," Keren moaned. "My life is over. There is no way to keep this thing a secret."

Channah did her best to tame Keren's hair with the comb. "There, there. Things cannot be all that bad. Did someone rob you?"

"You know nothing." Keren snatched the comb. Then she began to cry. "Forgive me. I am so upset I cannot think. I am so frightened, Channah."

"You are home. There is no need to for fear now."

"But Enos." If Keren said more, her words were lost in her flood of tears. After many racking sobs, she took a breath and wiped her eyes. "You have to help me before he returns and finds out."

"Finds out what? You are not making sense, Keren."

"Maybe I can go somewhere and hide until his anger passes. If it ever does. But where could I go? What can I do? I only know Enos. Oh, Enos—"

As if he heard his name being called, Enos threw open the door.

Chapter Twenty-Nine

Enos's face was flushed. His eyes reminded Channah of a mountain lion about to pounce on its prey.

Not knowing what else to do, Channah stepped toward the door to offer her customary greeting. "How pleasant to be graced with your presence, husband."

Enos shooed Channah out of his path with an arm, never moving his stare from Keren. "Harlot!" he shouted. "Did you expect to get away with your betrayal?"

When he reached the corner where Keren cowered rolled up like a ball, Enos grabbed one of her hands and pulled her to her feet. "How could you do this to me?" He slapped across her face.

Keren's sobs filled the air, and Rachel began to cry also. Channah took the baby in her arms and retreated as far as possible from Keren and Enos.

"You are divorced," Enos yelled. "Divorced, do you hear me? Get out of my house. Now!" He continued to punctuate his words with open-handed blows.

Without speaking, Keren took a robe and tunic from their wall pegs. Enos snatched the garments from her and threw them on the floor. "You will take no possessions, not after you humiliated me in front of everyone in Jerusalem. You will leave with nothing but your miserable daughter."

"No, Enos." It was a moment before Channah realized it was she who screamed those two words.

"Well." Enos put his hands on his hips and turned to face Channah. "The silent shepherdess has found her tongue at last. Do you have something to say?"

The fear in Channah's core put a tremble into her voice. "Husband, please, surely you do not mean to send the baby away."

"At least the harlot gave birth, even if it was only to a girl. What have you ever done to give you the right to question my orders?"

"Rachel is not yet a year old," Channah answered softly, ignoring Enos's insults. Despite her apprehension, she approached her husband and put a hand lightly on his arm. "What is to become of her if you put her out? I beg you to have compassion on the child."

"What a very pretty word, compassion." Enos's eyes had lost nothing of their wildness. "Who has ever had any of it for me? Certainly not my wives." He turned back to Keren. "Get out of my sight, faithless woman, and take the brat, before I throw both of you into a vat of boiling urine."

"As for you." He whirled around and faced Channah. "Why are you so concerned? You need to think about whether that baby is worth more to you than your husband. If so, perhaps you should go out into the streets with her and her slut of a mother. I will not stop you." He crossed his arms and glared at Channah for a long moment. Then he spoke in a quiet voice. "But if you make the foolish choice to go, you are never to return to this house."

Her head told her to stay with Enos, where she had the security of a prosperous home. Nevertheless, her heart insisted she must protect Rachel. When Enos turned back to

156

shout curses at Keren, Channah swiftly stuffed whatever she could grab into the nearest bag. She strapped her knife around her waist, under the coat she donned earlier that day, when she thought the worst thing that could happen was a failed batch of pickles.

At last Enos seemed to tire of berating Keren. He slumped into a sitting position on his bed. He glanced toward the door, where Channah stood with Rachel in one arm and her bag of belongings slung over the other. "You, too? You would leave me after all I have given you?"

Although she was furious at Enos, Channah found a twinge of sympathy for her husband. He might be a decent fellow if only he could dispense with his enormous pride. "I cannot be separated from Rachel," she replied at last. "If she can remain, I will stay also."

"Go, then. What are you waiting for?" He hurled a kitchen pot in Channah's direction, barely missing her.

Keren stood and wiped her eyes. "I am glad to leave this house," she said as she crossed the room, moving to Channah's side. She touched a bruise that covered her left cheek. "I am relieved to be free of a man who cannot beget children."

"I made a daughter, and with a new wife I will have a son."

With a defiant lift of her chin as she followed Channah through the door, Keren turned and said, "No, Enos, you have no child. Remember Philip, the one they call the Greek, your former milkman? He fathered Rachel. A gentile, a slave, did what you cannot."

Through the closing door, Channah caught one last glimpse of Enos sitting on the bed with his mouth hanging open.

"We must make haste." Keren looked behind her. "Enos may come after us."

"No," Channah answered without bothering to look. "He is too proud to follow us in the sight of others. Surely you know that by now."

"I suppose so." Keren glanced backward once more. "It is getting dark. What shall we do? Where can we go?"

"Uncle Avram and Aunt Yael took me in when no one else would. I do not want to impose on them further, but I have no other possibilities."

"You mean to go back to the shepherds? If you want to live out in the country with a bunch of smelly animals and ignorant sheep herders, that is fine. But I will not go."

Much as she wanted to take refuge in Avram's tent, Channah was determined not to abandon Rachel to Keren's negligent care. "Do you have a better idea?"

"What about your other uncle? The one named Yakov?"

Channah thought for a few moments before answering. "Yakov sent me away when I was a little girl. He certainly will not shelter me now that I have the disgrace of being barren in addition to being turned out by my husband."

"Enos did not divorce you, Channah. You chose to leave."

"I fear to Yakov that would be even worse." She was certain her greedy, by-the-book uncle would not take her in. Even if he gave her temporary shelter, he would never extend his hospitality to Keren and Rachel. "What about your family? Is there someone who would let us sleep on their roof or in their courtyard tonight?"

Keren's shoulders slumped. "I have no family. My father's identity is unknown, and I have no idea where to find my mother. She makes her living sleeping with any man who offers her a coin." She gave Channah a sidelong look. "So now you know."

"I am sorry." Channah stood still and shifted Rachel to her other arm. "There is no reason to keep walking until we decide where to go. We must stop and make a plan."

Chapter Thirty

As the two women made their way to Shuwshan and Joab's house, Channah asked Keren, "What did you do to make Enos so angry?"

"It is complicated."

Channah insisted. "Try to make it simple for me."

Keren walked a few steps before answering. "I went into the city and wandered around, waiting for a suitable man to approach me."

"Suitable?"

"Try to think like a grownup, Channah. I wanted to please Enos, to give him the son he wanted so desperately. To make myself valuable to him again. But he betrayed me."

"Enos?" Channah had difficulty following Keren's story.

"No, the man I slept with in the city." Keren huffed. "The viper never even told me his name." She shifted Channah's bag to her other shoulder. "He took me to a place where he said we could be alone together."

"No."

"Yes." Keren rubbed her bruised cheek again. "As soon as the man got what he wanted, five others jumped out from hiding and seized me. I thought I was going to die." She fell silent for a few moments.

"Did they stone him? The man who—that is, the man you went with?"

"One of the five gave him a pouch full of coins. He laughed and left. Then the other men dragged me before a rabbi for judgment in the temple courtyard."

"How did you get away?"

Keren shook her head. "The rabbi shamed the men who said I should be executed. After he told them someone who was sinless must cast the first stone, they all skulked away. One by one." A single tear spilled from each eye. "Then he allowed me go."

"What? He let you escape without being punished?" Channah was astonished. "I have never met a rabbi, but Uncle Avram spoke of them as an unforgiving lot. You were most fortunate."

"He told me to quit sinning." Keren ducked her head. "All the way home I vowed to live a better life. I hoped Enos would not find out what happened." She put a hand on Channah's arm. "Why did he come home early?"

"He had to turn back because the Romans closed the road. There was some kind of trouble. Rebels, I think Enos said."

Dropping her hand, Keren moved ahead. "I was afraid sooner or later someone would tell Enos what happened, because the five men made sure everyone in the temple knew what I did." She sighed. "Still, I held onto the hope I would be safe for a little while, and maybe I would be pregnant before Enos found out. Then he would wait and see if I had a boy." She cut her eyes toward Channah. "Now I suppose you will tell me what a fool I have been."

"For what purpose? Angry words will not find food for Rachel."

While Keren stood at a distance with the baby in her arms, Channah tapped on the door of Shuwshan's house. She was about to give up and leave when the door cracked open.

"May Rachel and Keren and I sleep in your courtyard tonight?"

"No." Shuwshan spoke loudly. "This family refuses to shelter you." Under her breath, she whispered, "Meet me at the river in the morning. Early."

Channah stared at the now-closed door for a moment, then slowly turned away.

"I see Enos spread the news to our neighbors," Keren said as Channah approached her.

With a shrug, Channah reached for Rachel. "They probably heard him yelling 'divorced' at the top of his lungs."

"Now what shall we do?"

"Let me think for a moment." Channah jiggled the sleeping baby. She looked toward the dark house she still thought of as home. "We might be able to go toward the river and circle back to our house. That is, Enos's house."

"Why?" Keren's voice conveyed a brittle tone. "So he can beat me again?"

"No. We may be able to sneak into the stable."

"And sleep with a nasty donkey and that disagreeable goat? No. I cannot."

Hungry and exhausted, Channah ran out of patience. "We either sleep with the animals or out in the open, under the stars. Unless you have some other suggestion."

Sighing heavily, Keren took up the small bag of provisions, which Channah took to be a grudging agreement.

"Follow me." In the deep darkness, Channah relied on her memory to skirt around to the open field behind Enos's house. When at last she slipped open the creaky door to the shed, Channah spoke softly to the animals to keep them quiet. She felt around on the bare earth for enough straw to make a bed for herself and Rachel. "Find a spot and try to get some sleep," she whispered to Keren. Then, too weary to fear discovery, she snuggled the baby close to her chest and fell asleep.

When Channah's eyes popped open early the next morning, she was disoriented. It took a moment for her to remember where she was and why. She extended her arm and felt around. "Keren," she whispered. "Wake up. We have to get to the river."

Keren moaned. "I hurt all over."

"You will feel worse if Enos finds us here." Channah leapt up, brushed the straw from her tunic, and grabbed Rachel. She carefully pushed the shed's door open and peered outside. Seeing no one stirring in the pale pre-dawn light, she stepped outside. "Come," she whispered to Keren.

When they reached the river, Shuwshan was already there waiting. "Forgive me for refusing you shelter last night. Enos can make trouble for Joab."

"I understand," Channah replied, patting her friend's shoulder.

"I brought you as much food as I can spare." Shuwshan gestured toward a large crock. "I am sorry I have no extra bags. A relative of mine has a farm where you may be able to get work, but please do not say I was the one who sent you. Go down the road all the way to an old olive tree near a grove of four tall oaks. Ask for Matthias." She glanced around and re-wrapped her scarf. "I must get home before Joab and the children wake up."

"Thank you," Channah said. "I will never forget your kindness."

"God be with you." With those words, Shuwshan trotted away.

Keren was already pawing through the food. "I am faint with hunger. I have had nothing to eat since early yesterday."

"Rachel and I have not eaten either." Channah looked around. "Where is our bag?"

"I have no idea." Keren pulled out a date cake and began to munch on it.

Rachel pointed to the cake and whimpered.

"I hope you can chew this." Channah took a date cake from the top of Shuwshan's crock and offered a pinch of it to the baby. "I suppose we must give it a try." Turning her attention back to Keren, she said, "You were carrying the bag of provisions last night. Did you leave it in the animal shed?"

Keren finished off the date cake before answering. "That may be where it is. How would I know?" She licked her fingers and took another cake from the crock.

"Enos will find the bag when he feeds the animals this morning. We dare not risk going back to the shed." Channah sighed, took another date cake, and shared it with Rachel.

"Leave the crock for Shuwshan. Wrap the food in your scarf and guard it carefully." She drew a deep breath, determined not to weep.

"The cakes are messy. They will get me dirty," Keren complained.

Channah pressed her lips together. She wanted to leave Keren behind and make her own way, but she knew that would mean abandoning Rachel. "Everything we own is in that crock or on our backs. This is no time to be concerned with the appearance of your clothing."

With a dramatic sigh, Keren unwound her scarf. "You have no call to be so bossy. I am older than you, and I was married to Enos longer."

Chapter Thirty-One

"Look." Channah pointed toward a wooden pavilion sitting in the midst of the barley fields. She drew a deep breath, as if air in her lungs would bolster her courage. "We can go there and ask for work." Many workers swarmed over the barley fields, making her doubt the need for any more harvesters.

"Give me your scarf," Keren said. "I will go and get us hired."

Surprised that Keren volunteered to speak to the overseer, Channah unwound her scarf and handed it over. "Should we not go together?"

"No." Keren pinched her cheeks and teased a few tendrils of hair from beneath her mantle. "I know how to persuade a man to do what I want. You do not."

As soon as Keren turned away, Channah pinched a few bites of date cake and fed them to Rachel. Jiggling the baby on her hip, she wondered what to do if there were no wages at the end of this day. Her mind was stirred by unbidden memory of the plentiful food Yael always kept on hand. As Keren stood speaking with a portly fellow, Channah had a wild impulse to run away and take the baby with her. Immediately, more rational thoughts intervened. She doubted she could outrun the long-legged Keren, certainly not while carrying Rachel. Furthermore, where could she go? Even if Avram let her come home, she had no idea how to locate Bethlehem.

"We are to tie up the stalks." Keren's announcement jolted Channah from her idle daydreams.

The overseer led the women through the barley rows to a wooden platform where threshers were processing barley grain. As they worked, the workers tossed empty stalks from the platform onto a haphazard pile. Channah observed an elderly woman bundle an armful of stalks and tie them together with a thin rope.

Using her long scarf, Channah tied Rachel onto her back, leaving her arms and hands free. Following the old woman's example, she gathered as many stalks as she could manage. After tying and cutting the rope, she noticed how uneven her bundle was in comparison to the bales stacked into a flatbed chariot. The next one was marginally better.

"Channah, can you come over here and cut my rope?" Keren awkwardly straddled a bundle of stalks. "You were smart to bring a sharp knife."

When Channah leaned to oblige, Keren whispered in her ear, "If anyone asks, we are widows. And Rachel is your child, not mine."

The work was monotonous yet demanding. Within a short time, Channah's hands were rubbed raw and had numerous small cuts from handling the sharp stalks. She was grateful when Rachel quit fussing and fell asleep. Taking her opportunity to tuck the sleeping baby in the shade of the threshing platform, Channah tied bundles much more quickly without the baby's weight on her back. She worried about being discharged if she and Keren did not produce as many bales as the overseer expected. Noticing the capable routine of the old woman working beside her, she did her best to imitate the same efficient motions.

When the sun was directly overhead, everyone went to the central pavilion, where the overseer handed each worker a portion of sour wine. Rachel scrunched up her face at a sip from Channah's cup.

"I am sick of date cakes," Keren grumbled.

Before Channah could respond, the old women they worked with squatted nearby. "I am Talitha."

"My name is Channah, and this is Keren." Channah smoothed a hand across the baby's dark curls. "This sweet little one is Rachel."

Talitha nodded toward Rachel. "She is beautiful."

"Thank you." Channah smiled for the first time that day. "I think so."

"You have not been in these fields before," the old woman said. "Where do you live?"

"We have no place."

"We are newly widowed," Keren added, shooting a glance at Channah. "Our husband just died a few days ago."

Talitha drank from her cup. "Ah, you face a hard life. I should know. I have been a widow for seven years now. I tell you it is a scandal, how families refuse to support us." Her eyes darted from Channah to Keren and back. "You are young. Perhaps you will find husbands to take care of you." She used her cup to gesture toward Keren. "You will find someone."

For the first time, Channah was despondent about the future. She was almost out of food and had no place to sleep tonight. She continued feeding Rachel, but focused her thoughts on Talitha's words. Where could they find a man willing to take on two wives and a child, all at the same time? Furthermore, Keren was clearly free to remarry, because Enos had proclaimed their divorce. Her own status was unclear. Was she still technically Enos's wife? Channah sighed, tied Rachel on her back, and returned to work.

Late in the afternoon, Talitha stood straight and used a rag to wipe perspiration from her brow. "If you can pay for lodging, I will show you a place. The widow next door to me takes in boarders. I must warn you, she requires a week's payment in advance and her rules are very strict."

"Thank you." Channah pondered whether the day's wages would be enough to pay the rent. And above all, she had to get Rachel some milk. Weary from the unfamiliar bending position, she untied her scarf and sat the baby next to her. "Keren, help me watch Rachel."

Keren glanced at her child, but then she turned away and continued to bunch stalks together without comment.

Realizing Rachel needed something to keep her from crawling away, Channah removed her knife's holster and gave it to her. "Here, play with this." Channah hurriedly gathered and tied bales while Rachel was occupied. With one eye, she watched while the baby examined and then chewed on the leather scabbard. The rhythm of Channah's movements went smoothly for a brief time. Then, suddenly, she realized Rachel was choking.

169

Channah was on her knees in a flash, instinctively using her fingers to dislodge the object in the baby's throat. To her relief, Rachel gagged and spat out a coin. In the dirt beside the baby lay a topaz necklace and another coin. As recognition dawned, Channah stared at the objects Yael tucked beneath her knife the day Yakov took her away to be married. How could she have forgotten for so long?

For the remainder of the afternoon, Channah worked with a lighter heart. One of the coins should certainly be enough to cover both lodging and a few necessities for Rachel.

Later that evening, the widow Elisheba showed Channah the room she paid to share with Rachel and Keren for the duration of the barley harvest. The mud brick walls jutted out from the widow's house, obviously a later addition. There was no window, only a door leading into an austere chamber where two narrow beds took up most of the floor space.

"It is dark in here," Keren said as soon as the widow left. "And that soup she fed us was mostly water."

"There is nothing to be gained by complaining," Channah replied. "We are fortunate to have a safe place to sleep and something other than date cakes to eat." She shook out Rachel's new blanket and spread it on one of the beds. Since they were alone, she whispered a question that had bothered her all day. "Keren, why did you tell the overseer we are widows?"

"So he would have compassion on us. Everyone assumes a divorced woman did something to displease her husband. Widows, on the other hand, do not deserve their hard lot."

"He will discharge us if he finds out the truth."

"He will never know." Keren sounded confident. Then, with a quaver in her voice, she asked, "Oh, Channah, what shall we do when the barley is all harvested?"

"If we are careful, we will be able to live on our wages from the barley field. Then perhaps the farmer will hire us to help bring in his wheat. It will ripen soon."

"And what then? Sooner or later we will have to sell our bodies."

"No," Channah said with all the conviction she could muster.

Chapter Thirty-Two

Avram stopped a woman in the street. "Woman, can you tell me where the man Yakov has gone?"

She set her pitcher down and wiped her forehead with the sleeve of her coat. "Yakov is no longer among the living. His wife Adah—I should say his widow Adah—went to live with relatives after he died. That was maybe a year ago."

"Do you know where she went? Adah, I mean."

The woman looked Avram up and down. "Why do you ask? If Yakov owed you money, I doubt you will ever collect. Many other creditors have come ahead of you to ask about him."

"No, I am searching for a young woman," Avram explained. "She is the daughter of Yakov's brother and my niece Rebecca." He touched the pouch attached to his sash. "I am willing to pay for information."

The woman shook her head. "I know nothing. Adah kept to herself. She had no close friends that I know of. As for Yakov, I can only suppose no one mourns him except possibly Adah, and maybe not even her. If you ask me, the neighborhood is better off without that greedy jackal."

"Yakov arranged the girl's marriage to a tanner, but I cannot remember his name. Do you remember the wedding? Perhaps there is a tanner who lives nearby?"

The woman wrinkled her nose and hoisted her pitcher to her shoulder. "As you know, tanners have to live outside the city walls. They are unclean." With those parting words, the woman ambled away.

After distributing many coins and visiting several small tanneries, Avram was discouraged. However, as he walked along he encountered a shepherd taking a tiny flock of sheep to market. The fellow shepherd described a large tanning operation south of the city, owned by a man named Enos. As Avram walked through Jerusalem, he thought "Enos" sounded familiar. Or was his aging mind confusing hope with factual memory? He was uncertain. If only Yakov had given him time to attend Channah's wedding. He pushed away his negative thoughts, preferring to engage in prayer as he continued his journey.

It was midafternoon when Avram's nose told him he was nearing a place where animal hides were processed. He took some consolation that he was going toward Bethlehem's pastures. If he did not locate Channah at the home of Enos the tanner, he could look forward to going home later. Home. It was not the same without his sweet Yael. He passed a short time re-living memories of his dearly departed wife before turning his attention to the tanning yard looming ahead.

"Good day. May I assist you?" The young man looked up at Avram expectantly.

Avram wondered if he was about to meet Channah's husband. "I want to see Enos the tanner."

"Is he expecting you?"

"No."

The young man raked a hand through his hair. "Sir, Enos the tanner is a very important man. He normally does business through appointments."

Something emboldened Avram to take a risk. "I want to speak with Enos about his wife."

With widened eyes, the fellow turned and ran into the tanning yard. Avram saw him pluck at the sleeve of a short, well-dressed man. They glanced at Avram several times as they spoke.

"I know everything about the whole incident," the well-groomed man said as he approached Avram.

The old shepherd sized him up as a man highly impressed with himself. If this tanner was not the right one, he would simply plead ignorance. "Enos the tanner? You are married to a woman Channah, are you not?"

"Channah? I thought. Never mind." Enos waved the younger man away. "Let us walk outside the yard."

As they exited the gate, Avram spoke. "I am Channah's uncle. I want to see my niece. I trust she is well."

"Channah is the niece of a man called Yakov."

"Yes, I know. Yakov arranged her marriage, but my wife and I raised her. Channah belongs to my brother's daughter Rebecca, who was married to Yakov's brother. That may seem complicated. Said another way, Yakov is on Channah's father's side of the house and I am related to her mother."

Enos chewed his lip. "Why do you wish to see her? I heard Yakov died. Is she due an inheritance?"

"I did not know of Yakov's passing. I expect he owed more money than he left behind, but I am here on another matter entirely. You see, when my wife and I raised the girl, I did not teach her of our Messiah. I was wrong. I now seek to undo my error and tell her about Jesus of Nazareth."

"I have heard of him. He is a rabble rouser in my opinion." Enos stared downward at his own feet for a moment before adding, "In any case, you cannot speak with Channah. She is dead."

"No!" Avram put his hands on the shorter man's shoulders. "Channah? So young and full of life? It cannot be."

"Yes. It is sad, I know. She caught a fever, something like a plague I suppose. In fact, both of my wives took sick and died on the same day, Channah and Keren."

Avram dropped his arms to his side, stunned. "When did this happen?"

"Only three weeks ago." Enos stepped back. "You can see that I have suffered a great loss." He cleared his throat and shifted his weight from one foot to the other. "Forgive me, but I must get back to work. My tannery is all I have left now. Good day." He turned and walked swiftly through the gate into the tanning yard.

Avram tore his tunic and sat in the road, sobbing and heaping dust on his head. He wept for Channah, for Yael, and for himself. A woman passing by asked if he wanted a drink of water. Avram accepted a cup from her hand, thanked her, and did his best to dry his tears. When the sun was low on the horizon, he stood on shaking legs and slowly began his journey home.

Chapter Thirty-Three

The morning light filtered through the thatched roof of the widow Elisheba's house while Channah arose and made her final preparations to go to work. Harvesting wheat was not much different from working in the barley fields. Instead of cutting the wheat stalks, the farmer ordered his workers to leave the bare plants standing for his livestock. Keren was assigned to cut and bag the grain from the plants, while Channah winnowed away the chaff from the wheat.

"I cannot go to the field today," Keren mumbled from her bed. "I am too tired."

"Everyone is tired." Channah dressed Rachel in the darkness. "We will rest tomorrow, on the Sabbath."

"No."

"Keren, we need both our daily wages to buy food. You must go to the field."

Keren sat up on an elbow, then fell back flat on her bed.

Attempting to remain patient, Channah said, "If I can carry Rachel on my back besides doing my share of the labor, surely you can get yourself to the field."

With a moan, Keren turned her face toward the wall. "But you are not pregnant."

"Are you?" Channah sank to Keren's side.

A moment passed before Keren answered. "That cursed jackal who betrayed me to the temple Pharisees. He did this to me." She began to sob.

"If you are with child, that is even more reason for us not to miss any wages. Come to the field with me." She patted Rachel's heaving shoulder. "You will feel better as the morning wears on."

Channah and Keren were the last of the workers to arrive at the wheat field. When the overseer met her nod of greeting with a stone face, she wondered about the security of their jobs. She was only too aware the more experienced harvesters were more capable than she, and Keren's productivity always lagged even further behind. She concentrated on working hard that day. However, she was distracted too often by having to encourage Keren or deal with Rachel's restlessness. By late afternoon, she was exhausted. The promise of a Sabbath day of rest was all she could think about.

As Channah stood in line to receive the day's wages, the old widow she met earlier in the barley fields stood behind her. "Thank God for the Sabbath tomorrow," Talitha murmured.

Channah nodded her agreement, too tired to summon the strength to speak.

"You are a hard worker, and surprisingly strong for one so small." Talitha leaned nearer. "But you should distance yourself from that friend of yours, the one named Keren."

Surprised, Channah glanced back at Talitha. "Why?"

"She is a slacker," Talitha replied. "I am surprised she was kept on for the wheat harvest, and I suspect if she was not so pretty she would already be gone."

Channah shrugged and stepped forward to receive her pay, knowing Talitha spoke the truth.

The next morning, Channah took Rachel outside, into the widow's courtyard, leaving Keren asleep. She sat in the shade of an acacia tree, watching the baby laughingly collect pebbles into a cracked bowl. For a while, she flirted with offering to part ways with Keren and take Rachel with her. Although Keren exhibited no interest in her child, Channah suspected she would hold onto her daughter for selfish reasons if nothing else. If they split up, Keren would be left to fend for herself.

Keren emerged into the courtyard and sat next to Channah on the wooden bench. "I have something unpleasant to tell you."

"What is that?" Channah asked.

"The overseer only gave me half a day's wages for yesterday."

Channah sighed. "We have already spent everything from the sale of my necklace. When I pay for next week's lodging, there will be nothing left from the two coins I had." She thought for a moment. "We must cut down on what we eat."

Keren surprised her by not protesting. "There is more."

"More food?"

"No, more news." Keren swallowed hard. "The overseer told me not to come back to the wheat field again. I am no longer employed."

Channah stretched her fingers, made fists, and flexed her hands once more. "Oh."

"I tried, Channah. You know how to do manual labor, and it does not seem to bother you. I am not like that. Can you understand?"

"It is not a question of understanding or not understanding. It is simply a matter of surviving."

"So what do we do now? Perhaps we should go down to the river and drown ourselves and her." She tilted her head toward Rachel.

Channah bristled. "Never say such a thing again. I intend to see to it that Rachel grows up well-fed and healthy."

"How?" Keren lowered her head and cupped it in her hands.

"I have worked very hard these past few weeks, but I am not a farmer. I know you think of me as ignorant, and I suppose you are right. But I do know about sheep. When the wheat begins to ripen, it is also time to harvest wool, and I can shear a sheep better and faster than anyone." Channah paused, expecting a reaction from Keren. There was none.

"And so," Channah continued, "I am going to find my way to the hills of Bethlehem. My aunt and uncle have food to eat and a place to live. I will beg them to hire me to help with their shearing."

Keren sat for a long while with her head in her hands. At last she sat straight. "Will they welcome me along with you?"

"Auntie will never turn me away. I cannot say for certain about Uncle Avram. He knows my work, and that may convince him to allow us to remain at least until the sheep are shorn. After that ..." Channah shrugged.

The widow Elisheba wandered into the courtyard. "Good Sabbath." She pulled a loaf of yesterday's bread from the outdoor oven and started to munch on it.

"Good Sabbath," Keren and Channah replied in unison.

Following Elisheba's lead, Channah took a loaf of bread. She pinched off small pieces for Rachel, who was instantly more interested in eating than in playing with her broken bowl.

"Do you perhaps know which direction Bethlehem lies from where we are now?"

Elisheba stared at Channah for a moment. "My hearing is not what it used to be. I thought you asked about Bethlehem."

"Yes." Channah took her first bite of bread. "Bethlehem."

With a snort, Elisheba pointed. "You know the road you take to work each morning? Instead of stopping at the wheat fields, keep walking down that road and you will come to Bethlehem."

Letting her gaze follow the widow's gesture, Channah asked, "Is it very far?"

"If I leave at sunrise, I can arrive in Bethlehem around midday, and I do not walk fast. It is too far to travel on a Sabbath, of course. Why do you ask? It is a worthless village. There is no work there unless you want to do business with shepherds."

"I have relatives who live near Bethlehem," Channah said. She carried Rachel to the courtyard wall and looked in the direction of home. "I had no idea we were so near."

Chapter Thirty-Four

At sunrise, Channah gathered her meager belongings and roused Keren. "Wake up. It is time to go." She wrapped sleepy Rachel in her blanket and tied her onto her back for the journey.

When they passed by the wheat field, Channah detoured off the road. She told the indifferent overseer she was leaving and hurried back to join Keren. Before the coolness of the morning faded, the territory began to look familiar. Although uncertain about the reception they would receive, she was excited when they crossed a row of low hills she recognized. In the distance, Channah heard a shepherd's pipe playing a tune she knew meant "three peaceful strangers." In her mind, she rehearsed her speech. "I have fallen on hard times. Would you be so kind as to permit me to work for wages to help you shear your sheep?" She wondered how to explain the responsibility she had assumed for Rachel. Perhaps that could wait until she offered to sleep outside and give Keren her place in Yael's tent.

Channah breathed in the hill country air. "What a beautiful place," she murmured.

"Beautiful?" Keren exhaled noisily. "Are there snakes out here?"

Before Channah could answer, she whirled toward the sound of pounding footsteps.

Avram never ran, but he was running toward her now. "Channah?"

"Uncle, I have fallen—"

Her words were lost as Avram pulled her into an embrace. "Oh, Channah, my darling child. I thought you were gone forever." He stepped back and held her at arm's length. "Praise God. It really is you."

"Uncle, I have—"

Again, Avram buried her in a hug. "You have a baby! How wonderful. And who is your friend?"

"This is Keren. We have fallen—"

"Greetings, Keren. You must join us for food and wine. Have you come far? Are you tired?" Avram continued asking questions without waiting for answers. "Let me carry the child for you."

As they unwound Rachel's blanket, Channah tried again to explain her situation. "Uncle, I have fallen on hard times."

"Thank God you came to me, then," Avram interrupted. "Your old uncle will take care of you, all of you." He lifted Rachel as if she had no weight at all. "Now this is a fine-looking little lamb. Boy or girl?"

Channah could not stop her smile. "A little girl. Her name is Rachel, and Keren is her mother. Uncle, there is so much I must tell you."

"Rachel? Well, she really is a little lamb with that name." Avram put his arm around Channah. "Come. There will be plenty of time to talk after a good meal and some rest."

For the first time since Yakov fetched her away from the hills, Channah felt as if she was somewhere where she was welcome, perhaps even wanted.

As they walked up and down the hills, Channah asked, "I cannot wait to see Auntie."

She felt Avram tighten the arm draped over her shoulder.

"Yael was too good for this world. And she was never strong." There was a catch in Avram's voice.

It took a moment for Channah to understand the meaning of her uncle's words. "Auntie is no longer alive?"

"Not on this earth, but I believe she is more alive than ever. She is able to sing again. I have always been the one to want proof and logic. Yael simply believed." He hugged Rachel to his chest. "I had a life-changing experience as a young man, and now God has blessed me with another in my old age. There is so much I need to tell you."

Channah fought to hold back tears. "I wish I could have been here to say goodbye to Auntie."

"She went peacefully, in her sleep." Avram sniffled. "And now she has no more pain or weakness."

"How do you manage the herd all alone?"

"My friend Caleb and his son Nathan are my partners now." Avram withdrew his arm from Channah and chucked Rachel under her chin. "She is too solemn."

"How much further?" Keren asked. "My feet are tired."

"Just over the next rise," Avram said, with a searching look in Keren's direction. "I need not return to the pasture today. Caleb and Nathan will bring the sheep home later. Meanwhile, we will sit and visit. You must tell me all that has happened since we parted, and I will do the same." He turned his face to Rachel and wiggled his eyebrows. "Perhaps the best baker in the hill country will make us some fresh bread. Would you like that, little one?"

Rachel giggled and grabbed at Avram's beard.

"Oh, no," he said, easing hair from Rachel's tiny fingers and laughing. "You have already discovered how to subdue an old man."

As they approached the paddock, cave, and tent where Avram lived, Channah felt sorrow welling up. How long she had cherished the hope of seeing Yael once more, but now she knew that was impossible. "I can almost see Auntie, welcoming us home from a day in the pasture." She brushed aside the unbidden tear that insisted on rolling down her cheek.

Avram swallowed hard and ducked his head. "Yes. I miss her, too." He held Rachel toward Keren, who stepped backward with a surprised face.

"I will take her." With one easy motion, Channah slung the baby onto her hip. She followed Avram through the small gap in the stone fence. How peaceful she felt, being in a place she understood and belonged. She took in every detail, while Keren stood with folded arms.

Pulling the tent's front flaps over tall stakes, Avram opened up the living area to the bright sunlight. In the center of the sheltered space he began to set out bowls of plain food—nuts, dried fruit, cheese, and wine.

"Let me help you." Channah sat Rachel on the smooth earthen floor, not comfortable allowing her old uncle to serve her. She hoped Keren would also offer assistance, but instead she stood silently apart, barely inside the tent flap's shade.

The baby crawled to a pile of sheepskins. She thrust her hands upward, but could not reach the top of the heap. With a grunt, she tugged at the ragged edges of the hides and pulled herself into an upright position.

"Look at Rachel! She is standing!" Channah hurried to put down a bowl of figs to rush to where the baby stood.

With all eyes on her, Rachel thumped onto her bottom. She sat grinning, appearing to understand what she had accomplished. After a moment of sitting, she tugged at the stack of hides again, and once more stood on her unsteady legs.

"Her first time to stand?" Avram asked.

Channah nodded, too choked up to risk speaking. However, this time the tears that threatened to spill were because of her unspeakable joy. She glanced toward Keren, whose face remained unreadable.

"This is good." Avram took a cross-legged sitting position at his low table. "It means the little one likes this place. Come, I will speak a blessing and then we will eat."

"Lord, we thank you for our food, and I thank you especially for bringing my precious daughter Channah to me." Avram completed his prayer and proceeded to pour wine, as if his words were perfectly normal.

Breaking off bites of cheese for Rachel, Channah kept her eyes low. She did not know what to think. Avram had never referred to her as his daughter, even though he and Yael took her in and raised her as their child. Furthermore, her uncle was obviously praying, which she had never known him to do. Perhaps her uncle's age was beginning to weaken his mind.

To Channah's relief, Keren did not mention the community dishes they all ate from without benefit of individual serving bowls. On the contrary, Keren ate with the enthusiasm of a starving beggar.

Avram took a few sips of his wine and leaned his head back for a moment with his eyes closed. "Do you want to tell me of the hard times you mentioned earlier?" His voice was soft, his words gentle, almost sad.

"Keren and I were wives to a tanner named Enos." She paused to consider how to be avoid being dishonest with her uncle without revealing Keren's wrongdoing. "One day our husband became angry with Keren and pronounced her divorced. He told her to leave his house and take her daughter." Channah fed Rachel another few bites while gathering her thoughts. "I know a divorced woman can barely make a living, let alone support herself and a baby. I could not stand the thought of Rachel going hungry, and I tried to get Enos to relent and keep Rachel. He told me I should leave, too, if I wanted to be with the baby."

"Was that this morning?"

"No, six or eight weeks ago. We found work harvesting barley, and then we went to the wheat fields." Channah pressed her lips together and took a deep breath before going on. She could hardly hear her own next words. "Keren is expecting a child, and I cannot make enough wages for all of us by myself."

"You will always be welcome here, Channah. You may stay as long as you like, and you may consider everything I own to belong to you."

"Thank you, Uncle." Channah was afraid to ask about Rachel or Keren, uncertain what she would do if Avram refused them shelter.

"What kind of viper casts out a woman who is carrying his child?"

To Channah's way of thinking, this was dangerous territory. She framed her response carefully to sidestep an outright lie. "Enos did not know of Keren's pregnancy."

"Tell me." Avram turned his cup around and around. "Did this man ever strike you?"

"No. Never."

Keren stopped eating long enough to interject, "Of course not. He was too busy hitting me."

Avram peered at Keren for a moment, then turned back to Channah.

"And your husband did not force you to go? You departed of your own free will?'

"Yes, Uncle. I chose to leave." She offered Rachel another bite. "To protect this child."

Chapter Thirty-Five

Rachel fell asleep in Avram's lap while Channah and Keren put away the dishes and the remaining food. The old man reached for a sheepskin, used one arm to spread it beside him, and gently laid the baby on the soft fleece. After resettling himself, he beckoned to Channah. "I have so much to tell you that I hardly know where to begin."

"About Auntie?" Channah guessed.

"Not exactly, though she played a part. I want to tell you about Israel's savior."

Keren stood. "Perhaps I shall take a walk."

Avram gave her a steady stare. "Do as you like, but have no doubt. What I have to say affects you as well as Channah."

While Keren edged away slowly, Avram focused his fierce eyes on Channah. "When I was a young man, I studied the Holy Scriptures diligently. In my youthful arrogance, I even considered myself something of a scholar." After another sip of wine, he continued. "Because of the words of the prophets, my generation knew we were privileged to live in the time when our Messiah was to come. Due to family economics, I had to find work. So, I became a shepherd. I loved being in the fields with the animals, as did, eventually, my beautiful young wife Yael." Avram brushed his hair back with both hands. "We were filled with joy when a baby completed our little family. You never knew we had a son, did you?"

"Yes." Channah saw surprise register on her uncle's weathered face. "Once, when we were bringing the herd down from the mountain at the end of summer, we shared our campsite with a family. That evening, I heard you tell the other shepherd an amazing story. You said soldiers killed your baby." She put her hand over his. "I was sorry for what happened, in my childish way. Now, when look at Rachel, I do not know how you and Auntie survived such a heartbreak."

"Yael fought the soldiers. Her bare hands against their swords. She was never again able to speak." Avram ducked his head and covered his face with his hands for a long moment. "That is another story, for another day. I was out in the fields with a small group of shepherds when an angel announced the Messiah's birth. I never doubted the baby born in the stable that night was the chosen one, because I was an eyewitness to many miracles that night."

Channah was transfixed. "You saw a real angel, Uncle?"

"I saw him and he spoke to me, as clearly as you and I are speaking to each other right now." Avram looked upwards, almost as if he expected an angel to materialize above him again. "I will spare you the grisly details about the babies. Suffice it to say, I thought the soldiers killed our Messiah along with my son and every other baby boy in Bethlehem, but I know now I was wrong. After Yael was well enough to come home, she would shake her head in disagreement when I said the chosen one was dead, but of course she was unable to explain."

When the baby made a mewing sound, Channah moved next to where she lay and lightly patted her back. Rachel sighed, turned to curl on her side, and quieted.

192

"You behave more like the mother of this child than your friend," Avram observed.

Glancing around, Channah saw that Keren was no longer in sight. "Keren is not exactly a friend." She passed a hand lightly over the little one's head. "But I love Rachel more than words can say."

Avram nodded and refilled his wine cup. After a few sips, he continued speaking. "I was angry after the slaughter in Bethlehem, and I did some terrible things I hope you never know about. Hear me, Channah, the Messiah, the savior of our people is not dead. I went to Galilee and heard him teach. I saw him cure a leper who was beyond all hope." Avram wiped his eyes and continued with a quivering voice. "He healed me."

"You were sick, Uncle?"

"Yes, the worst kind of sickness, the kind that bored its way deep inside my soul." Avram's voice grew stronger. "Over the years my anger at God hardened into bitterness. I blamed him for the evil in this world, and I relished being labeled a lunatic because that gave me an excuse for separating myself from other human beings. No longer. I may look like the same old man you remember, but I am different now. The teacher changed me." He tapped his chest. "On the inside, where it really matters."

When Rachel turned over, opened her eyes, and began to babble, Channah took her into her arms. "You have given me much to think about, Uncle."

"Yes," Avram agreed. "Let all of this settle. I will try to answer questions as you think of them, although Nathan can explain things better than I. He spent time studying with the teacher." He glanced left and right.

"What happened to your—that is, to the one you call Keren?"

"She is probably taking the measure of this place. She has lived all of her life in the city." Channah kissed Rachel and sat the wiggling baby on the earthen floor.

"Why does she leave the care of her child to you, if I may ask?"

"Our husband wanted a son, and Keren hoped to give him one. When Rachel was born, both of them were disappointed. They seem to hold the baby responsible for not being a boy." Channah pulled the inquisitive child away from the cooking pots. "Tell me, Uncle. How can Keren not love Rebecca? I truly do not understand."

Avram shook his head. "I cannot answer that question. Perhaps I would have tried when I was a younger man. I thought I knew everything back then." He swirled the last of his wine before draining the cup. "Have you considered the possibility this woman may depart from you and take Rachel away with her?

"That is my greatest fear, Uncle." Channah chewed her lip. "But Keren has no family, and nowhere else to go."

"That may be true for now. After she has her next baby and regains her strength, I expect she will go looking for a husband to take care of her."

Chapter Thirty-Six

Channah smiled at the familiar sound of the sheep returning to the fold for the night. She hoisted Rachel onto the low stone fence near Keren, and then took a seat between them. "I love this time of day," she said, resettling Rachel into her lap. "The sheep are coming home, and the hard work of the day is done. I have baked fresh bread and warm lentil soup is ready and waiting for our evening meal."

"Who are those men with the sheep?" Keren nodded toward the approaching herd. "Your uncle mentioned he has a partner. Is he a relative?"

"Caleb is a distant cousin, but not closely related. He is Uncle Avram's oldest friend. I suppose the other man bringing in the herd is Caleb's son, Nathan. I saw him once or twice when I was a little girl."

As the sheep filed into the enclosure, Keren looked intently at the approaching men. "How old is Nathan?"

"Who knows? Younger than Enos, perhaps about your age. Why?"

Quickly dropping her eyes, Keren said. "Curiosity." She adjusted her scarf. "Is he married?"

"How would I know?" The questions unnerved Channah. She suspected Avram was right that Keren hoped for another husband.

"Remember to move slowly and speak in a quiet voice around the sheep," Channah warned. "Remain near one of the shepherds until the animals get used to you."

"I am always sedate." Keren nodded toward Rachel, who alternately pointed at the sheep and wiggled wildly. "How will you restrain her?"

Channah laughed at Rachel's enthusiasm. "I have no idea."

As soon as the sheep were somewhat settled inside the pen, the men went to the tent. The routine of serving the evening meal was familiar to Channah, except the woman at her side was Keren, not Yael. When Avram scooped Rachel into his lap, the baby did not object. Instead, she babbled at him and examined his beard with interest.

"We have not had such bread for—how long ago was it you were married, Channah? Two years?" Caleb chomped on a chunk of nicely browned loaf.

"Something like that," Channah murmured. She glanced up to catch Nathan's eyes fixed on her. Although she dropped her gaze immediately, the sudden warming of her face and neck told her she was probably blushing.

"I absolutely agree, Caleb. Channah's bread is even better than I remembered." Avram grinned and fed Rachel a bite. "And wait until you see how fast she can cut away a sheep's winter growth of fleece."

"You know how to shear?" Nathan looked surprised.

Channah concentrated on pouring wine. "Yes, but I am out of practice." She wished the attention would shift away from her. As soon as everyone had food and wine, she took Rachel from Avram and sat with her head bowed, hunched over the baby.

Avram offered up a prayer of thanks for their food, and Channah alternately fed the baby and ate while the men talked.

"Will you attempt to go to the synagogue in Bethlehem again, Nathan?" Avram pointed his wine cup at the younger man.

"No, I think not." Nathan tore bread from his loaf. "What do you think of gathering with a few likeminded shepherds in a pasture to celebrate the Sabbath?"

Avram lifted his eyebrows. "That would be different."

"The men of Bethlehem have no business telling us not to come to the meeting house," Caleb said.

"I agree, Father, but no good can come from stirring up dissension. Perhaps I should go into the city and confer with followers of the Way there."

"Good idea," Avram said, nodding his head in agreement.

Caleb studied his food for a moment. "I would prefer to have it out with those stone heads in Bethlehem, but Nathan is right. Those men will not listen to us. They think shepherds are ignorant and dishonest, as well."

Channah stole a quick glance at Keren, who had recently expressed that same low opinion of sheeperders. Did she recognize her error, after hearing how well-spoken these men were? However, Keren displayed no emotion. How lovely she was, as the soft lamp light heightened the glow of early pregnancy on her beautiful face.

A subtle motion from Avram caught Channah's eye. Soon thereafter, he mumbled something about checking on the sheep and exited the tent.

Nathan rose and extended a hand to his father. "Shall we assist Avram?"

Caleb nodded, drained his wine cup, and accepted Nathan's assistance to stand.

"They think themselves clever," Keren commented as soon as the tent flap closed behind Nathan.

Channah's bowl was only half-emptied, since she had been feeding Rachel as well as herself. "What do you mean?"

"They have not gone outside to tend their sheep. They are talking about us."

Glancing toward the tent flap, Channah asked, "Us?"

"Certainly. Whether to allow me to stay here or not. People will talk if they allow two women to live with them. You may be safe, since you are a blood relative to one of them. But I am not. They know there will be a scandal when my belly begins to grow."

Channah ate in silence, realizing she had not considered how her arrival impacted Avram's household. In her desperation, she thought only of coming home to the hills and pastures. But then, Avram was never one to consider the opinions of his neighbors. However, he seemed somehow different from the way he was when she left to be married. She pondered the change. It was something she could not exactly define.

Keren's voice broke into Channah's reverie. "I fear they will decide to turn me out. I dread the thought of following in my mother's footsteps, but what else is there for a divorced woman with a child and another one on the way?"

Channah's stomach turned over at the thought of Keren taking Rachel away to live in the streets of Jerusalem. "Uncle Avram is a kind man, despite what you think of shepherds."

Keren sighed. "I can only hope he will show me compassion, then."

Chapter Thirty-Seven

When Channah awoke at daybreak the following morning, she heard the familiar sounds of the sheep milling outside their cave, ready to go to the pasture and graze. Leaving Rachel and Keren asleep, she slipped outside and breathed in the cool morning air. She saw Avram and went to his side. "Good morning, Uncle. May I go with you to the pasture today?"

"Good morning. I am delighted for you to go with me, but I think it best if the woman remains behind." Avram leaned against the low stone fence and gestured for her to take a seat beside him. "Caleb and Nathan did not spend the night here. I will meet up with them this morning. Do you understand the concern?"

"Yes. You want to protect everyone's good name."

Avram nodded in agreement. "Nathan's in particular. He is a devout follower of the Way, and he cannot tolerate the thought of bringing disgrace on the name of Jesus—even if based on unfounded accusations. So Caleb and Nathan will make their home in the pastures for the time being."

"Uncle, I am sorry to bring trouble down on you. I did not foresee this difficulty."

"No, Channah." Avram put a hand on her shoulder. "You have warmed my heart by coming to me for shelter. I count you as my daughter, and there is nothing I would not do for you." He removed his arm and stood straight. "Besides, you did not know of Yael's passing or that I had taken business partners."

Channah gathered her courage for her next question. "Will it be all right for me to bring Rachel with me to the pasture?" She hesitated before adding an explanation. "Keren is not especially maternal."

"You mean she takes no responsibility for her daughter." Avram's face softened. "Yes, bring the child along if you wish. I trust you can see the mother uses your concern for her child to gain an advantage."

"I know," Channah admitted.

"Your attachment to her baby may lead to heartbreak. The woman cares nothing for your feelings."

"What you say is true, Uncle. But I cannot help loving Rachel." Channah moved as quickly as possible through the paddock of waiting sheep. She gathered the sleeping baby into her arms and then roused Keren. "I am going to the pasture with Uncle Avram, and I will care for Rachel there. Your only responsibility is to have an evening meal prepared when we return at sundown."

"All right," Keren mumbled. "First I need to sleep." She turned away and pulled the blanket over her head.

Channah rushed to gather food to sustain herself, the baby, and the other shepherds through the day. In her haste, she almost forgot to pack the wine. She did not want Avram to perceive having a child in the pasture as a detriment to her work. She tied Rachel onto her back and hurried to join her uncle. She walked beside him as he led the herd through the familiar countryside. How safe she felt in Avram's company. "Do you think the sheep remember me?" she asked, taking extra steps to keep up with his long stride.

Avram shrugged. "Perhaps. They do not treat me like a stranger, but I have never been separated from them for more than a month."

Channah found tending the herd easier than harvesting grain. With the sheep, she did not have to constantly bend over. Additional relief came from knowing what needed to be done and how to do it. Without any discussion, she diverted the stream to fill the stone trough with water. The sheep exhibited no fear of her or—to her surprise—of Rachel. While the animals satisfied their thirst, the baby sat in the dirt and chewed her fist. Channah was not certain which of them was more thankful Rachel did not have to remain tied to her back all day.

When the sun was high, Channah took Rachel and went to the shady spot she knew so well. When she began to unpack food, Nathan appeared and took the bag from her hand. "Sit and rest for a while," he said. With no further comment, he arranged food on a tray which he set between Avram and Caleb. To Channah's astonishment, the young man served her a portion before squatting to eat with the other men.

"Thank you," she mumbled, not understanding why Nathan's kind smile embarrassed her.

While sharing food with Rachel, Channah ate in silence, concentrating as much as she could on the men's conversation. She made up her mind to learn more about the one they called Jesus, even daring to hope she might someday be able to go and hear him speak to his followers.

Only a few days slipped by before Avram declared the time was right for shearing. Channah reluctantly left Rachel with Keren before sharpening her knife and setting off to help the men. She found the setup exactly as it had been before. As soon as the sheep were positioned near a shallow stream, a publican arrived to do a head count. To her surprise, Channah realized Avram presented his entire flock for the publican's review.

"You are a hard worker," Nathan said to Channah at the end of the long day of shearing sheep. "You collected more fleece than anyone."

Channah smiled. "I think the sheep enjoy shedding their winter coats."

In the middle of the following afternoon, Caleb and Nathan left for Bethany. "They are going to celebrate with other followers of the Way tomorrow," Avram explained. To Channah's surprise, Avram took the sheep to the fold well before sundown. "We will put out enough food and water for the animals this afternoon. Tomorrow, when we observe our holy day, we will not take them out to the pasture."

The Sabbath at Avram's home differed dramatically from the way Channah remembered it in Enos's household. After eating food prepared the day before, Avram spoke words from the Holy Scriptures. Then he explained how he understood what was written. Finally, he encouraged Channah and Keren to ask questions or discuss what they heard.

"How do you know these words, Uncle?" Channah asked at the first opportunity.

Sitting cross-legged, with hands folded in his lap, Avram did not immediately answer. When he did respond, his words were tinged with sadness. "As a boy, I studied the law and the prophets diligently. I had ambitions of becoming a scholar. When my father Abijah died, instead of continuing to go to school I became a shepherd." He looked into the distance and shrugged with his eyebrows. "By that time, I knew all of the books of Moses and the Psalms by heart, plus a good portion of the writings of the prophet Isaiah."

"And you can recite them still?"

"I cannot seem to memorize more now, but what I learned as a youth has never left me."

"I will meditate on what you have said." With those words, Keren rose and ambled away.

Smoothing Rachel's hair while the child sat in her lap, Channah watched Keren retreat from the conversation. "Perhaps she will think about the rabbi who was very kind to her not long ago." Turning toward Avram, she asked, "Will you tell me again about the teachings you heard on your journey to Galilee?"

Chapter Thirty-Eight

For weeks, Channah wrestled with her conscience. She withdrew several times each day to the overlook where Yael went when she wanted to be alone. The more she prayed, the clearer the answer became. With a sigh, she went to sit by Avram in the shade of a great boulder.

After a brief but companionable silence, Avram took a small stick and began to scratch in the dirt. "What is troubling you, my child?"

Channah tucked her skirt over her ankles. "I do not know if I am still Enos's wife or not. For many days, I have wondered what is right, and now I believe I must ask him. If he pronounces me divorced, so be it. If not." She drew a deep breath. "If not, I will return and live as his obedient wife."

"He is not good enough for you." Avram made circles with his stick.

"Enos has his failings, as all of us do. If I rightly understand the teachings of the Way, my concern has to be with what I do, regardless of what my—that is, how Enos conducts himself."

"It breaks my heart to think of this."

"Mine also, Uncle. Yet I must do what is right in God's sight if I am to be a true follower of Jesus."

"You have been listening to Nathan." Avram turned his face to her. "You know Caleb's son thinks fondly of you. For the first time in his life, the young man has begun to speak of taking a wife."

Feeling warmth spreading upward from her throat to her cheeks, Channah ducked her head. "I cannot think in that direction until I know I am free to do so."

"I see." Avram tossed the stick away. "I will accompany you to Enos's house whenever you wish. Before that, consider what a momentous step you are taking. It may affect the rest of your life."

"I have already thought, Uncle. And I have prayed. Let us go tomorrow." *Before my resolve weakens.*

"What about the woman Keren and her daughter you love so dearly?"

Channah brushed away a tear. "Enos is a proud man. I doubt he will welcome me back. When he tells me I am divorced, I will return home with you."

Putting his arm around her, Avram said, "There is always the risk things may not go as you expect. Nevertheless, I cannot find the words to say how greatly I admire your determination to live in a way pleasing to our God, dear child."

Early the following morning, Avram led the sheep to the pasture and returned to escort Channah to the city. When she joined him in the paddock, he said, "I have been meaning to give you this." He held out a scarf she knew once belonged to Yael.

"Thank you, Uncle. I will love wearing something to remind me of dear Auntie." When Channah tossed the scarf across her shoulder, she noticed the hems were weighted. "What is this?" She lifted one end to examine it. "There is something inside."

"Silver coins." Avram followed her through the gap in the stone fence. "I hope you never need them. However, it is best to be prepared."

As they trekked through the hills, Channah began to sing a Psalm Avram recently taught her.

> *I will lift up mine eyes unto the hills, from whence cometh my help.*
> *My help cometh from the Lord, which made heaven and earth.*
> *He will not suffer thy foot to be moved: he that keepeth thee will not slumber.*
> *Behold, he that keepeth Israel shall neither slumber nor sleep.*
> *The Lord is thy keeper: the Lord is thy shade upon thy right hand.*
> *The sun shall not smite thee by day, nor the moon by night.*
> *The Lord shall preserve thee from all evil: he shall preserve thy soul.*
> *The Lord shall preserve thy going out and thy coming in from this time forth,*
> *and even for evermore.*

Avram joined in, his tuneless bass rumbling against her sweet, clear soprano. They sang for a while and then walked on in silence. When they reached the road, Channah asked, "Will you tell me again of the night you heard the angels sing?"

"Have you not grown tired of that story, since I have repeated it so often lately?" Avram's smile belied his gruff voice.

She shook her head. "Never."

The closer they drew to her former neighborhood, the more unsettled Channah became. How grateful she was that Avram chose to make this journey with her. Although she expected Enos to shout at her, she was confident her uncle would brook no violence.

At the bend in the road, Channah gasped. Her hand flew to cover her mouth.

"What is this?" Avram stopped moving and gaped at the sight before them.

Where the main building of the tannery once stood, there was now nothing but a burned-out shell. The surrounding yard was scorched, with broken tools and pieces of equipment haphazardly strewn here and there. Except for a goat munching grass nearby, the whole area appeared deserted. Channah shifted her eyes to Enos's house, which to her relief still stood.

"A fire," Channah whispered. "I wonder if Enos ..." She could not bring herself to complete her thought.

"We shall find out." When Avram pushed at the door, it sagged open.

"Who is there?" a woman's voice called out.

"It is I, Channah."

"But I thought you were ... Never mind. Come in, and welcome. Do you remember me? Peninnah, whom you have not seen since your wedding day."

Channah entered the once-familiar home and began her rehearsed speech, "I have come—"

Peninnah interrupted. "No doubt you are worried about my poor nephew." The old woman waved a hand toward the bed, where Enos sat motionless. "He is fortunate he was not killed, as many were. But he was outside and did not suffer the full blast."

No emotion showed on Enos's face, but he rasped, "Channah? My wife, at last you have come home to take care of me. I hoped for your return."

Channah's mind was unable to take in the situation all at once.

Peninnah hobbled to the table. "I have little to offer you to eat. Perhaps you will take some wine?"

"No, nothing, thank you." Channah glanced toward Avram, who stood just inside the entrance, arms folded. She did not know what to say or do.

Peninnah used her walking stick to push a stool near Enos. "Come, Channah, visit with your husband."

Feeling as if her legs were carved from stone, Channah breathed a silent prayer for courage. After an awkward delay, she crossed the room and perched on the stool. She reached a hand toward Enos, but withdrew it. Despite the shadows, she could see his face was scarred. "I am sorry for your accident."

"It is good you have returned," Enos said without turning toward her. "My care is too much for my great aunt, and she is the only one who stands by me."

Channah tried to choose her words carefully. "Enos, when last we saw each other, you gave me the choice to stay with you or go away. I take that to mean I am divorced."

"I never said that," Enos replied. "I divorced Keren, but not you. You are my wife, and I need you to take care of me. It is your duty."

Channah realized Enos was desperate for someone to serve his needs. Therefore, he would claim they were still married, regardless of what intention he may have had the day she departed. She removed her head covering as an indication of her resigned intention to resume her life as his wife.

From across the room, Avram's voice growled. "Why did you tell me Channah was dead?"

Enos jumped as if startled. "Who is there? Identify yourself."

"I believe you know." Avram crossed the room and squatted near Enos. "Do you remember my face now?"

Enos continued to stare straight ahead. "Have pity on me, sir. I am blind."

Chapter Thirty-Nine

Avram stood, glaring down at the top of Enos's head. "Blind, you say?"

"Yes," Peninnah answered. "He lost his eyesight when his tannery exploded and burned." She made a clucking noise. "Then everyone deserted him. I have been doing what little I can."

"It is your choice, Channah." Avram took her hand in his. "Do you want to return home with me?"

"I cannot leave," she replied, barely above a whisper. She stood and hung her scarf on a peg. "I will prepare a meal." She pulled out the flour crock and began to mix dough for bread.

Avram stood against the wall with his arms folded for a time. "I will go now."

"But Uncle, you have had no food."

"I will find sustenance somewhere. Come, Channah. I will speak to Enos, and I want you to hear."

Wiping her hands on a towel, Channah returned to the stool beside Enos's bed. Avram knelt in front of the blind man. "To honor God, I forgive the lie you spoke when you told me Channah was no longer alive. Hear me well. I will return from time to time. If I do not find your sweet wife being well treated, I will hold you responsible." Avram leaned near Enos's face. "Blind or not, you will answer to me."

211

Avram stood, helped Channah to her feet, and embraced her. "The Lord bless you and keep you, my beloved child." He pulled his coat closed and nodded toward Peninnah. "Good day. May you be blessed." On his way out, Avram paused long enough to knock the door's drooping hinge into place with his shepherd's rod.

"Wait." Channah ran to Avram as he began to walk away from the house.

His eyes searched her face. "Have you changed your mind?"

"No, Uncle. I cannot." She looked downward and shuffled her feet. "Will you deliver a message to Nathan for me?"

Avram nodded his agreement.

"Ask him to search his heart to find compassion for Rachel and Keren."

"It is not proper for the woman to continue living with me."

She pressed a palm against his chest. "They can stay if Nathan takes Keren as his wife."

"Channah, you cannot mean that."

"I do, Uncle. Please tell Nathan if he has any regard for my wishes, he will marry Keren and give Rachel a father."

"I will deliver the message."

Despite the presence of Enos and Peninnah, Channah had never felt more alone than she did as Avram walked away. She stood and watched until her uncle disappeared around the bend in the road. Then she squared her shoulders and returned to her husband's house.

***

After walking a short distance beyond the bend, Avram sat on a stone by the side of the road and wept. He shed tears for his losses—Channah, Yael, his son, and his wasted years of unbelief. After a while, he wiped his eyes and stood. Tipping his head toward the sky, he said, "Doing the right thing is hard."

It was almost sundown when Avram arrived at the pasture where Caleb and Nathan tended the herd. His first words to them were, "Channah has returned to her husband."

Nathan looked as if he had been struck. "No."

With a glance toward his son, Caleb said, "Then it is settled."

"Enos, the man Channah was sold to for a bride, was blinded in an accident." Avram sank to sit on the ground. "The cursed liar only wants her so she can take care of him now." He rested a hand on his forehead, realizing he had consumed nothing since early that morning. "Do you have anything to eat?"

While Nathan ran to fetch food, Caleb sat next to Avram. "Shall we keep the sheep outside tonight?"

"Yes." Avram stretched his neck and rubbed his shoulder. "The woman is at the cave." He turned to look at his friend. "Channah asked me to plead with Nathan to marry Keren, out of concern for the child."

Caleb lifted an eyebrow. "You know his heart was set on your niece?"

"It is Enos who is blind, not I." He sighed. "And she was kindly disposed toward Nathan as well. Yet she has chosen to do what she believes is pleasing to God. I cannot fault her for that."

"There are times," Caleb said, "when I think we would be better off if Lord had not decided to make us male and female. There is too much wasted energy between us."

"Without a wife, you would not have your son," Avram pointed out.

"God can do anything. He could make people grow on trees, like walnuts. Want two sons and three daughters? Go into the forest and pick them. Put them in your basket and go home. It could work." He grabbed Avram's sleeve. "There is too much fretting about selecting a woman, then worrying about how to please her family. Perhaps wives, also, should grow on trees."

"I will overlook your foolishness, and I pray the Lord will do the same." Avram worked his shoulder round and round. "How will Nathan respond to the suggestion of marrying Keren? It appears she has no family to make demands."

"My son is deeply disappointed. I have seen how his eyes follow Channah in the pasture. He has told me how he admires her absolute commitment to the Way. As for whether he will accept the other woman now?" Caleb shook his head. "I do not know."

"What are your thoughts on the matter?"

"He is a grown man. Let him decide for himself." Caleb sighed. "I will only say I would like to see a grandson before I sleep with my fathers."

Leaning against the rock, Avram closed his eyes. "I will give Nathan Channah's message tonight. If he agrees to marry the woman, well and good. If not, I shall evict her from my home in the morning."

"Where will she go?" Caleb bolted upright, and began to wave his arms in the air. "What about the little girl and the child to come? It cannot be pleasing to God to turn out helpless children to possible starvation."

The trace of a smile played around Avram's mouth. "Perhaps you should be the one to marry Keren and rescue the little ones."

Caleb's grin lit up his face. "Or you."

Chapter Forty

As Avram performed night patrol among the sheep, Nathan caught up with him. The two walked in silence until Nathan said, "I am saddened that Channah is no longer with us. I know you will miss her."

Though he grunted his acknowledgment, Avram did not speak.

After a short distance, Nathan said, "I hope your niece's husband is a good man, a follower of the Way."

Avram stood still. "I have no regard for Enos. He is of low character." Reading shock on Nathan's face in the moonlight, he added, "He turned out his child and wives. Now he wants Channah to take care of him in his blindness."

"He is blind?" Nathan poked at the ground with his shepherd's crook. "He should go to Jesus."

"Perhaps he will agree to do so. I will speak to him in a few days when I take a gift of five sheep." Avram resumed his stroll.

Striding along with Avram, Nathan said, "Channah will take pleasure in having sheep around her, but she will pine for little Rachel. Your niece has a soft heart for the child."

"I agree." Avram gave Nathan a sidelong glance. "I suppose that is why she asked me to convey a message to you."

"Channah spoke of me?" Nathan's joy was obvious, but his voice became quieter with his next words. "What did she say?"

Avram stopped and put his hand on Nathan's shoulder. "She asked that you marry Rachel's mother so that you give the girl, and the child yet to be born, a father to care for them."

"Marry? Keren?" Nathan's eyes fell to the ground. "For Rachel, of course."

"You are in no way bound to do this thing, my son." Avram dropped his arm to his side. "In the morning, I will tell the woman she can no longer dwell in my tent, due to Channah's departure."

They walked many steps without speaking. At last Nathan said, "She has nowhere to go. A woman with a baby and another on the way. What will she do?"

"I cannot say." Avram scratched a stray hair from his forehead. "To be honest, I prefer not to think on her future."

"I will consider this." Nathan looked over his shoulder. "If you will excuse me, I must go and pray for guidance."

Tucking his staff over an elbow, Avram stood with arms akimbo. "Do you mean to say you may truly consider this thing? Do not be swayed by Channah's love for the child. Marriage is a lifelong commitment, Nathan, and I doubt this woman is all she should be. Think what you would be letting yourself in for."

"The teacher commands us to think of others first, ahead of ourselves."

Avram watched Nathan retreat to the far side of the herd's perimeter. "Would that I had half the faithfulness of these young ones," he whispered into the crisp night air.

Knowing he should get some rest, Avram angled toward the hollowed-out cliff where the shepherds kept their bedrolls. He pulled his bedding a short distance away, preferring a view of the sky to the shelter of the overhang. Try as he might, he could not still his mind enough to drift into sleep. When Caleb came to sit nearby, Avram said, "I am awake. I cannot sleep for thinking of tomorrow. Either I send the woman and child away or your son rescues her. Either choice is dreadful."

"Nathan is guarding the sheep and praying about the woman." He sighed. "The boy is so like his mother, kindhearted to a fault."

Avram sat up on his mat, cross-legged. "His dedication to the Way is commendable, as is Channah's. But they cannot save the whole world."

"I told Nathan as much," Caleb said. "Do you know what he told me?"

"I have no idea."

"He said he knows he cannot help every destitute child, but he can save this one." Caleb spread his hands. "How surprising that such a noble young man has sprung from my contemptible loins."

"You have raised Nathan well. This loose woman is not suitable for him."

218

"Nor from what you say is that fellow Enos worthy of Channah." Caleb lifted an eyebrow. "We have taught our young ones lofty values, not realizing how painful it can be when they believe and act on them."

"Things were clear under the law. An eye for an eye and a tooth for a tooth. Stone the adulteress." Avram settled into a prone position with an arm under his head. "The Way is difficult to live up to, trying to do for others what you would have them do for you."

Caleb rose and took up his staff. "Ah, we worry for no cause. Perhaps after he prays Nathan will reject her. I will go and make sure no predators approach the sheep."

Avram stared up at the night sky, the starlight dimmed by the brightness of the full moon. When he lost his wife and believed his niece was also dead, he thought there was no more heartbreak awaiting him. What could touch a man who had no one to care for? Then Channah returned, only to leave again. He sighed. It seemed allowing his heart to course with love inevitably led to a shipwreck of pain. Even as he vowed not to let it matter what happened to the child named Rachel, he knew he could not keep that resolve.

Midmorning the following day, Caleb walked with Avram to the paddock. "Did you sleep, my friend?"

"Not at all," Avram admitted. "How about you?"

"Very little." Caleb tightened his belt. "I dread this."

Avram nodded. "It must be done."

Keren was inside the stone fence, grinding grain outside the tent. Avram averted his eyes from the little girl, who played with a length of rope nearby. While Caleb and Avram entered the enclosure, Rachel crawled toward the men, babbling "knuckle"—or was she attempting to say "uncle?"

Continuing to push the roller against the grain, Keren kept her eyes on her work. "Good morning, sirs."

Against his better judgment, Avram took Rachel into his arms. The men stood with their shadows covering Keren and her grinding trough. After a moment, she wiped her hands and stood, eyes downcast.

"Channah has returned to Enos."

Keren's hand flew to her throat. "He allowed her to come home?" Surprise was written on her expressive face.

"Enos was injured in an accident. There was an explosion at the tannery, and he is now blind. Channah has returned to his house to care for him." Avram hated hearing his own words, since speaking them aloud seemed to confirm their truth.

When Caleb cleared his throat, Keren's eyes shifted to him. "Have pity on me," she pled. "I have nowhere to go."

"To say nothing of your daughter," Avram said.

"My son is willing to take you as his wife."

When Keren opened her mouth, Caleb held up his hand to stop her.

"Let me finish. Nathan will provide for you and your children. In return, you must promise to be a good and faithful wife to him." Nathan emphasized the word "faithful," causing Keren to duck her head. "We are followers of the Way. No one will force you to believe, but I do expect you to live up to our high moral standard. If you agree to these terms, I will make the arrangements."

Using her scarf to wipe tears, Keren nodded. "Yes, I promise to do everything you say. Only do not cast me out, please."

Chapter Forty-One

The morning after she returned, Channah worked diligently to set Enos's house in order. Busily putting away a massive amount of clutter and taking stock of the household provisions, she prepared to go to the market. She opened the kitchen chest to count out coins, only to find the money pouch missing. "Where are our coins?" she asked Peninnah.

The old woman's eyes darted toward the bed where Enos lay. "He keeps them."

When Channah moved toward the bed, Peninnah grabbed at her sleeve. "He will be angry if you wake him." Dropping her hand, she added, "Then he will demand to know why you need coins. I must plead and beg before he will give me even one. It is hard for me to walk all the way to the market. Yet he does not allow me to take the donkey and then complains I take too long for the trip."

After patting out loaves of bread to rise, Channah returned inside from the courtyard. "Is he still sleeping?"

Peninnah nodded, continuing to darn a tunic.

For a brief time, Channah considered whether she should risk Enos's wrath. In that moment, she realized she did not wish to provoke her husband unnecessarily. Yet she no longer feared his moods. She went to the bed and began to feel around the covers.

"What are you doing?" Enos did not sound sleepy, merely grumpy.

"I am searching for coins. I must get food for us and for your poor skinny donkey. I cannot find the goat."

"The goat ran away more than a month ago," Peninnah interjected.

Enos propped his upper body on an elbow. "How much food do you want, and exactly what will it cost?"

Channah exhaled noisily. "I will not know the full accounting until I return. I do not even know what is for sale today."

"If you are too foolish to know what you need, then why should I give you any of my money?"

Standing with a hand on her hip, Channah replied, "If you give me coins, we will eat. If not, we will go hungry. It is your choice."

Enos pointed a finger into the air. "You have learned evil habits from that woman whose name is not to be mentioned in this house." He felt around the bed before withdrawing the coin bag. He put it under one arm, laid on it, and closed his eyes. "You will have no coins from me until you repent of your bad attitude."

"As you wish." Channah put on her mantle and covered her shoulders with the scarf Avram gave her the day before. With a nod and a smile toward Peninnah, she took the bag hanging by the door and departed for the market. After going beyond the bend in the road, she took her knife and liberated a silver coin from the scarf that formerly belonged to Yael, and tucked the hem back into place.

At the market, Channah paid for grain, a portion to take with her and the rest to be delivered by the farmer along with a load of hay. She admired the vegetables but restrained herself from buying anything other than provisions for the donkey.

Instead of going inside the house, Channah went directly to the animal shed when she arrived home. "Hello, old friend," she cooed to the donkey. "Your time of starvation is over now." She emptied her shopping bag of the grain and patted the animal's lean flanks. "The farmer will deliver more this afternoon."

Entering the house from the courtyard, Channah was determined to remain pleasant. "Greetings, husband, Aunt Peninnah."

"Where have you been?" Enos demanded.

"To the market, as I said earlier." Channah hung her scarf and mantle on a peg in the wall. Across the room, she replaced the shopping bag at its location near the front door. "I obtained food for your donkey."

Enos pulled himself to a sitting position. "How did you pay for it? Did you steal from me? Where are my silver candlesticks?"

"Your possessions are all in place, husband." Channah pushed down her anger, reminding herself how followers of the Way stressed the importance of kindness. "I bought hay and grain with a coin from Uncle Avram."

With a lift of the chin, Enos asked, "What did you bring for me?"

"We have enough provisions for me to bake bread, but nothing else. So I suppose we will eat bread." She went to the back door. "I will put the loaves into the oven, and they will be ready soon."

Peninnah followed Channah into the courtyard. "He is angry."

"It is unfortunate that my husband's choice of coins over food has upset him."

The old woman leaned on her cane while Channah slid the paddle into the oven. "Do you know what has become of Keren and the child?"

"They are safe and well cared for. May God grant they remain so." Channah stepped back from the oven and wiped her forehead.

Peninnah leaned closer. "He told me you left because of his blindness. I found a bag packed with food and baby things in the barn. I could see someone fled in haste." She looked left and right. "Tell me, what happened?"

"I left before the explosion." Channah reached to straighten Peninnah's shawl. "There was an argument. Enos declared Keren divorced, and he told her to go and take the baby."

"No." Peninnah shook her head. "I know what it is to be alone in this world. But with a child to feed?"

"I begged him not to send Rachel away with Keren. He said I could go with them if I wanted to. And so I went."

Peninnah's eyes were bright with curiosity. "When was that?"

"Months ago." Channah picked up her dough trough and turned toward the house. "I lost count of the days. I knew nothing of Enos's blindness." She slipped inside to avoid further questions from Peninnah.

As Channah served his evening meal in bed, Enos asked, "No lentils?"

"We ate the last of them last night," Peninnah said from across the room. "But the bread Channah baked is more than enough for me."

"Well, not for me." Enos tossed his loaf aside. "A man needs vegetables. And meat once in a while. Not bread only."

Channah offered a suggestion from the table where she and Peninnah reclined. "Perhaps you would like for me to go to the market and buy some of those things to cook for you."

"You used to be different, Channah." Enos asked. "What has happened to you since you left me?"

Although uncertain whether Enos wanted an answer, she considered his question. "I have learned to trust in God, and I suppose I have also grown up."

He grunted. "I liked you better before."

The following morning, she oiled Enos's body while he lay in bed. Taking great care with his wounds, she dared to ask, "Have you heard of the rabbi from Galilee, the one they call Jesus?"

"I have." Enos winced as she dabbed at a cut across the top of his foot. "One of my dead employees followed his foolish teachings."

"He healed Uncle Avram's friend Caleb. Perhaps he would do the same for you. I believe he is our savior."

Enos yawned. "Ridiculous."

After two more days of nothing but bread at every meal, Enos threw two coins toward Channah. "Go and buy us food before I starve."

"As you wish, husband." Channah bent and picked up the coins. "Do you want to come along, Aunt Peninnah?"

"No, dear," the old woman replied. "The walk is too much for me. I will stay and keep Enos company."

"Very well." Channah gathered her things, her mouth watering at the prospect of cabbages and leeks.

Chapter Forty-Two

"Channah! You have returned." Shuwshan stood on the riverbank with her three children.

Channah returned Shuwshan's smile. "Yes."

After the women embraced, Shuwshan held her friend at arm's length. "Let me look at you. I expected we would never see each other again."

"I thought the same," Channah replied, delighted to be greeted joyfully. "How your little ones have grown, even in the space of a few months."

"Yes, they keep me busy." She patted her tallest daughter's head. "Are Keren and the baby home now also?"

"No, I returned alone. Enos needs me to care for him now."

"I heard he was blinded when the tannery burned." Shuwshan wedged a crock of water among her children in a small hand cart. "I must hasten home. Will you come and visit me? I want to hear all about your departure and return."

"How will your husband feel about me coming to your home?" Channah remembered being turned away the day she and Keren were exiled from Enos's house.

Shuwshan frowned as she gripped the handle of her cart. "I cannot say. Joab is not a friend to Enos. And yet …"

Sensing the other woman's embarrassment, Channah patted her arm. "Perhaps we may walk together to the vegetable market one day."

"Yes. I would like that." Shuwshan's eye remained on her water jug. "Thank you for understanding. Joab is a good man. Only, sometimes he tends toward harsh judgment of others."

As her friend began to climb the shallow river bank, Channah said, "I will always be grateful for the food you shared when I was in desperate need."

Shuwshan turned and smiled. "I had almost forgotten about the date cakes. I am glad I was able to help." Pulling her wooden cart filled with children and water, she disappeared. Channah fought a bubble of envy at the sight of the Shuwshan's three little ones. Again, she wondered how Enos ever brought himself to banish Rachel, the only child ever to make his house ring with laughter.

While filling her jugs with water, Channah recognized how difficult it would be for her and Shuwshan to maintain a close friendship in the light of Joab's disapproval of her. Strangely enough, she realized she would miss Keren's mercurial companionship. And Rachel—she must not allow herself to dwell on how she longed to hold that sweet baby.

The first Sabbath after she resumed life in Enos's house, Channah went into the courtyard at sunrise and softly hummed the tune of several psalms the shepherds sang in worship. There were scrolls in the house, but they were of no use to a blind man and two illiterate women. Returning inside, she asked Peninnah and Enos if they would like to hear words she had committed to memory, words passed on from the teacher from Galilee. "Yes,"

Peninnah said. "I have heard talk of this man. Everyone is curious about him."

"I am not the least bit interested," Enos boomed from his bed. "I forbid his name to be spoken in this house."

"As you wish." As soon as Enos ate his portion of food prepared the day before, Channah went outside and sat in the shade.

After a short interval, Peninnah joined her and mentioned she thought a small group of Jesus followers met somewhere nearby. "I heard they allow the women to sit and listen to the teaching, right in the same house with the men," Peninnah whispered.

"Perhaps at the river or in the market I will encounter someone who knows about these people," Channah said. "If I locate them, do you want to go with me to a meeting?"

Peninnah shrugged. "If I do not have to walk too far."

Days melted into a week. Despite asking other shoppers at the market and varying the time she went to the river in the morning, no one seemed to know about followers of the Way in her vicinity. Channah busied herself with household chores, occasionally going across the road to clean away debris from the ruined tannery.

One day as she pulled bread from the outdoor oven, she heard bleating in the pasture behind the house. Channah straightened her posture and used a hand to shade the sun from her eyes. A short distance away, Avram led a flock of five sheep toward her.

"Uncle." She ran through the courtyard, then slowed her pace to avoid frightening the sheep.

Avram embraced her. "Are you well?"

"I am. And happy to see you again so soon."

He motioned toward the sheep. "They missed you." With a nod toward the shed, he added, "Your barn is not as spacious as the cave, but you have enough room to shelter your small flock."

"These sheep are for me? I thought you were taking them to be sold."

Avram smiled. "My wedding gift to you, albeit belated."

"Thank you. I am deeply touched by your generosity, Uncle." Channah smiled. "Enos's donkey will have some company now. Will you have some wine and something to eat? I have just now taken fresh bread from the oven."

"I will have some refreshment in your courtyard."

"Uncle Avram has brought us five sheep," Channah said to no one in particular, as she loaded a tray with wine and cups.

Enos grunted.

"What good news," Peninnah replied after a cautious glance toward Enos.

With her hands full, Channah used her head to motion Peninnah outside. The old woman nodded and followed her through the doorway.

Avram devoured half a loaf of bread in one bite. "No one can make bread like you, Channah." He lifted his cup.

"Yes," Peninnah agreed. "She is an excellent baker." Pointing with her walking stick, the old woman added, "She takes good care of Enos and me."

Channah ducked her head, embarrassed at receiving praise. "How is Rachel?"

"The child is flourishing. Trying to walk and talk." Avram averted his eyes and rubbed the head of his shepherd's crook. "Nathan is a good father to her."

"So he agreed." Channah ignored Peninnah's curious stare.

"Yes," Avram nodded. "Nathan has married the woman."

"Good." Channah forced a smile. "Very good." Searching for a way to redirect the conversation, she said, "I am trying to find other followers of the Way. Aunt Peninnah has heard some believers meet in this area, but I have not yet located them."

"I hope you find them soon." Avram drained his cup and stood. "We will move up to the high country in a few days. I will not be able to return until autumn." He put a hand on Channah's shoulder. "May the Lord bless you and keep you, my daughter."

"You will not go inside and speak with Enos?" Peninnah gestured toward the house.

"No." Avram brushed bread crumbs from his tunic, offering no explanation for avoiding Enos.

"Goodbye, Uncle." Channah stood to embrace Avram. "God be with you."

"Farewell," Peninnah said.

Avram herded the five sheep into the shed and walked away without looking back.

Chapter Forty-Three

As the summer months wore on, Channah found a house on the opposite side of the river where followers of the Way met. Each Sabbath thereafter she crossed the shallow stream, skipping from one rock to another to avoid getting her clothing wet. Although Enos was irritable when she went, he did not forbid her attendance.

"Do you wish to go to the meeting with me tomorrow?" Channah plunged her arms into the thick curd slush she was forming into balls of cheese. "You could ride the donkey."

Peninnah did not answer immediately. When she did speak, her voice was quiet. "I fear doing anything that may make my nephew the least bit angry with me." After shifting her eyes around the courtyard, she scooted closer to Channah. "You see, I have nowhere else to go if Enos casts me out."

Shocked at the mere suggestion, Channah wiped her hands and put an arm around the old woman. "What makes you think he would do such a thing?"

"He sent you away." Peninnah began to shed tears. "Since he did that …"

Channah wiped Peninnah's face with her towel. "You can never do anything to make Enos as furious as he was the day he sent us away."

"He threw you out, and you are the kindest person I know."

"Thank you, Aunt Peninnah." With one final hug, Channah returned to her cheesemaking. "Enos did not force me leave his house. He gave me a choice, and I decided to leave because I wanted to protect Rachel." She looked at the pitiful old woman sitting beside her. "The baby is safe now. So my life is looking after Enos. You have my promise that I will always take care of you also, to be best of my ability."

"Do you mean this sincerely?"

"I do." Unable to persuade any more balls to form, Channah dipped a cup into the remaining liquid and offered it to Peninnah. "Here, have some cheese milk." Although Enos's behavior was unpredictable, she knew he felt the need to be cared for. Therefore, she was confident she could successfully intercede if he threatened to drive his aunt away.

Accepting the cup with both hands, the old woman gulped it. When the last drop was drained, she wiped her mouth with the back of her wrist. "You know this is my favorite." Placing her hands on the head of her cane, Peninnah looked up at Channah. "I put up with Enos and his foul humor because I must. You can return to the shepherd's home. What makes you stay?"

"Enos is my husband, and I am bound to serve him." Channah wrapped the first of her cheese balls in thin cloth. "I try to follow the instructions of Jesus. We are to treat others as we wish to be treated."

Peninnah's eyes searched her face. "Are you content? With only an old woman and a disagreeable husband filling your days?"

After taking a moment to consider Peninnah's unusual question, she replied, "I am satisfied to be doing as I should. A child would be the greatest blessing I could ask, but I know that will never happen."

"Children can be a great gift." Peninnah sighed. "On the other hand, they can wound a mother's heart more deeply than anyone. Perhaps someday I will go with you to hear about the teachings of the healing prophet."

"I would like that very much." Channah smiled as she put away her cheese and stacked the utensils. "I must hurry and gather the animals into the barn before sundown."

In the pasture behind the courtyard, Channah untied the donkey from her stake. She led the animal to the barn, with the sheep following behind. In preparation for the following day, she filled the drinking trough with water and measured out enough food to sustain the animals through the holy day.

Inside the house, food sat waiting on the table. Channah took particular pleasure in the evening meal. She looked forward to meeting with other believers the following day, and she appreciated a day of rest from her household chores. The one problem that plagued her was working on the Sabbath. Sheep milk and cheese brought in enough income to buy food for the household without dipping into the shrinking number of coins Enos kept beneath his bedcovers. Since she could not afford to pay a gentile to milk once a week, Channah went to the barn before sunrise every day to do the milking. She did as little labor as possible on the Sabbath, taking some consolation that Avram and his friends did what was essential for their animals every day.

The following morning, Channah made the short trek across the river. She sat quietly with the other women and their children while the men spoke of the teaching of Jesus. Two of the men had heard the teacher himself preach. They relayed the master's words as well as they could recall them, while other men commented or asked questions.

As the meeting broke up, the women visited among themselves. Channah met a woman whose cousin had a ram available for breeding. Another was interested in buying cheese. On the way home, Channah took pleasure thinking about the possibility of new lambs in the spring. If she could expand her flock, she might be able to provide more than food for the household—a replacement for Peninnah's ragged coat, for example. So far, she was able to meet their expenses by selling milk and cheese. She hoped to maintain that status to keep Enos from being upset about his possessions.

The warm days of summer passed uneventfully. Since neither Peninnah nor Enos could climb the stairs, Channah slept inside the house instead of on the rooftop. Enos's first act upon awakening was to call out her name. When she answered, he often had no specific request. She understood that he simply wanted the reassurance of knowing she was nearby.

Satisfied that all the wounds to Enos's legs and chest were healed, Channah attempted to get him to leave his bed. "Husband," she asked one early autumn morning, "do you want to arise and perhaps go into the courtyard for some sunshine?"

Enos groaned. "Not today."

Channah did not press him. "When you are stronger, perhaps you would like to take a ride. I will saddle your donkey and lead her up the road."

"What then? Let everyone see me riding along, with my donkey's path controlled by a woman?" Enos snorted.

Although she normally kept quiet in Enos's presence, Peninnah ventured a comment. "I doubt anyone will pay attention."

Turning his head in his aunt's general direction, Enos sneered. "What do you know, old woman?" He settled under his covers. "Perhaps the two of you expect me to start sitting near the temple and begging all day? I will not humiliate myself that way. No, never."

Chapter Forty-Four

Avram and Caleb guided the sheep into their home paddock after the long trek down from the high country. Nathan rose from where he knelt, replacing a cracked rock. He embraced his father with the words, "Welcome home."

"It is good to see you," Caleb replied. "Was the child born?"

"Keren and the babe are well. The midwife said it was an easy birth. Now Rachel has a fine, healthy little sister."

With a clap to his son's shoulder, Caleb smiled before continuing to herd straggling sheep inside the stone wall.

Following the last of the animals inside the enclosure, Nathan turned and rolled the boulder that served as a gate into place. Keren stood near the outdoor oven. Her scarf was wound and tied to keep her infant daughter against her chest. Meanwhile, Rachel sat near the tent's entrance placidly filling a cracked pot with soil.

Avram emerged from the cave. "The sheep are settled in. I think they are glad to be home." He squatted next to Rachel. "What are you making?"

"Cake." She patted the top of her dirt-filled pot with a stick.

"Her speech is so plain." Avram grinned.

Nathan joined Avram. "Yes, Rachel is growing up. After all, she is the big sister now." He flipped a lock of Rachel's hair.

Avram pointed toward a cart sitting outside the fence. "We needed a replacement for our chariot. Did you make this one?"

"I did, and another smaller one we can pull by hand." Nathan smiled. "I also built a new water trough under the rock overhang in the north pasture."

"And the burial cave?"

"Yes. I hope not to need them for some time, but I did hollow out eight new niches, as you instructed me."

Avram raised an eyebrow. "Why so many?"

"That number fits the contours of the cave." Nathan shrugged. "Also, I wanted to do as much work as possible down here. I felt guilty, since I was not up on the mountain helping you and Father with the herd."

"It was better for you to be with your wife when she delivered her child." Avram absently patted Rachel's back. "There will be plenty for you to do now, as we begin the breeding season."

With a glance toward Keren, Nathan said, "I will have new regard for the ewes as they carry and birth their lambs."

Later that evening, the three men stood at the far corner of the paddock. "Is the woman always so silent?" Avram asked.

"Yes," Nathan answered with downcast eyes. "She is deeply disappointed that the baby is not a boy." He folded his arms and looked across the enclosure at the tent. "I have tried to convince her I am grateful we have a healthy daughter, but to no avail."

"She should be on her knees in gratitude for your acceptance of her and her fatherless children." Avram spat on the ground.

"She is not evil, merely misguided and confused. I believe patience will eventually win her over." Nathan rubbed his chin as if in thought. "My immediate concern is to persuade her to eat enough to nurse the baby."

After Nathan went inside the tent, Caleb turned to Avram. "I do not know if my son made the right decision concerning this marriage."

"I feel the same about Channah's choice to go and take care of her blind husband," Avram said. He rubbed the earth with the toe of his boot. "After the rams do their work, I will go again and check on her situation." He sighed. "If only we could live their lives for them."

Caleb grinned. "We would do no better than the children, probably worse."

"Perhaps so." Avram stared into the distance. "I hope Channah will tell me if that jackal Enos mistreats her."

"Why? To justify punishing him?"

"No." Avram shook his head. "I'm done with vengeance. I suppose I want to know so I can rescue her and bring her home again if necessary."

Caleb put a hand on his friend's shoulder. "Perhaps someday, if God wills it, she will return of her own free will."

Two days later, Avram and Caleb took a journey to fetch three frisky rams. With Nathan's help, they divided the herd, pairing each flock with one of the males. Keren continued to prepare food for the men, which she served in near silence. Avram noticed her hair had lost its glossy sheen, and she seemed thinner every day. He was tempted to admonish the woman to stop moping around and eat. However, he held his tongue. It was up to Nathan to manage his peculiar wife.

After returning the breeding rams to their owners, Caleb returned to the herd. Avram went to Jerusalem to see about Channah. He found her in the pasture behind Enos's house, singing to her little flock of sheep.

"Uncle!" she cried. "Just this very morning I was thinking what a long time it has been since I have seen you."

Avram closed his eyes as he embraced her. "I have prayed for you every day." He stepped back. "You look well."

"As do you." She waved an arm over her flock. "How can I ever thank you enough for your gift of these fine animals?"

"You have fattened them up."

"I enjoy taking care of them." Channah's face glowed with health. "Will you come and have some refreshment?

"I prefer not to enter your husband's house, but I will sit in your courtyard."

"I can keep an eye on my sheep from there." Channah led the way. "The donkey guards the flock also. She treats them as if they are her colts."

Avram settled onto one of the large square stones in the courtyard. "Did the old woman go home?"

"No, she is resting inside. Let me fetch wine and food for you."

While he waited, Avram noticed the courtyard fence had been repaired. The rows of a winter garden were neatly laid out, and the weeds were gone from around the house. "You have been busy," he commented when Channah came through the door bearing food and drink.

"Our house was neglected too long, but no more." She set a tray on his knees and handed him a generous cup of wine. "I hope you like the cheese. I make it the way Auntie taught me."

Avram broke the bread and sampled a chunk of cheese with it. "Good. Maybe better than Yael's."

"Your memory fails you, Uncle." Channah smiled. "No one can rival Auntie." She settled at his feet. "How is Rachel?"

"She is thriving. She runs without falling and jabbers all day long." Avram took a long drink of wine, followed by more cheese and bread.

"And the baby?"

"Another girl. Nathan named her Zara."

"I am glad to hear that." Channah rested a hand on Avram's knee. "That must mean he truly cares for the child, if he uses his own dear mother's name for her."

"Caleb's son is an exemplary father," Avram said between bites. "He compensates for the woman's inadequate mothering. Therefore, the little ones are well taken care of."

"Thank you, Uncle. You know how much that means to me." She shifted her position, locking her arms around her knees. "Keren once vowed to live a better life. I pray every day for her to love and protect Rachel." After a brief silence, she added, "I have found followers of the Way. They meet in a house on the opposite bank of the river."

"A house? Not a synagogue?"

"They were thrown out of the synagogue after one of the men proclaimed Jesus is Messiah."

"Poor blind fools, these religious leaders. They cannot see the light that shines in their faces." Avram sipped from his cup. "But I cannot fault them. I too was blinded for many years."

"I never knew you were blind, Uncle."

"I mean spiritual blindness, the worst kind. Far more dreadful than the physical loss of eyesight your husband endures."

Channah nodded. "You speak like the leader at the river house. He used to be a priest, but he was banished from all official places of worship because of the Way. His wife is bringing her cousin's ram to me this week."

"Ah, I was hoping you would be able to breed your ewes."

"More wine, Uncle?"

Holding his hand up, palm out, Avram declined. "No, but I will lie here and sleep before making the journey home." He moved into the shade.

Channah whisked the dishes away. "You are welcome to come inside and relax on a bed."

"This soft earth is more appealing to me." He yawned and stretched out next to the courtyard wall.

Chapter Forty-Five

Springtime brought the shepherds an abundance of lambs. "The publican will be delighted when he comes to assess our taxes," Avram commented, as he and Caleb stood overlooking their herd. "I have never seen a year with so many surviving young ones."

Caleb nodded in agreement. "We are blessed, my friend."

"I hope Channah's little flock is doing as well as ours." Avram leaned on his staff. "After the Passover, I will go and see about her."

"Speaking of Passover, Nathan will be delivering the lambs we owe the owner of the rams who begot them. I have told Nathan to go to Bethany afterwards. I want my son to spend time with his friends and have some respite from his labors," Caleb said. "I will stay behind with her and the children so Nathan can go without worrying."

"It is good for your son to go and celebrate the feast with his friends. He works hard, doing things you and I no longer have enough strength for. I will remain with you. We can always have our Passover meal with other shepherds who follow the Way."

"How I miss being young, when I took my family to the temple several times a year." Caleb pulled at his beard. "I always thought my Zara would be a widow someday, never suspecting I was the one to be left behind."

"Life seldom unfolds as we expect. Be grateful you have your son." Avram dug the tip of his staff into the earth. "I will walk around the perimeter to frighten away predators."

"I shall go around in the opposite direction and meet you on the other side."

As he strolled among his sheep, Avram continued thinking about his and Caleb's conversation. It seemed he was always in opposition to those around him. As a young shepherd, the other fellows teased him for his interest in learning. After the vision of the angels, he ceased going to the temple to observe holy days, even though that was the expectation for all Jews. Now, since his trip to meet the man of Galilee, he belatedly longed to worship at a synagogue. However, followers of the Way were not welcome. He batted small stones from his pathway, pondering how different his life might have been.

If Yael's mother had recovered sooner, his wife would not have been in Bethlehem when the soldiers came. If their child had been a daughter, the soldiers would not have murdered the babe. If only he had refused to allow Yakov to take Channah away to be married to the tanner. If only he had raised her to know about God. If, if, if. None but God was able to weave the threads of what is from what could have been. Avram determined to trust past, present, and future to the sovereign Lord. He thought of the gracious wisdom he heard from the lips of Jesus of Nazareth. Yes, as he remembered from the scroll of the prophet Isaiah, the Lord's ways truly were always higher and better than man's.

Seeing Caleb approaching him ended Avram's thoughtful reverie. "All is well," Caleb said. "I saw nary a wolf lurking."

"The same on this side." Avram pushed his hair back and smoothed his beard. "Go and sleep, my friend. I will keep watch."

Early the following day, the men separated the seven perfect yearling males chosen to fulfill the owner's bonus for the ram studs. Caleb ran a thumb over his pursed lips. "How did he know his rams were going to bring us so many lambs?" He shook his head. "I was certain we would never have to pay the extra premium."

"I have to admire a man who knows his business," Avram said. "He predicted our high birth rate, and he figured we were honest enough to keep account and pay up. Clever fellow."

After opening the back of the cart, Nathan spread plenty of fresh straw to pad the floor. "The young rams have ridden to and from the pasture several times. I hope they have lost their fear of the cart."

"Take it slow," Avram advised. "Stop frequently and give them extra grain to eat, and they will make the journey intact."

"I plan to return a week or so after Passover." Nathan flexed his fingers before looking at his father. "Please encourage Keren to eat enough."

"Take your time." Caleb embraced his son. "Avram and I will see to your little family."

After Nathan drove the donkey cart away, Avram turned to Caleb. "I do not understand why a nursing mother starves herself when there is plenty to eat. Perhaps I should not have delivered Channah's message asking your son to marry the woman."

"I believe he is content," Caleb replied. "In addition to her disappointment at bearing another daughter, I suspect she grieves for her former life."

Avram snorted. "She should be on her knees, thanking God that she has a home and a faithful husband. As to why she would mourn for that jackal who is married to Channah—"

"Oh, not so much him as city life, fine clothing, people to keep her company. She has hardly anyone to talk to but Nathan. He enjoys discussions of spiritual things, which do not interest her at all."

"What are we? Dumb animals?" Avram asked. "We speak during our meals, but she never responds."

"She knows you dislike her." Caleb lifted his eyebrows. "You will not even say her name."

Avram crossed his arms. "She has caused difficulty for Channah. I make every attempt to be forgiving, but the woman tries my patience with her selfishness. She uses her children to her advantage. Otherwise, I cannot see that she cares for them at all."

"I grant you my daughter-in-law is not the most attentive mother. But what is that to you?"

"When Channah's heart is wounded, I bleed."

Chapter Forty-Six

The bread merchant came a little later than usual. "How many loaves do you want?" he asked. "Quickly, please."

"Eight." Avram dug a copper coin from his pouch. "What is your hurry?"

"The whole city is in an uproar. You are my last stop." The merchant mopped his forehead with a square of cloth. "I usually go on to your neighbors, but I must make my way through the mobs before sundown."

"Yes, Jerusalem is always crowded before and after holy days."

The merchant counted loaves. "This is the worst day ever. The Romans crucified a prophet from Nazareth. There is much unrest. Here, take an extra loaf. There is no reason to let the bread spoil."

"Wait." Avram grabbed the side of the cart as the man flicked the reins over his donkey. "Did you say Nazareth? Not Jesus?"

"Jesus? That sounds familiar. Yes, I think that is his name."

Avram stood still, stunned. "Caleb," he shouted, not concerned if he frightened the sheep.

After a moment, Caleb came, walking so fast he almost trotted. "Wolves?" he asked, his eyes searching the landscape. "Avram, you have thrown our bread in the dirt. What is the matter?"

"It cannot be true." Avram sank to his knees.

"What? What are you talking about? Did the bread man cheat you?"

Avram's words did not convey the emotions raging within him. "The merchant said the Romans crucified a prophet from Nazareth. He thinks the man's name is Jesus."

"Ridiculous." Caleb looked toward the cart disappearing over a hill. "Jesus, our Jesus, has the power of life and death. The Romans cannot kill him. It is a common name. They must have crucified someone else from Nazareth."

"I have never heard of another prophet from there," Avram said. "Have you?"

"That merchant is a shameless gossip. He probably has no idea what is going on." Caleb stood for a moment. "I hope Nathan has already made his way to Bethany. It would not be good for him to be in the city if—"

Avram crumpled to sit on the ground. "Channah."

"Cursed Romans." Caleb sat beside Avram. "They will pay for all they have done when Jesus takes the kingdom."

Avram scooped a handful of dust and sprinkled it on his head. "We must do something."

"What?" Caleb poured dust over his scalp.

"I do not know. I cannot think. For the first time, I am glad Yael is no longer alive to see what a terrible thing has come to pass."

The shepherds who followed the Way led their sheep to the valley where they met every Sabbath. Before anyone spoke a word, Avram knew what the bread merchant told him was true. Sorrow was clearly displayed on every grief-stricken face. He and Caleb sat in silence for a long time with the younger men. At last, the shepherd known as John Simon whispered, "How could this happen?"

A tall young man cursed the Romans under his breath.

When Avram leaned forward, the shepherds turned their eyes toward him expectantly. "I did not sleep last night."

Murmurs of agreement rippled through the group.

"More than thirty years ago, I saw angels announce the holy birth of our Messiah. I went and worshipped him in a stable in Bethlehem. Not long afterwards, soldiers came to the village and murdered all the baby boys under two years old, my own son among them."

Ignoring the collective gasp, Avram continued. "After many years, I found out Jesus escaped Bethlehem before the soldiers arrived. Yes, the same Jesus of Nazareth, the one all of us believed until now to be the son of God, our savior, whose birth the Heavenly host proclaimed."

The tall shepherd asked, "Are you saying—?"

Avram held up a hand. "Hear me first. Then you may speak. In the years between the birth in Bethlehem and an encounter with Jesus in Galilee, I did unspeakable evil. In addition, I despised the temple and the synagogue. I was not able to prevent what the soldiers did to the baby boys of Bethlehem, but then I myself made the choice to abandon my devotion to God."

Tears filled Avram's eyes. Despite his resistance, one escaped from each eye to roll down his weathered cheeks. "Last night I reviewed the scroll of Isaiah in my head. I do not know why our teacher was crucified, but I believe if we study the holy scroll of Isaiah with open hearts and minds we will gain wisdom if not understanding. I know this one thing. I once allowed the acts of evil men to steal my faith. I will not make the same mistake again. I have the same belief in Jesus today that I did yesterday, and I pray every day for the rest of my life."

Some of the men glanced at each other, while others avoided eye contact.

"I trusted this Jesus," the tall shepherd said. "Either he does not have the power I once believed lived in him, or he decided not to exercise it. He has betrayed me by his death." The young man's voice broke. "Why? He was good to everyone." He stood and leaned on his staff. "I cannot return to the synagogue. I do not know what to do."

"Believe, my son," Avram said gently. "Do what Moses did at the Red Sea, what Joseph did during his years in prison. Did Joshua understand how he was to conquer the walls of Jericho? Believe God's ways are so far above ours that we simply do not have the ability to comprehend how he works."

"Pretty words." The tall shepherd turned and walked away.

As the men conferred in bands of three or four, Avram put a hand on Caleb's sleeve. "Now that my mind is settled, I want to get some sleep. I cannot explain why, but I feel some urgency about Channah. If you can manage the herd alone, I will go to her tomorrow."

"John Simon is a companionable young man, and he works alone. I will pasture our sheep with his until your return."

"Should I try to find Nathan as well?"

"No," Caleb replied. "I have peace about his safety. Jesus's death will break his heart. Let him mourn with his friends."

Chapter Forty-Seven

Channah stood outside the animal shed, watching Avram pick his way across the meadow behind her house. "Greetings, Uncle," she called out.

"Good day, Channah. Are you well?"

"I am enjoying this wonderfully crisp morning. And you?"

He came near and gave her a searching look. "Did you meet with the followers yesterday?"

"No. There must have been rain somewhere upriver. The water was too high for me to cross safely, and so I turned back." She stared at his gaunt face. "Why? Is something wrong?"

"Come and sit in the courtyard. There is something I must tell you."

"This is not easy," he said, once they were settled. "Jesus, our Savior, has died. He was crucified."

"I have heard crucifixion is the worst kind of death. What a cruel thing." She turned her face up to her uncle's. "But why?"

"I do not know much." Avram brushed away Channah's tears. "The people love him. Loved him, that is, and that generates envy and hate from people who crave power. It is possible the Romans or our own religious leaders will now persecute followers of the Way. You must be careful."

"Do you mean to say that I should not go to the meetings across the river?"

Avram hugged her shoulders. "You must make your own decision in that matter. However, I wanted to warn you of the possible danger."

"Will they crucify us also?"

After considering the possibility, he said, "I doubt it. Extreme punishment is usually for hardened criminals, but we know Jesus was innocent. So who knows? The people behind this horrible thing are capable of anything."

"Peninnah has gone with me to a few meetings. She agrees with the wisdom of the teachings of Jesus."

"Channah, we must hold to our beliefs, including our trust that Jesus is God's son."

Putting a hand on his sleeve, she asked, "Why would we not?"

"Some will say he was a false teacher because he was killed."

"Why?" Her wrinkled forehead bespoke puzzlement. "I do not understand."

"I can only say that is how some people think. I am relieved that you do not." Avram smiled for the first time in two days. "Do you have any wine?"

After Channah brought bread and wine outside, she pointed out the two new lambs with their grazing mothers not far away. Avram told of Rachel's expanding vocabulary, Nathan's journey to Bethany, and the amazing

256

number of lambs born within his herd. Then the pair fell silent for a while. "Your husband and his aunt are well?" Avram asked.

"Peninnah suffers with aching bones, especially when the morning is damp. I would like to say she never complains, but that is not the case. As for Enos." She drew a deep breath. "He spends most of his time in bed, although the wounds on his body have healed. It seems he has lost interest in life because he cannot see. What can I do to help him?"

After a glance at her open, trusting face, Avram swallowed the disparaging words about Enos that clamored to be spoken. "You are a good woman, Channah, a true follower of the Way. You cannot help the man until he decides to help himself. Such things cannot be forced."

"I appreciate the kind words." She twisted a dishcloth in her hands. "I so want to do what is pleasing in God's sight, but sometimes I have trouble knowing what that is." She chewed at her lip. "I must confess I milk my sheep on the Sabbath. It costs too much to pay someone else to do it, but I cannot stand to see my ewes suffer."

Placing a hand on her head, Avram said, "The few times I heard Jesus speak, I realized he emphasized mercy and kindness over strict adherence to rules. I do not believe he would condemn your choice."

"Thank you, Uncle." As Avram nibbled on bread, Channah asked him, "Will you stop meeting with the other shepherds who follow the Way?"

"Certainly not." He raised his cup. "Whatever gave you that idea?"

"You said it may be dangerous to gather together."

"That is no reason—" He stopped himself. "I can afford to defy the Pharisees and the Sadducees and even the mighty Romans. What can they do but kill me? I am an old man, and most of my years are behind me. Your situation is different. You are young, and I want you to have a long life."

Channah again twisted her dishrag, wringing it as if there were answers hidden among its loosely woven threads. "I will think on what you have said, Uncle. I cannot have the future I want, which is to bear a child of my own." She folded the cloth and patted it on her lap.

"In your youth and strength, you should have many sons and daughters."

"No, Uncle. Enos cannot." A delicate blush spread across her cheeks. "So I know my heart's deepest desire will never be."

"I see." Avram held his cup with both hands, staring into it. "Who can fathom the ways of the almighty? I do not know why God allowed my little boy such a short span on this earth."

"As Nathan explained, we simply trust." Channah stood and took the food tray. "Do not be concerned on my behalf, Uncle. I am content to serve Enos and now Peninnah as well. Without faith, where would I find the strength to care for them? Following the Way has given me an understanding of life's meaning and purpose."

"Even though you are my blood relative, not hers, you put me in mind of Yael more than anyone."

"She was a fine woman. It is most pleasing that you think me to be like her."

On his way home, Avram noticed how few people were coming and going. Crucifixions always put a temporary damper on commerce. Soon, however, vendors would offer their wares for sale. Women would venture out of their homes. Things would gradually return to normal in a few days, except for the families of those unfortunate fellows the Romans nailed to crosses to demonstrate their power.

As a young man, he expected to see the Roman conquerors thrown out of his land. Yet every rebellious uprising came to nothing. When he thought the possibility of freedom was gone, discovering the nation's savior—he was so sure Jesus was the one—revived his hope.

He had no fear for himself, but what of Channah? Once again, as with his son, then his wife, he felt unable to protect his family from the evils of a cold, dark world.

Chapter Forty-Eight

Making his way through the pastureland, Avram found Caleb and their herd. "John Simon is a good shepherd," Caleb declared. "Perhaps someday he will partner with Nathan when we are too old to work."

"We are already too old." Avram sat and pulled off his boots.

Caleb eased himself slowly to the ground beside his friend. "Today I feel as if I was never young. Did you find out anything more about Jesus?"

"No." Avram rubbed his tired feet with olive oil. "I only spoke with Channah. She has two new lambs."

Caleb jumped at the sound of John Simon's voice. "Greetings."

"Good day." Avram spoke with no enthusiasm.

"Try to give me some warning when you come up behind me," Caleb said. "Otherwise, I may think you a predator and react accordingly."

"I shall keep that in mind, sir." Although he smiled, John Simon's words had a serious tone. "Have you learned anything more about Jesus?"

"No." Avram stowed his boots in his knapsack and pulled out a pair of worn sandals.

John Simon stroked his dark, close-clipped beard. "If you are agreeable, I will separate from you and take my sheep to their next pasture."

"Go in peace," Avram answered. "I thank you for sharing the watch with Caleb during my absence."

"I was glad to be of help." With a casual salute, John Simon ambled away.

"Odd fellow," Caleb muttered as John Simon whistled to his sheep and led them away.

"In what way? Is he dishonest?"

"No, but too quiet. I can hardly get him to say a word." Caleb sighed. "Hard worker, though. Reliable. I like that in a young man. Have you considered taking vengeance for the death of Jesus?"

"No." Avram tossed a pebble away.

"Ah." Caleb sighed. "You are not as fleet of foot as you were thirty years ago."

Avram shook his head. "Revenge is completely contrary to his teachings." He leaned his head back to face the sky. "If Jesus was not our savior, then I have no cause to take up a weapon. If he was, then I must follow his commandments."

"So then what do we do now, old man? Simply carry on as if nothing happened?"

"I wish I knew the answer to that question, and many others." He drew up his knees to rest his elbows on them. "But I know nothing. Nothing."

"And yet you continue to believe?"

"Yes," Avram answered. "I must."

***

After three weeks went by, Caleb began to mention the imminence of his son's return to the herd. When more than a month passed with no word from Nathan, Caleb came to Avram and said, "I am considering going to Bethany. I must find out what is delaying my son."

Avram nodded. "That is what I would do. What of the woman?"

"Keren complains of spending her days alone in the tent by the cave with the children. However, as you know, she has food, access to fresh water, and shelter from the elements. It seems to me she should be grateful instead of restless. In any case, there seems to be no other option."

"I will keep the sheep at pasture and sleep under the stars." Avram rubbed his shoulder. "Perhaps I will mingle our herd with John Simon's until you return."

"I wish the young fellow had a wife to go and comfort Keren, but alas."

"When will you go?"

Caleb stood looking toward the setting sun. "Perhaps tomorrow at sunrise."

Two days after Caleb's departure, the bread merchant appeared for the first time in weeks.

"Greetings," Avram said as the merchant pulled the reins to still his donkey. "I hope you have extra bread today. I have had none since you last made your rounds."

"These are turbulent times. No one is certain of anything anymore." The man looked left and right as if to verify they were alone. "Have you heard the rumors?"

"About the crucifixion of the Galilean? It is true. The Romans executed him."

The vendor dismounted. He stepped to the side of his cart. "Oh, everyone knows that by now. How many loaves today? The usual eight?"

"Ten if you have them. I have developed a great hunger for bread during your long absence."

"Yes, my wife baked extra today." He counted the small, rounded loaves into the bag Avram held open. Although no other human was anywhere near them, the merchant leaned nearer and lowered his voice. "They say the body of the prophet from Nazareth has disappeared."

"No."

"Yes. The Romans, the Pharisees, the Sadducees, even his followers agree the tomb where they laid him is empty." The merchant accepted Avram's small copper coins and tucked them inside his belt. "The official word is that the man's disciples stole the corpse." He arched his eyebrows. "But some say Jesus is alive again, walking around, talking, and meeting with his followers. Can you imagine?" He leapt into the driver's seat of his cart. "I put no confidence in such wild tales myself, but my neighbor insists the prophet has come back to life." He flicked the reins over his donkey's back. "I plan to resume my regular routine now that the city is calmer. Be ready to buy bread again next week."

Avram watched the merchant slowly disappear around a rise. He felt as if his legs were tree trunks with deep roots, tethering him to the ground where he stood. For some time, his body remained still while his mind raced. He regretted Caleb's absence mightily. Calling to his sheep, he moved them toward the pasture where he hoped young John Simon was feeding his flock. He had to find someone to talk with about the bread merchant's report.

Chapter Forty-Nine

Sunset came before Avram and his herd reached the meadow where John Simon's sheep rested in the twilight. Grateful to be nearing his destination, anticipating rest for his weary body, Avram was surprised by a noise. The unmistakable growl of a wolf ripped through the air. Simultaneously, a straggling ewe at the edge of the herd cried aloud. Instinctively, Avram grabbed the rod from his belt and aimed it at the attacking wolf. He threw with all his might but overshot his target.

Avram rushed forward, noting the presence of several circling wolves. He swung his shepherd's crook with one hand while unsheathing his knife with the other. As he lunged to stab a threatening wolf, his foot slipped. He landed hard, face down on the ground. Avram rolled over, slashing the air around him with his knife. While he struggled to stand, a wolf yelped and fell nearby. One more animal shrieked, and the wolves retreated.

Looking upward in the dim light, Avram saw John Simon wipe blood from a sword. The young shepherd extended a hand to help the old man to his feet.

Brushing dirt from his clothing, Avram grunted, "Thank you." He retrieved his crook and rod.

"Come and sit." John Simon pointed toward a hillock.

Although his first thought was to resist, Avram recognized the wisdom of his young friend's words. "Yes, I will." He followed the young shepherd to a high spot overlooking the herd.

Without speaking, John Simon served Avram a cup of wine, then proceeded to pour more wine into a soft cloth. He dabbed at Avram's skinned knees, forearms, and face. When every wound was treated, he added wood to the campfire set a short distance behind them.

"I have never before needed help subduing a wild animal, but this night would have ended badly but for you. I am in your debt." Avram realized he was weak from the exertion of fighting the wolves. He nibbled at the fruit John Simon offered, glad for something to replenish his strength, but mostly grateful for another human presence. "I have always been the strong one, but old age takes its toll."

The young man acknowledged Avram's words with a nod.

"I did not stop to see how many sheep I lost."

"One to the wolf and perhaps another to fright." John Simon topped off Avram's wine. "I will get the carcasses. We will eat the meat."

While John Simon made his way through the herd, Avram attempted to stand. Finding his legs unreliable, he resumed sitting. This once, he would let someone else do what needed to be done. Soon, the young shepherd returned, dragging the bodies of a ewe and a yearling.

Avram watched as his companion skinned the smaller animal and threaded its body onto a spit for roasting. "I have never seen a shepherd wield a sword."

"Military training." John Simon began to remove the ewe's hide.

"I see. Yet now you follow the Way."

The young shepherd worked quietly for some time before responding. "To escape from a dangerous situation, I blended into a crowd and ended up sitting with a throng to hear the words of Jesus. I never returned to the Zealots' armed camp."

With food and rest, Avram felt himself slowly returning to normal. He was intensely curious about the young man's time with the rebels. However, he did not yet have the energy to pursue a conversation.

"You are not full of questions," John Simon commented. "I like that."

Avram considered the insight the young man gave him. Perhaps he would learn more by opening up about his own past. "I never joined an organized insurgent group myself, probably because I had no idea how to find them. However, as a young man I did much evil that I now regret."

John Simon stretched out the fresh sheepskins on the ground. He discarded the wounded area of the ewe's carcass. After cutting the remaining meat into chunks, he set it to boil in a great iron pot. At last he settled to the ground and laid on one side, half leaning on an elbow. "Seeing my sword covered in blood took me back to a different season of my life." His eyes scanned the sleeping herd from right to left and back. "It is one thing to talk about killing, something altogether different to actually do it."

Grunting his agreement, Avram remembered why he came to find John Simon. "I saw the bread merchant today. I have spoken with no one else from the city since the Romans crucified Jesus.

"You should walk some, to keep from becoming stiff from your injuries." John Simon sat up, keeping his face turned toward the sheep. "I avoid city people, including the bread man."

Avram wanted to argue about needing to walk, but he knew the younger man was right. He leaned heavily on his staff, groaning as he stood erect. "I will be sore tomorrow." Avram used his free hand to rub the small of his back. "The merchant said there are many rumors circulating in Jerusalem, including one that Jesus is alive."

"Does the merchant know Jesus?"

Bending his aching knees, Avram replied, "I think not."

"Then how would he know whether he is alive or dead?" John Simon stood and stretched. He stirred the boiling pot with his staff. "I will keep watch if you want to sleep."

Recognizing how tired he was, Avram leaned against a large stone for assistance in getting to the ground. Spreading his coat beneath him suddenly seemed like too much effort. He watched John Simon descend the little hill as nimbly as a mountain goat. "Cursed wolves," he muttered, as he closed his eyes.

The following morning, Avram awoke to find the sun already risen. As soon as he pulled on his boots, he detected an enticing aroma.

"Come and eat." John Simon dipped a generous helping of boiling broth, and then maneuvered a chunk of meat into the bowl. "How do you feel?"

Avram pushed his hair back. "I have been worse." He smoothed his beard. "I am good enough to water the sheep while you sleep."

With a lopsided grin, the young man said, "I will sleep when I am dead."

Contrary to his original intent, Avram decided not to separate his herd from John Simon's until Caleb returned. Hoping his old friend and his son were alive and safe, he thought briefly about the woman, alone with her children at his home cave. He had a gnawing feeling he should see about her, but he could not leave his sheep until one of his partners came to relieve him. For the first time in his life, he did not feel confident moving his herd through the hills without help. Much as he hated admitting his need for John Simon, Avram knew he had to depend on the peculiar young man for the time being.

Chapter Fifty

Channah hummed the tune of a psalm while she finished up her evening routine in the animal shed. After pouring water into the drinking troughs, she stopped at the open barn door to enjoy the late afternoon breeze. Movement across the meadow caught her attention. She strained her eyes to determine whether the distant figure was—as she thought—a human coming toward her.

Taking a few steps into the meadow, she made out a woman coming toward the house, carrying a baby and leading a toddler by the hand. "Keren," Channah gasped, breaking into a run. She slowed to a trot when she was near, realizing something was dreadfully wrong.

"I am sorry," Keren whispered. She thrust her baby into Channah's arms and slumped to the ground.

Channah knelt to gather Rachel into a hug with one arm, holding the infant with the other. She released the little girl to brush Keren's hair from her face. "What is it?"

"So tired and hungry." She grabbed Channah's arm with surprising strength. "My babies."

"I will take care of them." She looked at the baby nestled against her. "This must be Zara."

"Zara," Rachel repeated, pointing at her little sister.

Channah touched the top of Rachel's head lightly. "Keren, are you able to stand?"

Without answering, Keren struggled to her knees. Channah put an arm around her and helped her to her feet.

270

"Come along, Rachel." Thinking quickly what she should do, she steered the little group toward the barn. Once there, Keren collapsed onto the straw.

"Hungry." Rachel looked at Channah with big, trusting eyes that made her heart lurch.

She placed the baby beside Keren and told Rachel, "Wait here."

Rushing inside the house, Channah flew around gathering food and drink. She was relieved to hear Enos snoring. Peninnah also appeared to be sleeping, though she was not in bed. Channah smiled at the sight of the old woman snoozing on her stool, leaning against the wall. Peninnah's sewing lay at her feet, probably where it fell from her limp hands.

When Channah returned to the barn, Keren drank wine and ate cheese. Meanwhile, Rachel stuffed bread into her mouth faster than she could swallow it. Touching Keren's shoulder, Channah said, "You must nurse the baby."

"Too weak." Keren put her arm over her eyes.

Channah coaxed a cup of milk from a surprised ewe. Patiently dipping into the milk, then allowing the baby to suck her finger, she managed to feed Zara the full amount.

"Where is Nathan?" Channah put the baby to her shoulder and patted her tiny back.

"Who knows?"

"We ran away," Rachel volunteered through a mouthful of cheese.

Channah stopped patting Zara for a moment. "You did?"

"Yes." Keren turned on her side and pulled her knees to her chin. "I tried hard to be a good wife." She shut her eyes. "Too tired to talk."

Soon all three of her visitors were asleep. Certain she could not take Keren and her girls into Enos's house, Channah decided to spend the night in the barn with them. Thanking the Lord for mild weather, she fetched her blanket from the house and curled up with Rachel. Her last thought before falling asleep was how good it felt to hold the child she loved in her arms once again.

Channah was awakened before dawn by a nuzzle from Enos's donkey. She sat up, rubbed the animal's nose, and brushed straw from her clothing. Relieved to see that Keren and the children remained asleep, she removed her containers from the wall and did her morning milking. Before stoking the fire in the courtyard, she shaped loaves of dough into bread and set them out to rise. She put grain on for the morning meal, and then ran to deliver milk to Shuwshan and two other neighborhood customers. As the sun shot its first slanted rays over the horizon, she led the donkey to the pastureland behind the house, softly beckoning to her sheep to follow.

Inside the house, Channah bustled about, making sure everything was ready for her to serve food to Enos and Peninnah when they awoke. She carried a tray of dishes outside, and ladled bowls of roasted grain for Keren and Rachel. Normally she would have added loaves of bread baked the day before. However, her hungry guests consumed the breakfast bread last night, except for two small loaves she held back for Enos.

Keren ate while Channah fed Rachel. "You must nurse your baby now," Channah insisted.

With a sigh, Keren took the infant to her breast. "Have you told Enos I am here?"

"Not yet."

"Perhaps he will take me back. He allowed you to come home, why not me?"

"But Keren, you are married to Nathan now."

"That was a mistake." She shifted Zara to the other side. "He leaves me alone and sleeps in the pasture." She put a hand on Channah's arm. "I have tried as hard as I can. But I am not suited to live out in the country with a man who thinks his sheep and his god are more important than I am. I want to come home and buy pretty things in the market again."

"Keren." Channah wiped Rachel's chin. "There was an explosion in the tannery. Enos has lost his business and his eyesight. He is poor now. I sell milk and cheese to buy our food. You must return to Nathan."

"No. I will live as my mother did before I will go back to the shepherds and their endless god talk." She wrapped Zara in her little blanket and laid her on the straw. "I lived with a man in the city for these past weeks. I should have stayed there."

"Why did you leave?"

"There was a plague spreading through the area. Some died. When the man became sick—"

Memories of Keren's self-centered ways overwhelmed Channah. She heard the hard edge to her voice as she said, "He took you in, and then you deserted him when he fell ill?"

"He has relatives." Keren began to weep. "I have no one."

Rachel stood by Keren and hugged her.

Keren put her arm around Rachel and nodded, but the tears persisted. "You said Enos is blind? And poor? I am sorry to hear that. Perhaps he will take pity on us. Will you ask Enos if we may stay?"

"I must pray and think." Channah sprang up. "Right now, I need to see to the morning meal for him and Peninnah."

"Peninnah? What is that old raven doing here?"

"She came to help Enos after his accident. Now she lives with us." Channah closed the barn door behind her and scampered to the house.

In the weeks following the crucifixion of Jesus, the spring thaw kept the water over the river's steep banks. How Channah wished for the river to recede enough for her to attend a meeting with other followers of the Way. The older women among the group could advise her how to deal with Keren's reappearance.

Chapter Fifty-One

Avram walked behind the sheep, nudging stragglers along as he remembered Yael doing so often in the past. His lips moved silently as he reviewed the words of Isaiah, still puzzling over Jesus' death. Although he desperately hoped the rumor of his resurrection was true, he did not want to convince himself unless it really happened. All morning he searched the Holy Scriptures in his memory, but he reached no definite conclusion.

When the sheep were settled in their new pasture, Avram climbed to an overlook to join John Simon. There was lush grass for the animals to graze, but he suspected isolation was the real reason his companion chose this place. His mind drifted from the prophet Isaiah to wonder once more why John Simon avoided contact with anyone he did not know well. Again, he marveled that Caleb managed to get acquainted with the laconic loner. Caleb. What had become of him?

At midafternoon, Avram heard the strains of a shepherd's pipe. Both he and John Simon turned to face the sound. "I come bearing good news," Avram said.

"What is that you say?"

"Years ago, the shepherds in this area used our pipes to pass information," Avram explained. "We signaled each other when strangers were in the hills—soldiers, tax collectors, that kind of thing." He put a hand on his hip. "Some old shepherd is coming to tell us something he believes to be good."

Not long afterward, Avram clapped John Simon on his shoulder. "Caleb. At last."

Caleb climbed the small rise where the others stood. "He is risen," he said, not waiting until he reached the summit. "Jesus is alive."

Without regard for his bruises, Avram fell to his knees and lifted his arms toward Heaven. "Praise God."

"You are certain of this?" John Simon asked.

"I saw him." Caleb was out of breath, but speaking nevertheless. "He talked to us at several gatherings." Caleb giggled. "He has power over death. Hallelujah!"

Avram rose from his knees and danced a few steps.

"What happened to you?" Caleb pointed to the scabs on Avram's arms.

"I had an encounter with a pack of wolves." Avram laughed and shook his head. "I was actually afraid for my life." He lifted his eyes toward Heaven. "John Simon came to my rescue and drove them away. What a fool I am." With another laugh, he asked, "Where is your son?"

"Jesus told his followers to remain in Jerusalem for a gift. When I found Nathan, he was waiting for the promise with the other believers. I joined them. Fellows, I must tell you about the day of Pentecost." He put a hand across his heart. "You will be amazed." Dropping his hand, Caleb added, "I wanted to let you know we were detained in the city, but all of the followers of the Way were there waiting with us. Nathan has now gone directly to your cave to see his wife and children."

"How fortunate we are," the normally silent John Simon said, "to live in this age. To see Jesus for ourselves and witness his miracles. Think of it. We could have been born Greeks or Egyptians. Many people died before Jesus made his appearance on this earth, and others are just now being born. We are a blessed generation."

"We have a deep thinker among us," Caleb said, lifting his eyebrows to wrinkle his forehead.

John Simon grinned. "I must water the sheep. Then I will ask you to repeat everything you saw in Jerusalem for me." He sauntered away but turned and briefly rejoined the other two shepherds. "I expected our savior to lead us in battle against foreign oppression. Now I see he has triumphed over death itself—an enemy far stronger than all the legions of Rome."

Putting an arm around Avram's shoulders, Caleb said, "You were right not to doubt, my friend. What is there to eat?"

"Not knowing you were coming, we gave a roasted yearling to a neighboring group of shepherds rather than let it spoil. However, there is still a pot boiling with the flesh of the ewe the wolf frightened to death." He watched John Simon helping the herd drink. "The prophet was right. We are like sheep."

Caleb looked at him with narrowed eyes. "What do you mean by that?"

"Merely an observation." Avram smiled. "He is risen, just imagine it."

Nathan arrived at sundown. His first words were, "Keren is gone." He went immediately to the pot of stew.

After dipping a portion, he sat cross-legged with the other men. "There was no sign of her or my little girls."

"Perhaps they were attacked by wild animals," Caleb suggested.

Nathan shook his head. "There was no sign of a struggle. Nothing was missing except their clothing and … and the few coins we had set aside." He set his half-eaten bowl aside. "She threatened to desert me before, and now I believe she has done it. I have no idea where to search for her."

"You would go after her, knowing she chose to leave?" John Simon folded his arms. His skeptical look registered his opposition.

"Perhaps." Nathan turned his face to Caleb. "What should I do, Father?"

Caleb drew a deep breath. "I suppose she took the children back to Jerusalem. You may never find her there. Too many people."

Seeing Nathan's disappointment, Avram refrained from expressing his opinion the young man was well rid of a wayward wife. He chided himself for delivering Channah's foolish request for Nathan to marry the woman. How much better it would have been for Caleb's son to remain single, or better yet to become a husband to Channah. Yes, Avram admitted how he hoped for such a union. It made sense for the couple, for both families, and for the preservation of the herd of sheep.

Caleb's words pulled Avram away from his thoughts and into the conversation. "We waited in

Jerusalem, as Jesus commanded before he ascended back into Heaven."

"Wait." John Simon grabbed Caleb's wrist. "You have left something out. He ascended? You saw this?"

"Not me," Caleb tapped his chest. "His apostles were present. I heard the story from one of them, the man they call Peter. He spoke to a gathering of followers and told us all about it."

"And now you must tell us." Avram said. "Start over, beginning with the women finding the tomb empty, and this time tell us everything that happened. Every tiny detail, in order of occurrence as best you are able."

"All right," Caleb agreed. He put an arm around his son. "Nathan will have to help me, to make sure I forget nothing. Now, very early in the morning, on the first day of the week …"

Avram doubted any of them would sleep that night, but he had no regrets.

Chapter Fifty-Two

Two days after Keren arrived, Channah's day began normally. Keren, Rachel, and Zara remained in the stable. From inside the house, Channah occasionally heard the baby cry faintly, but neither Enos nor Peninnah seemed to notice. She knew their presence could not remain secret indefinitely, but she did not know how to approach Enos to ask permission for them to stay.

Something was amiss. Channah was sure of it when she delivered milk to Shuwshan's home.

The oldest child, her hair unkempt, stood in the courtyard alone. "Mama is sick," she told Channah. "Will you help her?"

Channah allowed the girl to lead her inside the cluttered house. When Channah touched Shuwshan's forehead, she felt the burn of a high fever. "How long has she been ill?"

"Two days."

"Where is your father?"

"Gone away."

"When will he be home?"

"He said never," the girl answered. "Can you help Mama?"

Channah sat by the bed and rubbed her friend's arms. "Shuwshan, do you hear me?" she asked. "Can you open your eyes?" Receiving no reaction, she wondered what she should do. She searched for something to feed the children, but found nothing. "Drink this," she instructed the little ones, as she gave each of them a portion of the milk she brought. "Stay inside the house. I will return soon."

At the nearest house, Channah explained that Shuwshan was ill. "Someone needs to look after the children."

The neighbor looked toward Shuwshan's house. "I have five children of my own and an ailing father-in-law. I am not able to help anyone else."

After receiving a similar reception at the other two nearby homes, she delivered milk to her other customer. She let the housewife know she could not bring milk again for a few days.

Channah used Shuwshan's bedclothes to slide her friend into the bed of the little water-hauling cart. "Come with me," she said, dreading her husband's reaction when she arrived home with a sick woman and three young children. Shuwshan's feet hung over the end of the cart, dragging on the ground all the way to Enos's house.

Peninnah stood leaning on her cane when Channah pulled the wooden cart through the front door. The old woman's eyes widened when the two little girls followed, one of them carrying a young boy. She and the children stood staring at each other while Channah maneuvered Shuwshan onto her own bed. Using their now-familiar hand signals, Channah motioned for Peninnah to meet her in the courtyard. The children silently followed the two women out-of-doors.

"Our neighbor Shuwshan is sick." Channah drew her friend's daughters to her side. "We must care for her and her children until she recovers. The first thing everyone needs is a good meal."

Peninnah nodded.

"We have three more guests. Keren and her daughters have been sleeping in our animal shed. Today, we will move them to the house also." Channah pushed strands of hair from her forehead. "Some of us may have to sleep on the rooftop."

From the side of her mouth, Peninnah muttered, "Enos."

Channah quickly gathered dried fruit and honey cakes and brought them outside. She stuck her head inside the barn. "Keren, you and the girls come and eat in the courtyard." As she walked by Peninnah, she said, "Keep everyone outside while I go and speak with my husband."

Channah mixed an extra batch of bread before awakening Enos.

"What?" he groaned.

"It is morning."

"Is that any reason to wake me up?" Enos rubbed his eyes. "I want to sleep a while."

"As you wish." Channah sat on the stool by his bed. "First let me tell you our neighbor Shuwshan is ill, and her husband has deserted her. I have brought her and her children here to stay with us until Shuwshan is better."

"Someone else needs to take care of these people. I am blind, and I dislike being around sick people."

"I asked among those living nearby, but no one is willing to help. We must do it. It is our responsibility as a neighbor."

Enos yawned and sat up. Channah fluffed cushions behind him and moved them to support his back. "You will have to keep the children quiet," he said. "You know how I hate racket in the house."

"I am aware of your feelings about noise, and I will do my best. However, children cannot be held silent for very long at a time."

"I do not like this." Enos folded his arms across his chest.

"There is something more. Keren has come home. She has nowhere else to go. We must care for her and her children."

"Children?" Enos yelled. "That harlot has gone and conceived another child? I will not have her in this house, and I certainly will not welcome her brats."

"Since you will not allow Keren and her daughters in your home, I will take them with me and leave." She waited a moment for her words to sink in. "Hear this, husband. I do not speak in anger, but in firm resolution. If I am forced to depart this house again, I will shake the dust from my feet. And I will never return."

"You would desert your poor, blind husband?"

"I will move to Shuwshan's house, taking Keren and the children with me. Peninnah also, if she wishes to go. When Shuwshan recovers or her husband returns, I will go home to my Uncle Avram."

Enos stuck out his bottom lip. "How can you be so cold?"

"The decision rests with you." Channah clapped her hands on her knees. "And now I will prepare your breakfast."

Chapter Fifty-Three

Two weeks later, Shuwshan died. Channah quietly exchanged one of Enos's silver candlesticks to pay for the burial. By the time the grave keeper collected the body, Keren, Rachel, Peninnah, and Shuwshan's two younger children were down with the fever.

With no one else to help her, Channah put Shuwshan's oldest daughter, Miryam, in charge of the animals. "The flock is important because it is our source of milk and the cheese and yogurt we make from the milk," she explained to the child. "You will do well. I was about your age when I began to take care of sheep. If you need me, run to the house." Channah wished she had more time to instruct Miryam, but she spent every waking hour taking care of the sick.

"What if I get this dreadful fever?" Enos clutched at Channah's arm.

Channah patted his hand. "Then I will nurse you as best I can."

"You will not leave me to die alone?"

"Rest, Enos. As long as you allow Rachel to remain with us, I will stay and take care of you."

"But the child is sick," he protested. "What if she dies? Shuwshan did."

"I cannot think of that possibility." Channah forced herself not to break down and cry. Instead, she dipped rags in water and replaced the compress on Peninnah's forehead. Then she propped Keren up in her bed and ladled broth down her throat. Moving constantly from one bed to the next, she tried desperately to keep strength up and fever down in each sick person.

There were no vegetables left in the house, but Channah did not dare take time to go to the market. Bread and cheese were the typical fare, with lentils and dried beans for soup. Using the donkey and Shuwshan's cart to make the trip more quickly, she managed to fetch water every other day. Though she knew it was the right thing to do, Channah cried as she slaughtered one of her lambs. Her feverish charges needed nourishing broth and meat.

Miryam slept in the barn, saying the straw was more comfortable than the floor of the house. "Are you not afraid to be out here alone?" Channah asked.

"The sheep are here with me," the child explained.

The following morning, Miryam leaned against Channah while she was milking. "I can learn to do that."

Too tired to turn down any offer of assistance, Channah guided the girl as she milked one of the ewes.

"I will do them all tomorrow," Miryam said.

"Bless you." Channah returned to the house, grateful for one less chore.

The following week, Shuwshan's little son Joshua, the breech baby Channah delivered, passed away. When Channah thought she could not keep going, Peninnah encouraged her by sitting up without help for a long moment.

286

Then Enos began to burn with fever. "This is your fault," he murmured to Channah. "You brought the sickness to my house."

Not feeling strong enough for a discussion of guilt, Channah wet a cloth and cooled his face. "We will talk when you feel better."

Channah knew day from night only because the sun kept track for her. She did not know or care how many days passed, except for her concern about the household food supplies. One day, Peninnah took up her cane and staggered to the courtyard, but Keren and Shuwshan's younger daughter seemed weaker every day.

"I am going to die," Keren whispered.

Channah smoothed the blanket beneath Keren. "Eat some broth and rest. You will recover."

"No." Keren turned feverish eyes to Channah. "I never wanted to do wrong, but I know I did." She seemed to struggle for breath. "Take care of Rachel."

"Always. And Zara as well."

"Zara will not live."

"Please, do not say such things."

"Tell Nathan I am so sorry. He deserved better." She closed her eyes.

Channah wet the cloth on Keren's head and moved to Enos's bedside.

The next morning, Channah's hands shook as she kneaded the day's bread. Finding it difficult to concentrate on any task, she went into the courtyard to take a short rest. While watching Miryam with the sheep, she wondered if the plague was widespread or confined to her neighborhood. What a warm day it was. She raised her arm to shield her eyes from the sun and was shocked to feel the heat of her own face. *I cannot get sick*, she told herself.

She willed herself to bake the bread. When she took it from the outdoor oven, she realized she must lie down for a moment. Just long enough to gain some strength. When she attempted to get up, she was unable to do so.

Chapter Fifty-Four

"Would you consider becoming partners with us?" Avram asked John Simon during the morning meal.

After a long moment, the young man replied, "I will think on it."

Chagrined not to receive an eager acceptance, Avram resisted mentioning the size and vigor of his herd in comparison to John Simon's little flock. Instead, he mumbled, "Good." He exchanged a look with Caleb, using a subtle hand motion to warn his friend not to join the conversation.

The men ate in silence as the sun broke over the horizon. "Another fine day," Caleb commented.

Avram grunted acknowledgment. "Every new day of life is a good one." He waited to see if their young companion had anything to say. The only sound was the chewing of bread. "Where is Nathan?" Avram asked, although he knew full well his friend's son was in Jerusalem.

"Gone to seek his wife, I suppose." Caleb's eyes remained on John Simon. "I doubt he will find her."

"She is a striking woman. Perhaps someone in the city noticed and remembers her. I will see to the sheep. Will you come with me, Caleb?" Avram turned as if to leave.

John Simon remained sitting. "I cannot give you an immediate answer." He looked downward. "It is not that I am unappreciative." He stood, gazing into the distance. "There are things you do not know about me."

Avram hesitated briefly and then made his way toward the sheep. Caleb waited for a few heartbeats before following.

Beyond John Simon's hearing, Avram said, "He will tell us what we need to know if we are patient. If you ask, he will bolt like a frightened lamb."

"Bah," Caleb snorted. "Why not say whatever this secret is, and be done with it? He is not old enough to have done much evil."

"That is not John Simon's way." Avram inspected a ewe's foot. "He does not trust easily."

"Nathan needs a dose of that distrust." Caleb sat beside Avram and took out his knife. "He honestly believes he will convince Keren to come home with him and that she will settle down and be a faithful wife."

Avram turned the ewe on her rump and trimmed her hoof. "I hope things happen exactly that way. If Jesus can walk out of his tomb and live again, who is to say that anything is impossible?"

A few days later, Nathan returned, crestfallen. At the evening meal, he sat with the other men, shivering. "I went to the house where someone told me they saw her, but it was unoccupied. A neighbor told me the man who lived here died of a plague." He pulled his coat tighter around his throat. "The same neighbor had seen Keren and the babies. She thought they left to go and be with relatives." He broke his loaf of bread in two but did not eat. "What a cold night this is for late spring."

"I feel no chill, my son." Caleb rested the back of his hand against Nathan's cheek. "You have a fever."

"That is how they say the plague begins. The people in the city said the fever kills many, and other suffer greatly before they recover. I hope I have not caught it." Nathan set his food aside. "Keren has no relatives, at least that is what she told me. Where did she go? What has become of Rachel and Zara?"

"You must accept that you may never know the answers to your questions." Avram felt sorry for the children and tried hard to generate a little bit of compassion for the woman. "Since she has nowhere else to go, it may be that she will come back to you."

Nathan wrapped a blanket around his shoulders and nodded. "God's will must be done in this matter. Perhaps I will go again to the city and search when I feel stronger."

Caleb put an arm around Nathan's shoulders. "Did you not have enough to eat on your journey?"

"No, it is not that." Nathan stretched out prone. "I must rest."

John Simon sat slightly apart from the other three shepherds, silently eating without looking toward the others. After Nathan closed his eyes and his breathing deepened, John Simon said, "He has the plague."

Immediately, Avram knew what the young shepherd said was true. He turned to Caleb. "Get on the donkey and go quickly to my cave. Bring the lidded iron pot high on the shelf in the cave. You will know which one I mean when you see it."

Caleb stood. "What is in the pot?"

"A vile concoction Yael made from plants and herbs. She swore by it. Take a few drops yourself to ward off the fever. Hasten, my friend."

After Caleb departed at a trot, Avram sat stroking his beard. "I wonder where the woman went. I am certain she has no family to turn to." He leapt up. "I must go."

"Leaving me with all of the sheep and a sick man." John Simon spoke matter-of-factly. "What strange men I have aligned myself with."

"Do you mean to say you will partner with us?"

"Someone has to take care of you crazy old men and your multitude of sheep. I suppose it falls to me." He spread his coat over Nathan. "First, I must trust you with my secrets."

"Not now. I have urgent business in the city." As he set out, Avram said over his shoulder, "Take some of my wife's medicine when Caleb brings it."

"Wait," John Simon called after him. "Take my horse."

Avram turned and walked to the young man's side. "No shepherd has a horse."

John Simon grinned in his off-centered way. "I will saddle him for you. Run away and hide if you see a soldier."

Chapter Fifty-Five

The big, muscular stallion delivered Avram swiftly to the meadow where Channah's little flock grazed peacefully under the care of a young girl. Feeling somewhat foolish, as if he worried for nothing, he dismounted and led the horse forward to keep from frightening the sheep.

"Good day," he greeted the child, pleased at the thought Channah could afford to hire a shepherdess.

The girl looked up, apparently startled, and ran to the house. Avram chuckled to find the child more skittish than the animals she tended. After guiding John Simon's horse in a wide arc around the sheep, he tethered the animal. The aroma of freshly-baked bread lingered around the outdoor oven.

As Avram cut across the courtyard, the door to the house cracked open. Peninnah's tear-streaked face poked through the narrow opening. "Avram," the old woman cried. "Thank God you have come."

Not waiting for a more formal invitation, Avram pushed the door open. He grabbed Peninnah as she sagged toward the ground. "What is wrong?" he asked.

"Plague." Peninnah spread her hand toward the opposite side of the house.

"Oh, no." As Avram's eyes adjusted to the transition from the bright sunlight, he saw bodies everywhere. "Are they dead or alive?" He feared the answer.

"Both. This girl and I took care of everyone as best we could after Channah fell ill." Peninnah's voice was flat, weary. "She—Channah, I mean—and Enos are the only two left alive this morning."

The girl who had been tending the sheep peeked from behind Peninnah's skirts. "No, Mr. Enos has stopped breathing."

One word flew from Avram's heart to his lips. "Channah?"

Taking Avram by the hand, the child led him to a bedside. Avram touched Channah's forehead. Then, in one swift motion, he scooped her and her sheet into his arms. "Get out of this house of death. Sleep in the courtyard or in the barn. I will return for you as soon as I can."

Avram rode the horse straight down the road, praying there were no Romans between him and Yael's elixir. Channah reclined in his arms, her eyes closed, with no sound other than an occasional moan. He urged the stallion from the road into open country, following the quickest route to John Simon's pasture.

In the distance, Caleb stood on the little hillock that commanded the best view of the grazing herd. Avram rode the horse straight toward his friend, barely managing to stop the steed from racing on by him. Caleb took Channah's limp body and laid her on the ground while Avram dismounted. "The medicine. Hurry."

Caleb complied immediately, ladling a small amount of liquid from the iron pot into Channah's throat. John Simon appeared and led his prancing horse away.

Channah coughed, moaned, and turned on her side.

"Here, take this." Caleb passed the small ladle to Avram.

The old shepherd swallowed the potion and made a sour face. "What a foul taste. Did you medicate John Simon also?"

"Yes." Caleb replaced the iron pot's lid.

"Good," Avram said. "We must partake of the mixture each morning and evening for the next three days. It should protect us from the plague."

"But will Yael's concoction cure Nathan and Channah?"

"That I cannot say." Avram pushed hair from Channah's face. "We must pray for them."

At sundown, Avram volunteered to keep watch. "I cannot sleep anyway."

"I will watch with you." Caleb scooted closer to his son.

"Staying awake never cured a fever," John Simon observed. He stretched out and closed his eyes.

Avram walked around the herd's perimeter wondering how everything could be different and still the same. The Messiah's arrival—even his resurrection—did not prevent a plague from coming upon people. The Romans still ruled the beautiful land with an iron hand. What was it going to take to banish evil from the world? Without coming to any conclusion, Avram returned to the hillock to find Caleb sitting by his son, head pitched forward, snoring. He pulled his friend's coat down to cover his feet.

"If you want to rest, I will take over." John Simon sat up and yawned.

Avram poured himself a generous portion of wine. "Perhaps this will help me relax. Do you never sleep?"

"Not as much as other people."

After they sat for a while, Avram said, "I am astonished that you own a horse and intrigued that you keep it hidden away. Is that the secret you referred to earlier?"

"Not exactly." John Simon picked up his coat from the ground, shook it, and put it on. "When I became a follower of the Way, Jesus forgave my sins. Caesar is not so gracious. I am a wanted man, and I keep the horse for a quick getaway if that ever becomes necessary."

"I see. That is why you keep to the hills."

John Simon nodded affirmatively. "And why I may simply disappear someday. Either on my horse or in chains."

"I am no friend of Rome. Your secret is safe with me."

"There is more. Something worse."

Avram lifted his eyebrows. "Worse than being considered a criminal by the government? I must hear this."

"My father was a Roman. I am only half Jewish."

"Oh."

"And I have not been circumcised."

Too stunned to speak, Avram gulped wine.

John Simon stood and took up his staff. "Now that you know these things, I will understand if you choose not be take me as your partner." He walked away, winding his way down among the sheep.

Chapter Fifty-Six

Three days later, Channah opened her eyes. She looked around and whispered, "Thirsty."

Caleb held her head slightly elevated and put a cup of wine to her lips. She took several swallows before closing her eyes. "Thank you."

The old man touched Channah's face with the back of his hand. He stood and waved his arms to get Avram's attention.

"What is it?" Avram was breathless from rushing to respond to Caleb's signal.

"The fever has left Channah. She asked for something to drink."

Avram fell to his knees. "Thank God. What about Nathan?"

Caleb shook his head and walked away.

Near sunrise the following morning, Channah opened her eyes. "May I have some?" She pointed toward the food the men were sharing.

Avram handed her a loaf of bread the size of his fist. Channah did not arise, but she consumed tiny bites until the bread was almost all gone. "How did I get here?"

"I brought you." Avram poured a cup of wine. "Do you want something to drink?"

"Yes, please." She slowly elevated herself to a sitting position. After drinking the wine, Channah asked, "Do you have any almonds?"

John Simon tossed a small purse to Avram, who loosened the string and poured Channah a handful of shelled almonds.

"Where is everyone else?" she asked.

Avram cleared his throat. "Peninnah and the child called Miryam are at our cave, gaining strength I trust."

"What about Rachel?"

Taking her hand, Avram said, "There was a plague."

"Yes, I remember. My neighbor Shuwshan and her little boy died from it." Channah's grasp on Avram's hand tightened. "Keren was ill, and Enos, and Zara. And my precious Rachel. Where is Rachel?"

"Only you, Peninnah, and Miryam survived. I am sorry. I know how it hurts to lose a child you love." Avram's tears rolled slowly down each cheek.

Channah laid back. "Poor little Rachel." She turned her face away and closed her moist eyes. "Zara, Keren, Enos, all of them gone from this life."

"When you have the strength, I will take you to Peninnah and the girl. Maybe tomorrow or the next day," Avram said.

Caleb's high, keening wail stung the air. "My son. No, Nathan, no, you cannot leave me."

Avram gently detached himself from Channah's grasp and put an arm around his friend. Caleb threw himself on top of his son's lifeless body and sobbed. "My son. Nathan. My boy. My only child."

John Simon sprinkled dirt on his head to signify mourning. "I will tend the sheep alone today." He made his way down the side of the hill without looking back.

After many tears, Caleb sat up, tore his tunic, and covered his scraggly white hair with dust.

"Nathan should never have married that woman." Caleb glared at Channah. "He caught the fever when he went looking for her. You must know that, Channah."

Channah closed her eyes. "I am sorry. I did not know how things would turn out. For any of us."

"Only God knows the future, and only he has the power of life and death, Caleb," Avram said. "We must take Nathan to my cave and prepare his body for burial."

While Avram led the beast of burden to the hill, Caleb bound his son's hands to prevent his arms from dragging. The two old men then laid Nathan's body across the donkey's back. "We will return as soon as possible," Avram told Channah.

"I will go with you," she replied.

"No, child." Avram held up a hand, palm outwards. "You do not have the strength."

"Thank you for your concern, Uncle. But I am no child. I am a grown woman, and now a widow. If I grow faint along the way, I will rest and catch up with you later."

Avram looked at Caleb and shrugged. "Although Channah is my blood relative, not Yael's, she puts me in mind of my wife more every day."

At the familiar stone fence surrounding Avram's cave, Miryam ran to meet Channah. "Look, we brought your sheep."

Sure enough, Channah's little flock lounged inside the fence, placidly munching straw. Avram spoke as he and Caleb laid Nathan's body on the low stone wall. "Peninnah rode the donkey while the child herded the sheep and I pulled a cart full of dishes and scrolls."

Channah pulled Miryam to her side and caressed her. "Thank you for taking your responsibility for the sheep seriously." She turned to Avram. "You brought Enos's scrolls? Why?"

"Peninnah insisted. She said they are worth at least a gold coin each."

"I never knew they were valuable." Channah smoothed Miryam's hair. "You must watch and learn while Peninnah and I prepare this dear young man's body for burial."

Peninnah came tottering from the tent. "What is this about a body? You know we will be considered unclean if we touch it."

"Shepherds do what must be done," Avram said. "There are linen strips in the tent, left over from Yael's preparation. The spices and herbs are on the high shelf inside the cave." He put a hand on Caleb's back. "Let us go and remove the stone from the place where your son will rest near my wife."

Although it was late afternoon before the burial cave was sealed, Avram announced his intention to return to the pasture immediately. "It is too late," Caleb protested. "You cannot get there before dark."

"I know," Avram agreed. "But John Simon must have help managing the herd. We have put too much on him for too long. I will go."

Channah took up a loaded food bag. "I will come with you."

Avram raked his unruly hair into place, albeit temporarily. "Are you not tired?"

"Exhausted," she replied. "Are you ready to go?"

"May I come?" Miryam asked.

"No," Channah said. "You have to remain here tonight. Then tomorrow, you must bring your sheep to the pasture to join the main herd."

Miryam beamed. "I will take good care of them."

"I cannot stay here alone," Peninnah protested.

"Then you must go with us," Caleb said. "I will lead the donkey while you ride and the child looks after the flock."

Chapter Fifty-Seven

"I have made a decision," Channah said, as she and her uncle marched quickly toward the pasture.

"Oh?"

"I will take Miryam and bring her up as my own. I always wanted to bear a child. After I knew that would never happen, I set my affection on Rachel. Then God took her. Now I will care for this little one who has no one else."

"What about her father?"

"If he ever comes to claim her, I will have to give her up. If not, she is mine."

Avram stepped over a stone in his path. "That sounds like a worrisome concern that will not go away until the girl is grown."

"I am willing to risk my heart in exchange for a daughter. As you told Peninnah, shepherds do what must be done. If I can be half as kind to Miryam as you and Auntie were to me, it will be enough."

"Do you wish for me to find a husband for you? I am more aware of my age every day. When I am gone, you will have no one to help you raise the girl. Caleb knows many followers of the Way in Jerusalem."

"Thank you for your concern, Uncle, but no. I am done with the city. I want to live out here, in the open country, with your sheep and Miryam. I suppose I am through with marriage also. I expected Enos to treat me as you did Auntie. But ... no, I do not wish to become subject to another husband."

"You are young, no older than most women when they first begin to think of getting married. Perhaps with time you will change your mind."

By the time they reached the pastureland camp, Channah noticed Avram's breathing was labored. "Rest now, Uncle. Sleep for a while," she said. "I will take care of the sheep."

"No." Avram panted as he climbed the little hill.

Without acknowledging her uncle's protest, Channah picked up Nathan's rod and staff. She grabbed a package from her food bag and made her way into the herd. When she met John Simon, she said, "You may go and rest now. I will stand watch."

"Alone?" he asked, with one elevated eyebrow. "In the blackness of the night?"

"Have you noticed the full moon?"

"What if a wild animal creeps up and grabs you?"

"Predators go after lambs or stragglers. They attack the weak and alone."

John Simon gave her a lazy salute. "I could use a little sleep."

Channah walked about the perimeter of the herd, almost hoping to encounter a wolf to demonstrate her skill with shepherds' weapons. However, the night passed quietly. Whether strolling or perched on a boulder, she felt at peace. When she was certain the men were asleep, she stopped and shed a great many mournful tears for those who died in the plague, especially her beloved Rachel. Afterward, she wiped her face and carried on.

The next day, Caleb, Peninnah, and Miryam arrived. At Peninnah's insistence, the donkey not only carried her but dragged along the small wooden cart packed with scrolls and dishes. No one objected when Peninnah announced she would do the cooking for everyone.

Channah showed Miryam how to oil the heads of the sheep. When she was satisfied the girl could do the job without supervision, she trimmed the overgrown hooves of her small flock of six. "You actually know how to use a knife," John Simon remarked as he walked by.

Channah pointed her knife at him. "I am good with all kinds of weapons." She expected an impertinent retort.

Instead, John Simon put his hands on his hips and grinned. "I will bear that in mind."

While moving the herd to a fresh pasture, Caleb tripped over a lamb. As he bounced down a hillside, he cried out. Channah quieted the sheep while her uncle and John Simon rushed to help the old man to his feet. After several failed attempts to stand, Caleb slumped to the ground with a pained expression. "I am afraid my leg is broken," Channah heard him say.

Avram motioned Channah to join him and John Simon. "Caleb cannot walk," Avram said, "Neither can Peninnah, not for any distance."

"I have feared such an accident for some time." John Simon glanced toward where Caleb sat hunched over.

"I know. You warned me, and I did not listen." Avram hugged himself. "The immediate problem is to get him where he can stay off his feet until the leg heals. I am thinking my cave. There is food there, water is near, and he will have the tent and the cave for shelter."

"Why not send Peninnah to cook and fetch water?" Channah asked. "She has trouble moving about in the pasture also. They can take care of each other."

"Good idea," John Simon said. He looked directly at Avram. "Forgive me, sir, but you are only one slip away from being in Caleb's condition."

"Anyone can break a leg any time." Avram pressed his lips together for a long moment. "I will take Caleb to my cave on the donkey. As soon as he is settled, I will return and take Peninnah to him." He winced. "She may balk at the improper living arrangement."

"I will speak with Peninnah to get her prepared," Channah said.

Peninnah fussed a bit, not—as Channah expected—about living at the cave with Caleb, but because of Channah and John Simon being thrust together. "Avram will have to sleep sometime," Peninnah cautioned. "You will be in the field alone with that young man. How will that appear to a prospective husband?"

Knowing Peninnah would never understand her intention to remain single, Channah merely replied, "Miryam will be with me constantly."

"She is only a child."

"I will be careful, Aunt Peninnah. This is the only practical way."

The old woman sighed. "I suppose you have no choice, any more than I do. I must admit I am dreadfully weary of sleeping out in the open and moving from place to place every other day."

Chapter Fifty-Eight

"What did you do to the bread?" John Simon held up his half-eaten loaf, studying it intently.

"Baked it as usual." Channah replied. "There is other food if it is not to your liking."

"No." John Simon raised his other hand. "Not at all. The bread is superb."

Channah shrugged. She packed her food bag to prepare for the first night watch.

In the distance, Avram and Miryam walked toward the campsite. "Your daughter learns quickly," John Simon said between bites.

"Uncle is a good teacher." Channah spread a blanket on the ground. On it, she set a tray of food for Avram and the girl to share.

John Simon looked at her over the rim of his wine cup. "You do not talk much."

"Only when I have something to say." She was not sure if he was criticizing her or making light of her quiet ways.

He smiled and continued eating without comment.

Avram flung himself down on the blanket Channah had waiting, breathing hard. Miryam sat beside him. As soon as he took bread, the girl did the same. "Mmm, I forget what good bread you make, Channah," Avram said appreciatively.

John Simon twirled his cup. "We must take the herd to the high country soon. We cannot wait any longer."

Avram nodded in agreement. "Yes. Tomorrow."

John Simon sat his cup aside. "Are you sure you can tolerate the altitude?"

Avram's eyes darted to Channah. "I will be fine. I wish Caleb could join us, but I know he cannot."

"Tomorrow, then," John Simon said. "I will be ready at sunrise."

When Channah returned from patrol after midnight, everything was packed and waiting to be transported to the mountain. "You have been busy," she said to John Simon.

He grunted and took a food bag. "I am taking the rest of your bread, if that is all right."

"Certainly." Channah scooted Miryam to one side of the blanket and curled up beside the girl. She watched John Simon disappear into the darkness. Several times he and Avram stopped talking abruptly when she joined them. She spent a moment wondering what they could have been discussing. Then sleep overtook her.

The next morning, Channah awoke with the dawn. She quickly roused Avram and Miryam, then folded the blanket. John Simon's horse stood tossing his head, while hitched to a loaded chariot. As prearranged, Channah took the lead. Miryam helped Avram keep the herd together from either side. John Simon led the horse and guarded the rear.

The journey to the mountain went smoothly, except for Channah's gnawing apprehension for her uncle. Rather than move at his normal brisk pace, he walked more slowly. He stepped tentatively on inclines, not displaying his customary agility. "Are you well, Uncle?" she asked him at their first evening meal in the high country.

"Of course. Why do you ask?"

"No reason," Channah mumbled.

The summer camp had a fine cave, with a thick stone wall encircling its entrance. This arrangement made night patrols unnecessary. Instead, the shepherds brought the herd inside the wall at sundown. The sheep passed the night in the paddock or inside the cave's shelter. Avram and John Simon slept next to a large stone that served as a gate. Channah's preference was to bed down near the mouth of the cave, with Miryam cuddled next to her.

Channah sang as she led the sheep to their pasture each morning. She thought of Yael often, especially when teaching Miryam how to sling a stone or shoot an arrow. She was unprepared for the words Avram spoke to her one beautiful summer morning. "Channah, do you remember why you asked Nathan to marry Rachel's mother?"

"I am sorry, Uncle. I meant well. It seemed like the best thing for everyone. At least I thought so at the time."

"My question was, why did you want him to do it?"

"I wanted him to take care of Rachel. And Keren, too, but mostly the child. Why do you bring this up now?"

The old man put a thumb perpendicular to his lips for a moment. Then he drew a deep breath and exhaled. "I want you to think about marrying John Simon."

"He dislikes me. He is too self-contained to want a wife. Besides, I thought you agreed not to seek a husband for me."

"I did not initiate the conversation with John Simon. He asked me if you would consider becoming his wife. And he likes you very much, or so he says. He admires your skill at shepherding, your strength, and even your stubbornness. I am satisfied he is a devout follower of the Way."

Channah frowned. "I never wanted to admit this, but I do like John Simon. He will be a good husband to some woman. But I do not want a man ruling my life. Always telling me what to do. He has no right to ask this of you."

Avram settled into a sitting position. "Forgive me, but I cannot stand all day as I once did." He patted the space beside him on a flat stone, indicating Channah was to sit beside him. After she did, he said, "You felt Rachel needed someone to take care of her. I feel the same way about you."

"She was a baby. I will fend for myself." Channah looked away from her uncle.

"No, Channah. Not in this world. You work hard, with great determination, but you cannot deal with a publican. A wool merchant—if he does business with you at all—will cheat you at shearing time. Sellers of grain all take advantage of widows." He used his hand to gently turn her face to him. "I will not live forever, Channah. You see how I cannot balance myself going up and down the hills." He dropped his hand. "I love you the way you loved Rachel, and I have the same desire for you to be looked after. Please, if you have any regard for your old uncle, marry this young man. For my sake if you cannot do it for yourself and Miryam."

She saw John Simon watching her from across the pasture. "He knows what we are discussing," Channah said, lowering her eyes.

"He asked me to speak with you, to find out if there is any chance you will accept him."

"Men want sons, Uncle. Does he know I am barren?"

"John Simon knows nothing about you other than what he has observed and what you may have told him." He jabbed the air with his finger. "I know things about him I will never reveal. The two of you can work all of that out. I never knew Yael snored until after we were married, nor that her mother was a constant nag. There is no perfect husband—or wife, for that matter—but in my opinion John Simon will be far superior to most."

The longer Channah sat by Avram, the more she realized the wisdom of his words. "He is to understand that we are partners. He must allow me a voice in every decision. Also, he must treat Miryam as his dearly beloved daughter. If he consents to my terms, I will be his wife."

Avram embraced her with one arm, and beckoned with the other.

John Simon's speed sent sheep scattering before him. After Avram repeated Channah's requirements, the young shepherd took her hand and swore on bended knees to uphold each condition faithfully. She saw tears gathering in John Simon's eyes, and she knew her uncle had made a good match for her.

At twilight, after the herd was settled for the evening, Channah rested from the day's labors. She sat near Avram and John Simon with her arm around Miryam. Although her little family had been drawn together by necessity, she was certain they cared for each other deeply. She was content as she looked forward to a life of faith, hope, and love. The shepherd woman did not speak, but her heart swelled with a song of thanksgiving.

If you enjoyed reading *Song of the Shepherd Woman*, please consider posting a review on Amazon. Your opinion matters!

About the Authors

Carlene Havel has a degree in English from the University of Texas at San Antonio. She writes Christian-themed romances and historical novels. Carlene has lived in Turkey, Republic of the Philippines, and numerous US states. After a career in human resources and software development, she began writing in 2005. The Havels make their home in Texas, surrounded by their extended family. You are invited to connect with Carlene through her FaceBook author page,

https://www.facebook.com/AuthorCarleneHavel

Sharon Faucheux was born in New Orleans, Louisiana. Raised in Austin, Texas, she graduated from the University of Texas with a degree in Psychology. After living in several others states and countries, she now resides in San Antonio, Texas. Sharon's favorite activity is traveling with her always-entertaining family.

View other Books by these authors at http://www.amazon.com/Carlene-Havel/e/B008M9J8JA/

A Hero's Homecoming by Carlene Havel

Colonel Rich Martino returns home from overseas to find everything has changed and nothing makes sense. His wife Rita has disappeared. His credit cards are invalid. A stranger is living in his house, and he keeps running into people who are convinced he was killed in action months ago. Worst of all, his wealthy father has suffered a stroke.

Psychologist Charlotte Phillips claims to be his comatose father's legal guardian. Rich is determined to learn what has happened, gain control of his father's money, and unmask Charlotte as the gold-digging schemer he's certain she is. He is shocked to find his father's crusty old attorney has been taken in by her along with everyone else.

Baxter Road Miracle by Carlene Havel

Henry Youngblood is determined to plant a new church in Buffalo Creek, despite seemingly insurmountable obstacles. Meanwhile, his pregnant wife worries about paying the bills. One daughter longs for a college education she cannot afford, and the other wants nothing more than popularity. It will take a miracle for the Youngblood family's dreams to come true.

Daughter of the King by Sharon Faucheux and Carlene Havel

Princess Michal was the youngest daughter of Saul, the first king of Israel. In an age when fathers arranged marriages, Michal dared to fall in love with a handsome young musician named David, from the little town of Bethlehem.

As recounted in the Bible, Michal helped David escape from her insanely jealous father. King Saul punished his daughter with a forced marriage to a distant war lord. Princess Michal unexpectedly returns from seven years of exile to find a changed world. Most of her relatives are dead. David has become King of Judea. He has acquired six additional wives, one of whom is a princess from Geshur. Michal longs to have a son to reign over Israel and reestablish the rule of King Saul's heirs. But each royal wife has hopes of placing her own son on the throne.

Can Princess Michal's love for King David survive war, madness, infidelity, and betrayal?

Evidence Not Seen by Carlene Havel

Although attorney Jeff Galloway's career is in high gear, his personal life is a mess. Just before his father returns home from a twenty-seven-year stretch in prison, his girlfriend dumps him. When a chance encounter begins to blossom into new romance, soft-hearted Melanie Clark encourages Jeff to find a way to forgive his father's long absence.

Here Today Gone Tomorrow by Carlene Havel

Disappointed, dumped, divorced. Everything Casey Slaughter counted on is gone. While contemporaries start their families, Casey works two jobs to haul herself out of debt. Friends and family recommend a new husband to solve her problems, but Casey resists. Although she longs for a soul mate, the last thing her flattened self-esteem needs is more rejection—and comparisons to her beautiful, talented older sister do nothing to enhance Casey's confidence. Unable to have children, she feels she has nothing to offer in marriage. Will bitterness and insecurity destroy her, or can renewed faith in God provide some measure of comfort for this wounded heart?

Texas Runaway Bride by Carlene Havel

In 1849, Ruth Van Ruekle is an orphaned teenager stuck in a frontier town, working in a saloon. A strange set of circumstances send her on a journey that includes meeting one of her own time-travelling descendants. When she reaches California and reveals her past to her prospective husband, Ruth finds out George has a secret of his own.

The Scarlet Cord by Sharon Faucheux and Carlene Havel

Rahab, a resourceful beauty, struggles to survive in the pagan culture of ancient Jericho. As years of harsh labor begin to lift her and her family from poverty, a foreign army threatens the well-fortified city. Rahab is forced to make an immediate decision. Will she put her

317

faith in the fabled walls of Jericho or the powerful God of the Hebrews? Either choice may cost her life.

A Sharecropper Christmas by Carlene Havel

The Great Depression left the Shoemaker family hungry and homeless. Their desperate prayers are finally answered when Herbert Shoemaker finds work as a sharecropper. Alice makes the best of the hard times without complaint, though she dreams of giving her little family a special Christmas.

The Twice-Shy Heart by Carlene Havel

Monty Chapman returns to Polson's Crossing, Texas, claiming to be a changed man now that he's a Christian. While continuing to work as a song-writer, he dreams of establishing a rescue mission. More than anything, Monty longs to put his family back together. Can he overcome the shady reputation he earned in his home town and persuade the love of his life to give him another chance?

Lacy Chapman was devastated when Monty deserted her to pursue a career in music, but that was ten years ago. Now her life consists of running Pearl's Roadhouse and taking care of her teen-aged daughters. As others begin to accept Monty's new-found piety, Lacy remains unconvinced. She is certain he has come home to take the Roadhouse away from her. This charming rogue broke her heart once, and she does not intend to let him do it again.

Discussion Questions

1. How did believing a lie shape Avram's life?
2. Did you gain or lose sympathy for Avram as the story of his past unfolded?
3. Why do you think Avram refused to deny what he saw?
4. Should Channah have told Enos about Keren's indiscretion with Philip the Greek?
5. Why do you think Enos was so protective of his honor?
6. How do you feel about Channah's decision to leave when Enos turned Keren and Rachel out of his house?
7. Did Keren become more or less sympathetic as the story unfolded?
8. Did you agree with Channah's return to Enos?
9. Did "Song of the Shepherd Woman" change how you think about the

"shepherds abiding in the fields, keeping watch over their flocks by night" in the Bible (Luke chapter 2)?

10.   Do you think Keren fits the story of the woman taken in adultery in the Bible (John chapter 8)?

11.   Who was your favorite minor character and why: Caleb, Peninnah, or Shewshan?

12.   Was Avram right to convince Channah to remarry?

13.   Why did Avram believe John Simon would make a good husband for Channah?

14.   Would you want to live in the place and time when Avram and Channah lived?

15.   Do you think there is significance in the main characters' names?

Channah is a variant of Hannah, which means grace or favor.

Avram is a variant of Abraham, which means high father.

Yael means mountain goat.

Rachel means ewe, which is a female sheep.

Made in the USA
Middletown, DE
01 June 2020